Praise for ~~Gill Hartzmark~~'s previous Kate Millholland novels

ROUGH TRADE

"Hartzmark . . . offers substance with excitement."
—*Publishers Weekly*

FATAL REACTION

"Exceptional: Hartzmark paints a fascinating picture of the world of drug research with characters who are believable, varied, and likable (even the villains are the kind you love to hate). The intensity of the complex plot never wavers, and the ending explains just enough to satisfy without being too pat."
—*Publishers Weekly*

FINAL OPTION

"A cleverly plotted and convincing inside look at freewheeling financial crooks and wizards . . . Hartzmark keeps the story moving swiftly to an explosive conclusion."
—*San Francisco Chronicle*

BITTER BUSINESS

"A page-turner."
—*People*

By Gini Hartzmark
Published by The Ballantine Publishing Group:

PRINCIPAL DEFENSE
FINAL OPTION
BITTER BUSINESS
FATAL REACTION
ROUGH TRADE
DEAD CERTAIN

DEAD CERTAIN

Gini Hartzmark

FAWCETT BOOKS • NEW YORK

A Fawcett Book
Published by The Ballantine Publishing Group
Copyright © 2000 by Gini Hartzmark

Fawcett is a registered trademark and the Fawcett colophon is a trademark of Random House, Inc.

www.randomhouse.com/BB/

Library of Congress Catalog Card Number: 99-91032

ISBN 0-8041-1900-7

Manufactured in the United States of America

First Edition: January 2000

10 9 8 7 6 5 4 3 2 1

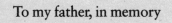

To my father, in memory

ACKNOWLEDGEMENTS

I'd like to thank all the usual suspects: Susan Randol, Don Maass, and Lisa Collins for their help in shaping the manuscript; Drs. Heather Raaf and William Morgan for always being happy to help me kill people—at least on paper; Dee Hartzmark and Elizabeth Gardner, who cheerfully answered all questions without asking why; and my husband, Michael, who is always there to help me find the way through my own plots after I've succeeded in confusing myself. Finally, special thanks to Steve Garrity, computer wizard, for solving problems real, fictional, and digital.

CHAPTER

1

As a lawyer I'm not usually interested in the truth. I know that sounds appalling. But if it's absolutes you're interested in, you'd better stick to physics. At its heart the law is all about human behavior, and human behavior is by definition messy. Which not only explains why lawyers make their living in the gray spaces between differing versions of the truth, but also why there are so many of us. But, that morning I wasn't interested in truth, physics, or the dark inner workings of the human heart. All I wanted was to make a deal.

After six months of letters, meetings, and conference calls, after months of missteps, frustration, and false hope—it all came down to this: three days and three nights at the negotiating table and still no deal. Not only that, but I was running out of tricks. I was too frustrated to be persuasive, and after being up all night, the lawyers for the other side were too sleep-deprived to be intimidated—which was probably okay, because I was also too tired to care. All I wanted was to make a deal, take a shower, and climb into bed—in that order. Considering that I'd spent the last seventy-two hours in the same set of clothes, I didn't think that was too much to ask.

It didn't help that the air in the conference room was

ripe with the scent of yesterday's sweat and the mahogany table was strewn with the wreckage of midnight coffee and fast-food breakfast. Jackets were off, sleeves were rolled up, and with a one o'clock deal-or-die deadline fast approaching, we'd moved past the point of being polite three ultimatums ago. When one of the Armani-clad wonders for the other side started going through his list of financial sticking points for what felt like the four hundredth time, I found myself alternating between fantasies of crisp cotton sheets and ripping his head off. I had just decided on the latter when my secretary sidled into the room and tapped me gently on the shoulder.

Cheryl was a petite powerhouse of a woman with a neat blond bob and a subversive sense of humor. She was also my rock, unflappable in any crisis and impervious to panic, which is why all it took was one look at her face for me to know that she hadn't come to bring me good news. As she slipped me a folded sheet of paper, I tasted adrenaline in my throat and scenarios for a half a dozen different disasters sprang full-blown into my head. In my line of work it helps to have a vivid imagination and a sixth sense for disaster, but this time it turns out I wasn't even close.

In Cheryl's tidy handwriting, the message was as brief as it was chilling. It said:

"Your mother is here to see you."

I raised my eyes from the paper and turned in my seat to face my secretary. A look of perfect understanding passed between us. Not only was the timing terrible, but we were both thinking the same thing. There was no way my mother would ever come to my office if she could possibly avoid it.

I scrambled to my feet and whispered something about an emergency to the lawyer sitting next to me. Then I started mentally running down the list of possible reasons for my mother's visit.

None of them were good.

As I made my way down the hall I tucked an errant strand of hair behind my ear and prayed that I didn't look as awful as I felt. The weight of my mother's disapproval is a burden under even the best of circumstances. The last thing I wanted to do today was give her fresh ammunition. Lately my personal life had been keeping her more than adequately supplied.

The love lives of corporate lawyers aren't usually a source of gossip-column fodder, but being Astrid Millholland's daughter has always made me something of an exception. Of course, splitting publicly with Stephen Azorini, Chicago's most visible and eligible bachelor, was hardly a move destined to avert the spotlight. Even so, I was completely unprepared for the months of lurid speculation my decision seemed to have fueled.

Mother, accustomed to the respectful worship of the society pages, made no secret of her mortification or the fact that she blamed me for it. In the meantime, I did what I always do, buried myself in work and prayed that someone prominent would turn up in bed with a barnyard animal, if only to give the gossip columnists something else to write about and get my mother off my back.

At Callahan Ross the room where clients cool their heels is everything you'd expect from a law firm where the letterhead reads like the passenger list of the *Mayflower*. With its clubby leather furniture and somber paintings of dead partners, it could have easily doubled as a stage set for a play about the establishment. Needless to say, Mother looked right at home there.

She also looked stunning. At fifty-three my mother had a face that most women would still kill for. Her signature dark mane was swept back from her forehead, framing her now-famous classic features. She was, as always, exquisitely dressed, this time in an elegant suit of charcoal wool subtly trimmed in black. It was just the sort of thing Coco Chanel might have designed for professional women, provided she could have found any willing to drop that kind of money on something to wear to the office.

At the sight of me an all-too-familiar flicker of disappointment crossed my mother's face. I tried not to let it bother me. It had taken a long time, but I'd finally come to terms with the fact that I am not merely a younger version of my mother, but a plainer one, and therefore doomed to forever fall short. The only consolation is that, of the two of us, it undoubtedly troubled her more.

"Mother! What a pleasant surprise," I lied, kissing the air beside her powdered cheek and smiling for the receptionist's benefit. In a place where minutes were reckoned, movements recorded, and absences noted, news of my mother's extraordinary visit was no doubt already crackling along the firm's synapses. I had absolutely no intention of giving anyone any more to talk about.

As I led the way back toward my office I did my best to make small talk, always tricky in our case since even neutral subjects had a way of quickly shifting to more dangerous ground. Playing it safe, I fell back on the usual attorney-client patter, prattling on about how we now had six hundred attorneys in Chicago alone and were in the process of opening a new office in Delhi. Mother, having been trained to feign interest practically since birth, listened politely. But I knew that my world, the world of people who work for a living, held little interest for her.

As I ushered her into my office I noted with silent amusement that Cheryl had made a whirlwind effort to tidy up my usual chaos. Not only had she carted off as many files as she could carry, but she'd shoved the rest underneath my desk so that when I sat down, there was barely enough room for my legs.

"To what do I owe the honor of this visit?" I asked brightly.

"I didn't know that I needed a reason to visit my own daughter," announced Mother.

"Of course you don't need a reason," I replied sweetly. "But that still doesn't mean you don't have one."

"If you must know, I've just come from the hospital," she declared, "and you and I have an important matter to discuss."

I felt my heart sink, but not for the reasons you might think. In my family, the word *hospital* meant only one thing—Prescott Memorial, the charitable institution founded by my mother's great-grandfather and supported by every generation of Prescotts and Millhollands since. But that didn't mean that Mother had dropped by to discuss medical care for the poor. The Founders Ball, the hospital's annual fund-raiser and the charity event that traditionally marked the end of Chicago's gala season, was this coming Saturday night. Having jettisoned Stephen from my life, my choice of escort had become the subject of seemingly endless debate. Mother, no longer content to plague me over the telephone, had apparently decided to intensify her efforts and begin harassing me in person.

"Mother, please," I began, appalled by how quickly I had been reduced to pleading, "this really isn't a very good time."

"It never is, Kate," she countered archly. "Perhaps you would have preferred it if I'd called ahead and made an appointment with your secretary?"

I was tempted to say yes, but I would have been lying.

What I really would have preferred was to not have this conversation at all. However, I knew the look on my mother's face all too well. Barring paid assassins coming through the door and killing us both, nothing was going to get her out of my office until she'd said what she had come to say.

"What's on your mind?" I asked, trying not to think about what was happening in the conference room in my absence.

"There was an emergency meeting of the Prescott Memorial board this morning. The trustees have voted three to two in favor of selling the hospital."

Mother waited in silence as I grappled with the news. I'm sure she was pleased not only to have caught me off guard, but to have finally captured my complete attention.

"To whom?" I demanded, when finally I managed to find my voice.

"Some company named Health Care Corporation of America that's apparently going around the country buying up hospitals."

I leaned back in my chair and considered what I knew about Health Care Corporation, which wasn't much. HCC was one of those companies that was much admired on Wall Street but reviled nearly everywhere else. They'd burst onto the scene a couple of years ago declaring themselves the messiahs of for-profit medicine and began making money hand over fist.

"Can they really do that?" I demanded, still trying to master my disbelief.

"Do what?"

"Can they vote to sell the hospital just like that?"

"They not only can," replied my mother, "but they did. As soon as the motion passed we signed the papers." She brushed a piece of imaginary lint from her sleeve.

"Four generations of philanthropy sold off like it was so much old furniture."

"What exactly did you sign?" I inquired, ever the lawyer.

"Only a letter of intent and a confidentiality agreement," she replied, as if these were documents that routinely passed through her hands. "The sale itself won't go through for another ten days."

"I can't believe the trustees would vote to sell," I muttered incredulously. Over the years the hospital's board had been deliberately kept small—just five seats. Two were held by family members—my mother and her younger brother Edwin—while the other three board members were individuals with close ties to both the family and the hospital. They were Kyle Massius, the president of the hospital; Carl Laffer, Prescott Memorial's chief of staff; and Gavin McDermott, the hospital's world-renowned chief of surgery. All were lifelong friends of the family.

"Naturally, Edwin and I tried everything we could think of to persuade them not to do this," continued my mother. "But we might as well have been talking to ourselves."

My mother was a very bright woman, but she was so used to getting her way as a matter of course that I wasn't sure if she could have persuaded a stranger to give her a glass of water if she were dying of thirst. On the other hand, just the thought of Uncle Edwin attempting any kind of higher level mental function was enough to give me chest pains. Edwin was a handsome ne'er-do-well who owed his board seat to the accident of his birth and the family's desire to give him something to do. His only talent, as far as I could tell, was for bad marriages and even worse divorces.

"But why? What reasons did they give that could possibly justify selling the hospital?"

"Oh, it was just all the usual rubbish about the hospital losing money and the skyrocketing cost of medical care," replied Mother. For once I thought her right to be dismissive. Money was always short at a charity hospital, and there would always be more patients than beds at an institution that didn't turn away people who could not pay. "Kyle Massius actually had the nerve to sit there and lecture *me* on the realities of the marketplace," she continued in a tone of voice that indicated that if he'd ordered her to get up on the table and perform a striptease, she would have been no less offended.

"So who gets the money?" I asked, wondering about the mechanics of buying and selling something that wasn't actually owned by anyone.

"The foundation will get the proceeds from the sale," Mother reported.

The Prescott Foundation was a family vehicle, an organization nominally headed by Edwin that existed primarily on paper. Through it, family funds were channeled to charitable causes.

Out of the corner of my eye I caught sight of Cheryl standing in the hall tapping the face of her watch to indicate that it was time to get back into the conference room.

"Well, I'm sure the family will have to put some serious thought into how best to redirect the money," I ventured, wondering how on earth I was going to manage to finesse my mother out of my office.

"I did not come here to discuss the relative merits of worthwhile causes," snapped Mother. "Prescott Memorial is not one of these companies that you seem to spend all your time buying and selling. It happens to be one of the finest teaching hospitals in the country and a place where poor people receive first-rate care. Not only that, but every brick, every piece of equipment, every dollar ever paid out in salary was a donation—a gift.

"When your great-great-grandfather Everett decided to donate the money to build the hospital, poor people were literally dying in the streets from influenza. There was no place else for them to go. And once it was built, he didn't stop. He convinced everyone he knew, his family and all the other prominent Chicago families, to open up their wallets and adopt his cause as their own.

"When your aunt Eleanor's baby died, the family donated the money for the neonatal intensive care unit. When Freddie VanCott developed kidney disease, his children endowed the dialysis center. Now, suddenly, some big corporation rolls into town and figures it can use those gifts to make money! There is a reason that the donors' names are on those buildings."

On some level I knew that she was right, but I couldn't help wondering whether my mother would feel quite so passionately about it if it didn't happen to be her name, too.

"Everyone always says that Everett Prescott was a man of tremendous vision," continued Mother, warming to her subject, "but I can tell you one thing for certain. There is absolutely no way that he could ever have foreseen this."

I was tempted to point out that I didn't think he could have predicted cable TV, the AIDS epidemic, or cell phones either, but I held my tongue. The Prescotts all looked upon Everett as if he were a god and not just the source of their wealth and position. But I knew that, like most robber barons, my great-great-grandfather's reputation had been rehabilitated over time. While the family was busy pointing to the hospital, there were still those who remembered that Everett had started out as little better than a pirate, running guns and opium into China.

I had even heard it whispered that he'd murdered a business rival in order to take over his trade, and it was well known that he'd been quick to champion any cause that benefited his own purse.

Despite my mother's calls for sainthood, I suspected he endowed Prescott Memorial Hospital not out of altruism, but in an effort to buy his way into Chicago society. I had no way of knowing how he'd have seen the sale of the hospital that bore his name—whether he'd perceive it as an outrage or see it as he'd viewed the opium trade, a function of the times. However, I didn't have the time to speculate about it right now. Cheryl had appeared at the door again, and this time she was taking the direct approach.

"I'm sorry to have to interrupt," she said smoothly, "but Kate's client needs her urgently in the conference room."

"I'm afraid you're going to have to go back and tell them that she's already busy with a client," my mother informed her.

"Pardon me?" I bleated. Out of the corner of my eye I could see a look of horror spreading across my secretary's face.

"Why else do you think I came here?" Mother demanded incredulously. "I'm hiring you to stop the sale of Prescott Memorial Hospital."

CHAPTER
2

I ended up saying yes just to get rid of her. There would be plenty of time to find a way to get out of it later. Besides, I told myself I hadn't agreed to anything I wouldn't have done for any prospective client—taking a look at the situation and offering an opinion. But in my heart of hearts I knew the truth: after thirty-four years I still hadn't figured out how to say no to my mother.

In the meantime I had to get back to the conference room and Delirium. By this I meant Delirium the client, not the state of mind, though after three days of caffeine and no sleep it was hard to be sure. Delirium was a computer company, a shoestring start-up on the cusp of either success or ruin, depending on whether I could keep its feuding partners from each other's throats long enough to make the deal that would make them rich. The company was the product of an unnatural alliance between a visionary professor of computer engineering and a venture capitalist whose time horizon extended only as far as the bottom line.

Normally, in my line of work, I expect to find my adversaries on the opposite side of the table, but there was nothing normal about Delirium. Even by the eccentric standards of the computer world, Bill Delius, the brains of the company, was considered deeply odd. To Bill, technology was his religion and the compromises of business were a painful anathema. On the other hand, his partner was purely a money guy. Mark Millman was a pragmatic opportunist who, if pressed, might confess to a certain faith in the free market, but whose more immediate concern was turning a profit.

For both men, Icon's interest in Delirium's technology was a dream come true. The only problem was that for each of them it was a different dream.

Founded by Silicon Valley legend Gabriel Hurt, Icon was the eight-hundred-pound gorilla of the computer industry. Its founder was Bill Delius's idol. To Delius, Hurt was an imagined soul mate, someone capable of understanding and sharing his vision of the world—a world in which information would soon replace money as the currency of power. However, Delius's partner was less interested in Gabriel Hurt's genius than in his bank account. Millman was a gambler, a man who saw his long shot approaching the finish line in the lead. The day Delirium and Icon signed a letter of understanding, the document that signaled the beginning of negotiations in earnest, Millman went out and made a down payment on a Ferrari.

As their attorney, my job was to lead them onto common ground, a task for which I'd begun to suspect a therapist might be better suited. As we neared the deadline for making a deal with Icon, I was beginning to feel like a realtor charged with selling the dream house of a couple now in the midst of an acrimonious divorce. My goal was to get the deal done and, if possible, avoid getting hit by the cross fire.

Contributing to an even greater than usual sense of urgency was the knowledge that I was dealing with quirky people in an idiosyncratic industry. Bill Delius might be weird, but Gabriel Hurt was arguably the world's most famous eccentric—probably because he could afford to be. Even though I'd spent the last three days in round-the-clock negotiations with Icon's handpicked transaction team, I had no idea of whether we were any closer to a deal than when we'd started. Gabriel Hurt might run an $800 billion company, but he still made decisions the same way he had when he was writing code in his parents' basement—alone.

I glanced at my watch and mentally cursed my mother's timing. Hurt was on his way to Chicago for COMDEX, the week-long computer industry expo held every year at McCormack Place. The Icon jet was due to touch down at Meigs Field any minute, where a limousine was waiting to bring him to Callahan Ross for lunch (a tuna fish sandwich and red Jell-O served on a plain white china plate per instruction) and hopefully the final round of negotiations. As I turned the corner to the conference room I rolled my head to relieve the tension in my neck and reminded myself that this is what I lived for.

I knew there was trouble the minute I pushed open the door. When I'd left the room in response to Cheryl's summons, there had been nineteen people at the table: myself, three other Callahan Ross lawyers, Delirium's two principals, and the thirteen attorneys, investment bankers, and officers that made up the Icon transaction team. Now there were only enough people to fill five seats. There was not one face from Icon to be seen.

Making matters worse, Mark Millman was pacing along the far end of the room as quickly as his ample bulk allowed. A fleshy man with thinning hair and flapping jowls, he'd obviously been at it awhile, because there were dark rings of sweat under the arms of his suit jacket and his face was a damp and unhealthy shade of red. By contrast, Bill Delius, wraith thin and dressed entirely in black, stood motionless at the opposite end of the room, staring out the window. I stole a quick glance at the trio of Callahan Ross associates who'd been working with me on the deal, but they were all too busy studying the surface of the table in front of them to catch my eye. Not a good sign.

"Where did everybody go?" I asked as I set down my legal pad and took my seat at the head of the table.

Mark Millman stopped pacing and slammed his meaty palms down on the polished mahogany of the table. The three associates actually flinched.

"They left," he growled. "Hurt called and said he wasn't coming."

"Why not?" I asked, saying a silent prayer for a benign explanation, like a plane crash.

"Nobody knows," reported Jeff Tannenbaum, the associate on whose broad shoulders I'd been heaping the grunt work of the transaction. "Hurt phoned from the plane and said he wasn't coming. We asked, but I don't think he gave his lawyers a reason. They just packed up and left."

"So we don't know whether the deal is off or on," I complained. I resented the lawyers' blind obedience to Gabriel Hurt less than the fact that they were probably back at their hotel by now, dialing room service and turning the hot water taps to full. I also reminded myself that it was too early to tell what it meant. Gabriel Hurt had a reputation for driving a hard bargain, and he was powerful enough to not have to play by the rules.

"I don't give a shit why they left," snapped Millman, furiously staring me in the face. "What I want to know is what you plan on doing to get them to come back."

When I got back to my office, I asked Cheryl to bring me a cup of coffee and a bag of M&M's. Then I started working the phones. The first thing I did was call and leave messages for the Icon people at the Four Seasons, where I knew they were all staying. According to the newspaper, Hurt and his retinue had taken the top three floors of the hotel, including the penthouse. Then I called everyone I could think of who'd had dealings with Gabriel Hurt. Of course, this wasn't the first round of calls I'd made to get the skinny on the famous software mogul, but now I had a better idea of what I needed to know. It wasn't until I dialed the third number on my list that I hit pay dirt.

Computer geeks, in general, make terrible liars. To them, the truth is too absolute to bend, and the one on the other end of the line was no exception. He was the computer guru for Stephen's company, Azor Pharmaceuticals, but he also did some independent consulting for me on the side.

"I told you that Hurt can be unpredictable," he observed as soon as I finished telling him what had just happened. "Who knows why he pulls this kind of shit? When you're Gabriel Hurt, you don't need a reason. However, I hate to be the bearer of bad news, but I just heard a rumor that there's a group out of Seattle that's developed this new input device that's twice as fast as Delirium's and is easier to configure with network applications."

"And that would mean in English?" I inquired.

"You're fucked. Somebody's built a better mousetrap than Delirium, and they're probably selling it to Icon even as we speak."

Cheryl stuck her head in the door to say good-bye. I'd forgotten that she told me that she had to leave early for an interview. I wished her luck and told her to switch me over to voice mail and shut the door behind her. I couldn't believe that in two more months she would be gone. Mrs. Goodlow, the firm's iron-backed office manager, had already begun sending me potential replacements to interview, but so far I found that I had little stomach for the task. Even though I'd always known that one day Cheryl would be leaving, somehow it didn't make it any easier. Cheryl had started in the night law school program at Loyola the same year that I'd joined the firm. Don't worry, I was told, with her working full-time, it'll take her forever to finish. Now suddenly forever was here.

The strange part was that her experience with me, doing the kind of deal-driven corporate work that characterized my practice, had made her one of the most sought-after candidates in her graduating class—a development I viewed with a kind of bittersweet pride. It was only a matter of time before the two of us found ourselves squared off against each other on opposite sides of some transaction.

For the rest of the afternoon I fretted like a lovesick teenager, waiting for the phone to ring, the roller coaster of my anxiety fueled by lack of sleep and a steady stream of irate phone calls from the two principals of Delirium. It was hardly remarkable that my clients were furious and looking for someone to blame. However, the fact that that someone should be me was the first thing they'd agreed on in a very long time.

But when I still hadn't heard from Icon by seven o'clock, I abandoned hope and decided to go home. I was so wrapped up in self-pity about Delirium tanking that I completely forgot about Prescott Memorial and my mother's visit. It wasn't until I had my coat on to leave for the night that I tripped over a box of files that my mother had apparently sent over. Cheryl had put it smack in the middle of the doorway so that I would be sure to not forget it. I rubbed my shins and cursed her efficiency.

I hoisted the box of files and made my way through the darkened reception room and out into the world. Wearily, I leaned against the back wall of the elevator as it carried me down to the basement. In the polished brass of the doors I contemplated my reflection, a pale face offset by dark hair, disheveled by the day and slowly working its way down from its usual French twist. It occurred to me that while I might be nearly two decades younger than my mother, it was I who looked older. I wondered what the female equivalent of the firm's balding and shriveled senior partners would look like and whether in thirty years' time that was going to be me.

The doors opened as the elevator deposited me on the lowest level of the parking garage—deserted this time of night. As my heels clicked across the smooth concrete I pushed the key-chain remote and heard the reassuring chirp of my car alarm being deactivated. I still hadn't quite gotten used to seeing the sleek bottle-green Jaguar in the place that had been for so long occupied by my recently totaled Volvo, but I was working on it. It helped that over the past few months the new-car smell had gradually given way to the more familiar scent of old running shoes and empty Starbucks containers. I'd also managed to accumulate enough Diet Coke cans on the floor of the backseat to replicate the Volvo's trademark rattle whenever I hit a pothole.

Of course, having an expensive new car wasn't easy in Hyde Park. The neighborhood that has been my home for the last half-dozen years isn't exactly a yuppie paradise, but rather the kind of neighborhood you get when you drop a world-class university in the middle of the ghetto, then allow it to be reshaped by every social tide of the last fifty years. White flight, the Jewish exodus to

the suburbs, race riots, urban renewal, and the vicissi-
tudes of the drug trade had all come and gone, leaving
their scars behind. Through it all the essential nature of
the place had remained remarkably unchanged. Hyde
Park was a real-life social laboratory, a place where the
affluent and the educated lived side by side with immi-
grants, criminals, and families where three generations
had lived from welfare check to welfare check. Needless
to say, it was a less than ideal environment for a luxury
car. That's where Leo came in.

Leo was an urban entrepreneur, one of those fringe
artists of economic survival that most people in their
leafy suburban neighborhoods haven't a clue even exist.
Nineteen years old, by day he was almost certainly employed as a numbers runner for Carmine Mustafa. Parking cars was a sideline, a way to pick up extra money
to help support his girlfriend, Angel, and their three
children.

It was a straightforward and strictly cash business. For
a flat monthly fee Leo met me at my door when I came
home at night, and parked my car behind the electric
gates of Carmine Mustafa's compound in Kenwood—
right next door to Louis Farrakhan's house. There, under
the double protection of a drug lord and a black suprema-
cist, my British luxury sedan safely passed the night until
Leo delivered it to me the following morning in time for
me to drive downtown to work.

As I pulled off Lake Shore Drive at Fifty-third Street I
called Leo's beeper number. By the time I pulled up to the
curb in front of my building, he was already waiting, his
baseball cap pulled down low over his face and his spot-
less Nikes iridescent under the soft streetlights.

"How do you ever expect to find yourself a new boyfriend, working as late as you do?" demanded Leo with a
smile as he held open the door for me.

"I think I've had enough of boyfriends for a while," I replied, shivering from a combination of the cold and my own fatigue. Even though it was April, in my world it still felt like winter. There was frost on the ground when I left for work in the morning, and by the time I came home at night, it was dark and I could see my breath. "I've been thinking it over and I've decided it'd be easier to just get a dog."

"I tell you what, until they catch the guy that's been breakin' into apartments around here, it wouldn't be a bad idea. Angel thinks maybe I should let you take Mona for a while." Mona was Leo and Angel's dog, an embarrassingly affectionate Doberman that sometimes came along with Leo when he met me late at night.

"That's sweet of you," I said, "but you need Mona to keep an eye on Angel and the kids while you're out watching over me. Besides, from what I heard, this guy follows little old ladies home from the grocery store during the day. I'm like Dracula, I only come out when it's dark."

"I just worry about you is all, two women living alone in this kind of neighborhood . . . ," Leo said as he slid into the driver's seat.

"You'd better watch yourself, Leo," I chided him sternly. "You're starting to sound like my father."

We both laughed, and I turned to make my way up the wide stone steps that led to the front door of my building. I waved at Leo to signal that I was all right and then climbed another six steps to the internal door to the first floor. As I turned the key in the next lock it occurred to me that if she lived for a thousand years, my mother was never going to meet someone like Leo, much less get to know him well enough to learn the name of his dog. And yet it was people like Leo—petty criminal, family man, and worrier about my safety—who were precisely the type who passed through the doors of Prescott Memorial Hospital every day.

As I made my way across the dimly lit first-floor landing I was greeted by the strains of Vivaldi coming from the living room. My roommate, Claudia, was not just home, but awake—a remarkable occurrence, especially given the relatively early hour. In the middle of a fellowship in trauma surgery, my roommate lived a life stripped down to work and sleep. One of only three doctors assigned full-time to what was arguably one of the busiest trauma units in the city, she not only spent every third night on twenty-four-hour call at the hospital, but was charged with supervising the follow-up care for every trauma patient admitted to the hospital during her shift. The irony of the fact that the hospital in question was Prescott Memorial was hardly lost on me.

I would have loved to tell her about the proposed sale of the hospital, if only to hear what she had to say about it, but I felt reluctant to raise the subject. Claudia had enough to worry about without having to keep my secrets. Surgery is a prickly meritocracy, a separate world filled with competitive people whose egos are as vast as their sense of entitlement. Like every other trauma fellow in her program, Claudia had hoped to be assigned to Prescott Memorial. It was considered far and away the best rotation, not just for the famous surgeons who left their prestigious practices to take their turn on trauma call, but for the high volume of patients—especially victims of person-to-person violence.

But Claudia had been equally determined to earn a spot on her own, without our friendship coming into play, and once she'd been chosen for the Prescott Memorial team, she was, if anything, even more anxious that her association with my family remain a secret. Having battled whispers about pulled strings and family connections my whole life, I understood her fears and respected her wishes.

And yet, as much as she had sought it, Claudia's rotation through Prescott Memorial had so far not been a happy one. They say that whatever doesn't kill you makes you stronger, but the stress was clearly taking its toll. Because the senior attending surgeons were all on staff at other hospitals, the burden of providing the bulk of care fell to Claudia and the two other trauma fellows. In addition, they were charged with supervising the work of a half a dozen interns and residents who were assigned to the service.

I set the box of Prescott Memorial files on the floor of the vestibule before following the sound of violins and the smell of pizza into the living room. I found Claudia in her favorite spot, an elaborately tufted cabbage-rose chintz armchair that was a hand-me-down from my mother. It was the most comfortable seat in the whole place. The rest of the apartment was furnished with a weird hodgepodge of pieces, castoffs from both our families and furniture we'd picked up over the years at the odd garage sale. The overall effect was less of a home than a resting place—somewhere where two women who conducted their lives elsewhere dropped in to sleep and change clothes.

"Did you leave any for me?" I inquired hopefully as I kicked off my shoes beside Claudia's bloodstained sneakers. By way of an answer my roommate lifted the lid of the Edwardo's box, revealing a large deep-dish spinach pizza with only one piece missing.

"You are going straight to heaven," I proclaimed over my shoulder as I made a quick U-turn into the kitchen. Returning, plate in hand, I shed my jacket and peeled off my pantyhose while Claudia served me up a slice and poured me a glass of wine.

Curled up in the big armchair, my roommate looked less like a surgeon and more like a little girl dressed for bed in a pair of green pajamas. With her curly black hair parted in the middle and pulled back into a single long braid, all she needed was a teddy bear to hold. Unlike lawyers, surgeons dressed for function, not success. Claudia's hairstyle was dictated by the fact that she could slip the braid down inside the back of her scrubs in the OR, and the scrubs, like prison togs, were institutional issue.

It wasn't until you looked closer, saw the fine lines of stress etched around her eyes, the splatter of dark stains that could only be blood, that you realized there was nothing at all childlike about her. Watching her dissect the pizza, I could not help but notice the exhausted slump of her shoulders. It was the cumulative effect of the years of sleep deprivation that are part of the surgeon's rite of passage, deprivation that no single night's sleep could ever erase.

But I knew her well enough to suspect that it was more than exhaustion that was getting her down. Whenever I asked her what was wrong, she invariably shrugged and reminded me that trauma was not a happy specialty. I worried that what had been damaged was not the heart of some poor innocent from the street, but Claudia's own.

During the winter, despite the demands of almost endless work, she'd begun seeing someone, a handsome paramedic named Carlos, one of the you-maul-'em, we-haul-'em crew that worked the neighborhood around the Prescott Memorial ER. He was a good-looking soccer player with an infectious grin and a sense of gallows humor that found its natural expression in practical jokes. He'd won her jaded New York heart by teaching her to bowl, drink beer, and watch kung fu movies. The only trouble was that he was married. At least that was the conclusion she'd been forced to draw when a pretty young woman, pregnant and with a toddler in tow, showed up and delivered a bouquet of brightly colored helium balloons to the emergency room as a surprise for her husband on his birthday.

Surgeonlike, Claudia had broken off the relationship cleanly, with a minimum of tears and few words spoken. However, as the weeks went by I'd suspected Carlos of trying to reexert his charm. In addition to a steady stream of cards and flowers, all of which Claudia had promptly sent back, we'd recently started being bothered by hang-up calls, always on nights when Claudia wasn't scheduled to be at the hospital. Somehow I doubted things were as over in Carlos's mind as they were in my roommate's.

"What are you doing home?" I asked, taking a sip of wine and feeling its warmth rush through me.

"Waiting for you," she replied. "I called you at the office, but the night operator said you were already on your way home. I need your advice about something."

"Well, if you thought you could buy it with food, you were absolutely right," I replied. "What's up?"

"We almost lost another patient today," Claudia said.

"Oh, no!" I exclaimed. "What happened?"

"We don't know. That's the problem."

"So tell me about the patient."

"She's a sixty-seven-year-old Caucasian female named Ida Lapinsky. Indigent. History of adult-onset diabetes. Smoker. Probable history of alcoholism. She was admitted through the OB-GYN service, complaining of abdominal pain, and was subsequently diagnosed as having an intestinal obstruction. She was resting in her room following surgery this morning to remove the blockage when she suddenly and for no apparent reason went into respiratory arrest."

"Were there any complications during the surgery?"

"None. I even tracked down the resident who assisted McDermott on the case and asked him. He said the procedure was completely unremarkable."

"So what happened to Mrs. Lapinsky?"

"Like I said, nobody knows. Mrs. Lapinsky's roommate woke up from her nap and noticed that she was turning blue and not breathing. Somehow she managed to call for help. I was at the nurses' station doing some charting, so I was the one who caught the code. I grabbed the crash cart and was in Mrs. Lapinsky's room in ten seconds flat. Even so, by the time I arrived, she was unconscious, not breathing, and had no reflexes to speak of."

"So what did you do?"

"I started 100 percent oxygen, gave her two ampules of sodium bicarbonate and five milligrams of intravenous epinephrine, and began mechanical ventilation."

"And?"

"I managed to resuscitate her to the point where she was eventually able to resume breathing on her own."

"So is she okay?"

"Well, there's okay and there's okay. It's too early to tell yet what kind of deficits she might have suffered."

"What do you mean by deficits?"

"Haven't you heard the joke? 'Congratulations, doctor, the good news is you saved the patient. The bad news is she's going to need to be watered twice a day.' "

"I don't know why they always say that economics is the dismal science when it's doctors who have such a bleak worldview," I observed.

"Do you know the three rules of emergency medicine?" inquired my roommate, proceeding to tick them off on her fingers. "One: all bleeding eventually stops;

two: all patients eventually die; and three: if you drop the baby, pick it up."

"I rest my case," I said, pausing to refill our glasses. "I take it you think that what happened to Mrs. Lapinsky is somehow related to what's been happening on the surgery service?"

"You mean that our patients are dying for no good reason?" demanded my roommate with a definite edge to her voice. "I guess I'd have to say that what happened to Mrs. Lapinsky definitely fits the trend."

"But she didn't die."

"No," replied Claudia, "but she should have. It was only a fluke that I was still on the floor and therefore able to get to her so fast. I was supposed to be downstairs in the clinic already, but I'd been running behind all day."

"It was lucky you were."

"I'm not so sure. The whole thing is so bizarre. I mean, finally clearing the surgical waiting list is supposed to be the best thing that ever happened to our patients . . . not a death sentence."

"How many deaths have there been?" I asked softly.

"Five, but six respiratory arrests if you count Mrs. Lapinsky."

"How many would you expect there to be?"

"Zero, which is exactly the number the unit had until three weeks ago."

"Maybe it's some kind of virus," I ventured, "or a faulty piece of equipment. There has to be some kind of common denominator. . . ."

"There is, but you're not going to like it."

"What?"

"All the deaths, they've all been patients of Gavin McDermott."

"You're kidding," I said. Gavin McDermott was considered the hospital's most highly skilled surgeon.

He was also a flamboyant character, as famous for riding his Harley to the hospital and his serial trophy wives as he was for his virtuoso performances in the operating room. "How's he taking all of this?"

"How do you think?" replied Claudia. "By making the lives of everyone around him completely miserable, starting with mine. You should have heard him this afternoon; you'd think I'd tried to kill Mrs. Lapinsky instead of saving her." She dropped her head into her hands as if trying to shield herself from the memory.

"But why are Gavin McDermott's patients dying?"

"Nobody knows. Some people are saying that McDermott's in a slump, that maybe there's something going on in his life that's affecting his judgment—you know, marital problems, booze . . ."

"Is there?"

"How would I know? I only see him once a week when he's on trauma call. But I've got to tell you, I've never seen anything from him in the OR that would indicate that his head is anywhere except where it's supposed to be. He's flat-out the best surgeon I've ever worked with."

"What about his patients at other hospitals? Are they dying, too?"

"How would I know that? It's not exactly the sort of thing that anybody's going to advertise. God knows we're doing everything we can to keep what's going on at our hospital a secret."

"So what do you think is going on? How do you explain it?" I asked.

"I don't know," groaned Claudia, shaking her head in frustration. "But I'm starting to think that either Gavin McDermott or Prescott Memorial is just plain jinxed."

CHAPTER
3

That night after Claudia went to bed, I hauled the box of Prescott Memorial files into the dining room. The only thing standing between me and a good night's sleep was my mother and her harebrained plan to block the sale of the hospital, and I was determined to spend as little time as possible on it. Indeed, I'd already come up with a short mental list of other lawyers to recommend in my place—lawyers who'd crossed me on deals past and whose suffering at my mother's hands wouldn't cost me any sleep.

I set the box on the dining room table, a scarred monstrosity inherited from a previous tenant who'd been forced to leave it behind when there turned out to be no room for it on the moving van. In the years that we'd lived in the apartment I don't think that Claudia and I had ever eaten a meal there. Instead it was our worktable, though what I was doing on it tonight hardly qualified as work.

What I was doing was just going through the motions. With the letter of intent already signed and the deal set to close in ten days, any attempt to stop HCC was sure to be a quixotic effort. Besides, engaging in a doomed campaign against an experienced and highly motivated corporate adversary was hardly my idea of a mother-daughter bonding experience. When it came to my mother, I figured I should probably stick with what I knew best, fighting about my choice of boyfriends and what I was doing with my hair.

I was also afraid that when it came to the sale of Prescott Memorial, her motives were suspect. Unaccustomed to being crossed, Mother was simply furious at the board members who'd betrayed her by casting their votes to sell to HCC; it had less to do with her concern for patient care than her own ego. I had no interest in using up my professional capital avenging my mother's injured pride.

However, there was no way I could avoid at least looking at what she'd sent over. Not if I knew what was good for me. Fetching a knife from the block on the kitchen counter, I slit the tape that sealed the box and opened up the flaps. What I saw inside was a nightmare, not an orderly compilation of documents pertaining to the proposed sale of the hospital, but rather every piece of paper in my mother's possession that was remotely related to the hospital dumped together into a box. I gave it a shake in disgust. It was obvious what importance my mother, whose social calendar was as meticulously laid out as the timetable for a NASA launch, attached to the affairs of Prescott Memorial Hospital.

Eager to be done with the entire charade, I picked up the box and dumped the contents out onto the table. Mixed in with the business documents were envelopes that had never been opened, scribbled notes for seating charts, and an assortment of to-do lists filled with such gripping entries as *lunch with Bitsy* and *fitting at Chanel*. The writing was all in my mother's characteristic backward slanting script. On several pages the margins were thick with the elaborate curlicues and fleurs-de-lis that she liked to doodle when she was bored.

The phone rang just as I was finishing up separating out the junk. I looked at the clock, deciding whether to answer. I was too tired to get up for one of Carlos's hang-up calls, but there was always a chance that it might be Elliott. Feeling optimistic, I got to my feet and caught it by the fourth ring and was rewarded by the sound of Elliott Abelman's voice, husky with fatigue, on the other end of the line.

"Are you okay?" he asked. It was his standard greeting, a holdover from the days when I called him only when I was in some kind of trouble.

I'd first met Elliott three years ago when I'd hired him as a private investigator. A former prosecutor and an ex-marine, Elliott had just struck out on his own and was as eager to please as he was happy for a piece of Callahan Ross's business. Since then, Abelman & Associates had become one of the premiere operations of its kind in the country. Employing nearly a hundred full-time investigators in three cities, Elliott's firm specialized in financial crimes—bid rigging, bribery, computer theft, and embezzlement—the kinds of bloodless offenses that police and prosecutors were ill equipped to handle.

"How's it going with the trial?" I asked, sliding my back down along the wall until I was sitting comfortably on the floor.

Now that Elliott and I were finally free to see what it would be like to spend time together, circumstances had conspired to keep us apart. A complicated fraud case he'd worked on for two years had finally gone to trial in the ninth circuit downstate in Springfield. In addition to providing testimony about the investigation conducted by his firm, Elliott had also been retained as a consultant by the counsel for the plaintiff. For the last four months he'd been living at the Ramada Inn with the rest of the legal team and trying to run his business on the weekends. Our only contact was made up of the occasional late-night phone call and one or two hurried lunch dates on days when he'd breezed back into town for a few hours.

"In terms of the trial, things are pretty intense," he replied. "We're actually just taking a ten-minute break. The defense gets our guy on cross tomorrow, and we still have a lot to do before we're ready."

"How did it go on direct?"

"I'll tell you when we're done with the cross."

"Doesn't it make you miss it?"

"Miss what?"

"Trying cases yourself," I replied.

"Oh, I don't know. Only when I think I'd do it better."

"And would you?"

"Right now, Carlson's doing a pretty good job for our side. I'll give you my final verdict after closing arguments on Friday."

"So you think you'll go to the jury on Friday?"

"Don't worry. I'll be there Saturday night. I promise."

"I'm not worried," I assured him. I let a beat pass. "Are you?"

"To quote my favorite modern existentialist philosopher, 'What? Me worry?' I mean, what on earth could possibly concern me about the evening? Just because it's our very first official date and I'm going to meet your entire family while dressed in a rented tuxedo—"

"So I guess you've definitely decided to go with the rental then?" I asked, unable to help myself.

"Oh, come on, Kate. You don't really expect me to drop that kind of money on a suit I'm only going to wear once, do you? Besides, I went to the tux shop down here by the courthouse, and I've got to tell you, the polyester ones look pretty good. I even got the guy to throw in a pair of shoes for free."

"I'm dying to see you," I said, pushing all thought of what my mother was going to have to say about rented shoes out of my mind.

"I know," replied Elliott, "I can hardly wait."

I sat on the floor for a long time, cradling the receiver in my hand and thinking about Elliott. Better than almost anyone, I knew that life turns on a dime. Even so, it seemed remarkable to me that it had come to this. In November it would be six years since my husband Russell died of brain cancer, a year for every month that we were married. What would he have thought of the mess I'd made with Stephen and Elliott and all the rest of it?

In my heart I prayed he'd have understood. Russell, even when he knew he was dying, believed the world was an enormous place, filled with limitless possibilities. The son of a Polish immigrant, a tailor who read philosophy at night and named his son after the philosopher Bertrand Russell, he'd laughed out loud as he'd swept me up the aisle after we'd said "I do." Later, on the church steps, as the four hundred guests strewed our way with rose petals, I'd asked him what he'd found so funny. He'd stretched his arms wide, taking it all in, the top hats and the limousines, his mother with her fresh perm and prim polyester dress standing beside my mother in her Givenchy, both women quietly sobbing. "If this isn't proof that God has a sense of humor," he'd declared, "then I don't know what is."

I'd spent six years trying not to ask what God was thinking when he'd given my husband brain cancer, six years filled with work and obligation spent trying not to think of how it all might have turned out differently. Russell had been dead two years before I was tempted back into Stephen Azorini's bed, but from the beginning I viewed it as an accommodation rather than an act of betrayal.

For a long time it had somehow seemed to work. Stephen was as committed to building his company as I was to my practice. Social obligations were strictly quid pro quo with the difference worked out in bed. On the surface we were the quintessential power couple, accomplished, photogenic (at least in Stephen's case), and unencumbered by the inconvenience of obligation or emotion.

I don't know what I was thinking when I agreed to move in with him. Certainly as an attorney I should have known better, but I think I was just dazzled by the view. In the hundred years since the building had been erected, the apartment had come on the market only twice. A Gold Coast duplex with lake views in three directions, its first owners had been my grandparents, who'd commissioned David Adler, the legendary architect, to design the interior. I'd lived there until I was six years old and my parents decided to forsake the excitement of the city for the sylvan pleasures of suburban Lake Forest. Convinced we'd never have the chance again, we wrote the check and embarked on a yearlong renovation. The only trouble was that by the time the plaster was dry, I knew that I would never live there with Stephen.

But as any lawyer will tell you, things only get more complicated when you start picking them apart. It had taken two months of negotiations to buy back Stephen's half of the apartment, longer still to straighten out the mess of contractors' bills and decorator's invoices. It was like going through a divorce without the benefit of ever having been married, and in the end the whole thing had left me emotionally exhausted.

So for now the big apartment on the lake sat empty and perfect, like a layout for *Architectural Digest*. For now, I was in no hurry to move in. The idea of taking up residence in a two-story apartment the size of a large house was going to take some getting used to. Besides, I'd agreed to stay on in the Hyde Park apartment with Claudia until her fellowship was over at the end of June. Her dream job was already waiting for her, a faculty appointment at Columbia's medical school.

I hoisted myself wearily to my feet and dragged myself back into the dining room. If the fact that I already have my dream job isn't proof that God had a sense of humor, I told myself, nothing else is.

I poured myself the last of the wine and gave myself over to the documents my mother had sent me. When I first started out at the firm, my old mentor, John Guttman, used to lecture me about finding the story of a file, the dramatic thread that ran through a particular matter. He believed that when you stripped away the dry terminology and the rigid structure of the legal forms, even the most unexceptional transactions contained the elements of drama.

Back then I thought he was crazy, that he'd spent so much time drafting prospectuses and parsing proxy statements that it had affected his brain. But lately I'd come to realize that he was right. Tonight I was even doing it myself, piecing together the fragments of the story and looking for the nuances in what had been left unsaid.

I began by reading through a sheaf of newspaper clippings I'd found at the bottom of the box. I don't know who was responsible for compiling them, but there was no doubt they presented an interesting picture of the Health Care Corporation of America. HCC was a company that likened medical specialties to product lines and had pioneered the practice of providing financial incentives to physicians and administrators for meeting

financial performance targets. Not unexpectedly, shareholders were ecstatic with the company's performance,
while the medical community was substantially less impressed. A *Wall Street Journal* profile of the company's
acquisition of a string of community hospitals in Duluth
seemed to exemplify HCC's style of operation.

Within an eight-month period Health Care Corporation, under the guidance of CEO Gerald Packman, bought
eight of the twelve hospitals serving the greater Duluth
area. Once they effectively controlled the number of beds,
they began slashing costs across the board, negotiating
discounts with suppliers, centralizing administrative operations, and dramatically cutting the number of beds. They
closed three hospitals completely. They also eliminated
overtime, cut the staff of registered nurses by a third, and
began limiting patient access to unprofitable tests and
treatments. The unspoken conclusion of the article was
that under the HCC system, profitability went up as the
quality of patient care came down.

But Prescott Memorial was not the same as a community hospital in Duluth. It was a charitable teaching hospital as committed to providing care to an indigent
inner-city population as it was to educating new doctors.
It was also a trauma center, one of the seven hospitals
within the city limits that was tied to the 911 system.
What that meant was that at Prescott Memorial they had
not just a ready operating room, but surgeons, anesthesi-
ologists, and a full blood bank ready round the clock.

Claudia had laid out the practical implications of this
when I'd questioned the efficiency of keeping a trauma
team on twenty-four-hour call. She'd explained that
when someone has a bullet in their heart, the only place
they can be treated is in an operating room. If they are
taken to another hospital in the city, they may have
equally skilled surgeons, but it might take them thirty-

five or forty-five minutes to mobilize their operating room, and with each minute that elapses for a critical patient, the potential for survival falls dramatically.

In the parlance of HCC, trauma care was one of Prescott Memorial Hospital's strongest product lines. It was also one of its least profitable. As I waded through the last three years' financial statements I could easily understand HCC's appeal to Kyle Massius, Prescott Memorial's president. For him, the sale represented deliverance from the constant begging and scraping for donations, a transition to operating on solid financial ground.

Indeed, the more I read, the less I questioned the three board members' eagerness to jump on the HCC bandwagon. Instead, what puzzled me was that HCC would want to take on the financial burden of Prescott Memorial Hospital at all. Did they really think that they could squeeze a profit out of providing trauma care, or were they planning on shutting down the trauma center altogether in order to provide moneymaking services to Medicaid patients?

While it did nothing to shed light on their motives, a careful reading of the proposed purchase agreement between HCC and Prescott Memorial Hospital made one thing perfectly clear: HCC was no novice when it came to this kind of transaction. There was none of the amorphous, let's-cover-our-asses-just-in-case language that you usually find in a company's first time through a particular kind of deal. Indeed, every document generated by HCC was an impervious construction, one that had obviously been passed through many hands and tightened by able minds.

The time frame that HCC had set out for the deal also disturbed me. Despite HCC's reputation for moving quickly, I still would have expected the purchase of an asset as complex as a hospital to take longer than ten days to complete. Indeed, two years before, when North-western Memorial Hospital had approached Prescott Memorial about merging into their system, the two hospitals had negotiated off and on for six months before deciding not to come to terms. Now HCC proposed to do a similar deal in less than two weeks. Not only that, but there were steep financial penalties built into the agreement for even the most trifling delays. Perhaps it was fatigue clouding my judgment, but the reasons for this eluded me. The use of this kind of fast clock was usually reserved for deals where there was another buyer waiting in the wings. But Prescott Memorial wasn't even up for sale, which meant that it was unlikely that HCC's haste could be attributed to the fear of competing bidders.

All of this was even more perplexing in light of the hospital's financial situation. Health Care Corporation was the self-proclaimed leader in the field of for-profit medicine. What did they want with a hospital whose balance sheet painted a picture that could best be described as hand-to-mouth? While all of this merely buttressed my decision to not get involved, as I slowly returned the documents to the box I couldn't help but wonder: What on earth did HCC want with Prescott Memorial Hospital, and even more importantly, why were they in such a big hurry?

CHAPTER

4

The next day was an exercise in frustration. While Cheryl kept my mother at bay with a series of increasingly inventive excuses, I found my efforts to reestablish negotiations with Icon deflected every bit as deftly. Under other circumstances I might have appreciated the symmetry of the situation or at least admitted that it served me right for being a coward. But the stakes for Delirium were much too high—something that Mark Millman and Bill Delius had both taken pains to point out separately and at great length.

Summoning the associates who'd been working on Delirium to my office, I set them to work drafting a tentative term sheet based on our negotiations so far, even though I didn't think we'd ever use it. Besides wanting to keep morale up, I needed to keep them busy. Whenever there was a lull in the action, there was a danger that one of my partners would snag them for another assignment, leaving me scrambling if things with Icon suddenly heated back up.

Afterward I asked Jeff Tannenbaum to stay behind. Jeff was an experienced associate who'd been working with me on Delirium from the beginning. Together we tried to figure out a way to reach out to Gabriel Hurt and rekindle his lust for Delirium's new technology. I used the word *lust* deliberately.

The truth is, even I had to admit that what Bill Delius had developed was sexy. It was a new integrated language-based input device designed to free the computer user from having to use a keyboard or mouse. A tiny video camera mounted on the edge of the monitor tracked the user's voice and movements and, using proprietary software, translated the visual and auditory information into commands the computer could understand. You could literally look at an icon on the screen and command the computer to open it.

Developing the technology had been a tremendous undertaking, Bill Delius's personal grail, the altar upon which he'd sacrificed everything: his marriage, his life savings, and sometimes, I feared, his sanity. Now its success or failure rested at the whim of a sole eccentric billionaire whose people wouldn't even return my calls. I was beginning to feel as though the term *computer business* was an oxymoron.

My thoughts kept turning back to sex. Maybe it was because it was the only thing I could think of that came close to the intensity and desire that fueled high-tech companies' search for the next big thing. Or maybe it was because I knew that it would take something besides stiletto heels and a leather miniskirt to capture a man like Icon's founder's attention. Besides, I wasn't interested in Hurt's body—I don't think anyone was—what I wanted was to catch his eye and kindle his desire.

I had Jeff pull out the file of clippings I'd had him compile on Hurt. We divided it in half and silently pawed through them, looking for anything that might be used as a lever.

I was about to give up when an old article about Hurt's days at MIT caught my eye. Describing those sleepless, seminal days as a graduate student whose Ph.D. dissertation would revolutionize software and the world, Hurt described his existence as a code-writing marathon punctuated only by pizza delivery and impromptu pinball tournaments. The interview included a two-paragraph quote in which he waxed with a mixture of lyricism and nostalgia about the Dark Invader pinball game he and his roommate played in the basement.

It took Jeff under twenty minutes to find one of the pinball machines on an Internet auction site that could be, by paying an obscene premium, delivered to Chicago by afternoon. I knew it didn't qualify as a great idea, but it was the only one I had, so I handed Jeff my American Express card and sat down to draft a letter to Hurt. Taping the interview to the bottom of my computer screen, I found myself looking at the photograph of Hurt that had run with the article. I knew he had to be in his twenties when it was taken, but he still looked like a little kid, the nerdy kind who accumulates a little cloud of spittle at the corner of his mouth and never gets picked to play baseball even though he knows every box score. Perhaps because he looked so goofy, I decided to go with an oddball approach. In less than an hour I'd composed a poem in iambic pentameter equating Delirium's quest for a joint venture with Icon to the quest of the hero of the Dark Invader game.

"No guts, no glory," I said out loud to myself as I typed in the command that sent it to the printer. "Now if only I could find something to rhyme with *orange*."

While Cheryl and Jeff tried to figure out the logistics of wrapping a pinball machine and having it delivered to the Four Seasons, I slipped out for lunch. After all, partnership *does* have its privileges. Besides, Joan Bornstein never asked me out to lunch without an ulterior motive, and as usual, I was dying to find out what it was.

Joan was a litigator, a high-priced, high-profile medical-malpractice attorney whose skill at defending prominent physicians and hospitals accused of wrongdoing was surpassed only by her talent for promoting herself. Joan had picked Nick's Fishmarket, a see-and-be-seen power-lunch spot whose deep, secluded booths have long been favored by LaSalle Street deal makers. It was the kind of place that Joan liked, a place where everybody from the busboy to the maître d' knew her by name and treated her like a celebrity. As I expected, by the time I arrived, I found her at the best table, holding court with a bunch of insurance types who'd stopped on their way out the door. At the sight of me they moved on, and she made a half-hearted effort to get to her feet, offering up air kisses and exclamations of pleasure at seeing me.

Joan always looked like she was about to step in front of the cameras. With her dark hair and telegenic red suit, she was less pretty than handsome, but struck a memorable figure nonetheless. She was also one of those people who somehow manages to look better on television than in person. Her strong features were somehow softened by the intervention of the camera, and as fond as I was of her, even I had to admit that hers was a personality best appreciated in sound bites. Today she was, as always, impeccably made up and expensively dressed. She was also, by the look of things, about seven months pregnant.

"Long time no see," I remarked, sliding into the booth across from her. "It looks like you and Adam have both been keeping busy." Adam was Joan's husband, a North Shore obstetrician with a gilded practice.

Joan patted her stomach. "I think this is going to be one of the hazards of being Adam's wife. He always tells people we're going to keep on having kids because the delivery room is the only place where I'll let him tell me what to do."

"So how does little Jared feel about all of this?" I asked.

"Oh, he's excited about having a little brother to push around," she replied. "But I didn't ask you out to lunch to talk about babies and potty training. That's what I go to the office to get away from." She leaned across the table conspiratorially. "I wanted to talk about the sale of Prescott Memorial to HCC."

I was so surprised I practically choked on my ice water.

"Oh, come on," she continued. "Don't pretend you don't know that the board of trustees signed a letter of intent yesterday."

"If they did, then I'm sure they also signed a confidentiality agreement," I pointed out. "You wouldn't be telling me this as if it's an accomplished fact, hoping to trick me into confirming it's true?" I asked, being all too familiar with Joan's courtroom wiles.

"Believe me, Kate. Being a mother has made me a much better lawyer. After all, medicine is a lot like nursery school. No matter what, somebody *always* tells."

"So what makes you think I'd want to talk about it?" I asked.

"Because your mother has been publicly associated with raising funds for the hospital her entire adult life. Because your family is the biggest single financial supporter of the hospital."

"And?"

"And if they knew what I know about HCC, they would turn and run the other way."

"In that case I think you'd better tell me what you know about HCC," I suggested.

"For one thing, they're evil."

"Oh, well, I'll just go right ahead and take that to the

board," I said, helping myself to rolls and butter. "I'm sure that'll persuade them."

"Okay, Miss Smarty Pants, why don't you tell me what it is that you know about HCC?"

"Not much," I replied truthfully, "only what I managed to read last night."

"In that case, let me test the limits of your knowledge. Question one. Why does HCC have its headquarters in Atlanta?"

"I have no idea, but I'm sure you'll tell me."

"I'll give you a hint. They don't own any hospitals there, but it's where Quickie-Mart, Circle Seven, and French's New Orleans Style Fried Chicken all happen to have their national headquarters."

"I still don't get it. What does any of that have to do with HCC?"

"You really weren't kidding when you said you don't know much, were you? Those are all the companies that Gerald Packman worked for before he decided to strike out on his own and start Health Care Corporation. It only seems natural, doesn't it, that having conquered the world of convenience markets and fried-chicken franchises that he'd want to share his unique vision with the health care industry?"

"What vision is that?"

"Oh, you know, the usual. Cost cutting, consolidation, taking the paper clips off your memos before you throw them in the trash—all the stuff that gives accountants hard-ons and is pretty much meaningless when it comes to medicine."

"What makes you so sure it's meaningless?" I demanded.

"Because in health care what is ultimately at stake is lives, not dollars."

"A business is a business," I countered, not at all

happy with the direction this conversation was taking. "It doesn't matter whether it delivers bagels or babies."

"Tell that to Adam's patient, the one whose baby was born with a heart defect last night. Her insurance company refuses to cover the cost of a new, less invasive surgery to correct it because it costs too much."

"Okay, I grant you the difference between babies and bagels, but that still doesn't mean that health care isn't a business."

"Then I guess it's time for quiz question number two. In one sentence or less, describe the mission of Prescott Memorial Hospital."

"To deliver high-quality health care to patients in need, regardless of their ability to pay," I answered, repeating the catechism without hesitation.

"Very good. So now tell me, what's HCC's mission?"

"I don't know," I replied, growing weary of this interrogation. "To deliver cost-effective health care to people who *can* pay?"

"Wrong answer. You just said it a minute ago. A business is a business. HCC's mission is to maximize profits for their shareholders. Period."

"So?"

"So that's what makes them evil," declared Joan passionately. "Medicine may be a business, but it's not like any other business. If you walk into Saks to buy a dress and you don't like the way they treat you, you can always walk down the street to Neiman Marcus. But when you're sick and helpless, you're in no position to go down the street. That's why, whether you can pay for it or not, you pray you're in a place like Prescott Memorial where everyone is working their butt off to give you the best possible care instead of an HCC hospital where all they're worried about is squeezing the maximum profit out of you in the shortest amount of time."

Suddenly I thought about Claudia, who attacked her job with a selfless dedication approaching mania.

"The doctors I know wouldn't have anything to do with a place that treated patients like that," I protested.

"You'd be surprised," said Joan in a tone of voice that told me she'd long ago been stripped of such illusions. "Doctors have their price just like anybody else. If they didn't, HCC wouldn't have been able to do what they've done. Everywhere they've gone, the company has made it worthwhile for the docs to roll over for them."

"In what way worth their while?"

"Kickbacks and insider contracts. Everyone knows that HCC gives bonuses to the doctors who perform more of the procedures that provide the highest profit margins and to the administrators who have the fewest empty beds. That's why HCC hospitals take more X-rays, do more MRIs, and perform more hysterectomies on average than other hospitals. Conversely, they see fewer emergency patients and have a policy of shunting off the indigent to noncompany facilities."

"Then what on earth could they possibly want with Prescott Memorial?" I demanded. "All they have is indigent patients."

"Oh, HCC isn't looking to make money from Prescott Memorial," answered Joan, "at least not in the short run."

"Okay, now you've really got me confused," I protested. "Just a second ago you had me convinced that all HCC was interested in was making money."

"They are. You're just not looking at the big picture. Don't you see? Acquiring Prescott Memorial is just the first part of a much larger plan."

"Which is?"

"To buy the company a foothold in Chicago. Think about it. HCC may be a $16 billion company, but they're doing all their business in places like Omaha and Dubuque. By buying Prescott Memorial, HCC is making their first move into a major metropolitan market."

"Why? What does it matter where they make their money?"

"You want to know why? Because Gerald Packman is an arrogant son of a bitch who actually believes that he's found a better way, and like every other arrogant son of a bitch who's come before him, he wants to shove it down everybody else's throat whether they like it or not."

After lunch I took the long way back to the office, pausing to admire the Chagall mural on the First National Bank Building as I tried to sift through everything that Joan Bornstein had just told me. The trouble was that Joan was a partisan by profession, a well-known and outspoken opponent of the constraints placed on the traditional freedoms enjoyed by physicians. Just like my mother, she had her own agenda.

When I finally got back to my office, I was surprised to find my door shut and the sound of voices coming from within. Puzzled, I shucked off my raincoat and ventured toward the door. Turning the handle slowly, I pushed it open to reveal a vaguely disturbing tableau—Cheryl, dressed in a dark blue suit that had once been mine, looking very much at home behind my desk. From the looks of things, she appeared to be conducting an interview with a very animated young woman whose hair looked like it had been cut by a poodle groomer.

I caught my secretary's eye and offered up an inquisitive glance. In response she shot me one of her don't-even-ask looks and promptly turned her attention back to the fascinating young woman with the strange hair. "Now, were there any other questions I can answer for you about the kinds of work involved?" she asked in an obvious effort to draw the interview to a close.

"Well . . . ," began the young woman rather tentatively, but it was too late. Cheryl was already on her feet and moving toward the door.

"It's been a pleasure meeting you," continued Cheryl, shepherding her toward the door.

"It's been really neat meeting you, Ms. Millholland," gushed the young woman, ignoring me and speaking to my secretary. "I just want you to know that if I *do* get the job, I know it would, like, work out to be super for both of us, you know?"

"I'm so sorry I'm late coming back from lunch, Ms. Millholland," I piped in, my voice dripping with contrition. "I promise it won't happen again. Would you like me to show the job candidate out?"

"That would be very nice of you," replied Cheryl, struggling valiantly to control her face.

I took my time showing the hapless young woman to the door, ducking through the library and taking a detour through the trusts and estate department to give us time to chat. As we walked I managed to learn that her name was Amber and that she wanted to work as a legal secretary only until she'd saved enough money to pay for electrolysis school. I must confess, I entertained myself further by regaling her with stories about what a harridan "Ms. Millholland" really was to work for, complete with anecdotes about temper tantrums and punitive overtime.

By the time I got back to my office, I found that my secretary had not only resumed her usual seat but also fetched fresh coffee for the both of us.

"It would almost be worth hiring her just to see her face on the first day," I announced as I settled in behind my desk.

"No, it wouldn't," replied Cheryl. "I guarantee you

you'd strangle her inside of a week. The woman has the IQ of a rutabaga. I hope you don't mind what I did, but you still weren't back from lunch and you're already on Mrs. Goodlow's shit list."

"What makes you say that?" I asked, wondering what on earth I'd done this time to get on the wrong side of Callahan Ross's imperious office manager.

"I'm afraid you've violated the three-strikes rule."

"And what, pray tell, is that?"

"One of the things I'm really going to miss about this place is the way that the lawyers are always the last ones to figure out how things really work around here. The three-strikes rule, as in three strikes and you're out, means that you're expected to choose one of the first three applicants that Mrs. Goodlow sends you to interview."

"And if you don't?" I demanded, doing some rapid calculating in my head and ending up in double digits.

"Then she decides that you're just being unreasonable, and to prove her point, she starts sending you terrible applicants until you come crawling on your knees to her office and beg for mercy, which, by the way, is exactly what she always wanted in the first place."

"Great," I complained. "So what you're telling me is that unless I pick somebody soon, I'm going to end up interviewing Chi-Chi the Chimp Girl and her fun-loving family of primate personal assistants."

"I'd say that pretty much sums up your current situation."

"Wonderful. Now tell me the good news."

"Your mother's called twice since you came back from lunch." I meant to groan, but instead it came out as a kind of plaintive keening sound. "She sounded even more annoyed than usual. What's going on with her, anyway? Are you really going to try to stop the sale of the hospital?"

"Do I look like an insane person to you?" I demanded.

"I elect to exercise my rights under the Fifth Amendment on the grounds that a truthful answer may have an adverse impact on any future job-performance evaluations."

"Thanks for that vote of confidence," I cracked, "but in response to your question, no, I am not. Not only is my mother's name to be found in the legal dictionary under the heading *client from hell,* but trying to block the sale of Prescott Memorial would be like trying to stop a locomotive by standing on the tracks."

"Then what do you want me to tell your mother when she calls?"

"I'll give you fifty bucks if you tell her that I've fled the country under an assumed name."

Cheryl gazed balefully around the office, her eyes traveling from the pink message slips that littered my desk like confetti to the stacks of files that lay in ramparts, covering every available surface.

"I have a better idea," she suggested. "Why don't I give you a hundred and you take me with you?"

CHAPTER

5

Now that the pinball machine was on its way to the Four Seasons, I found myself having second thoughts. It wasn't so much that I was afraid that Hurt wouldn't want it. If he didn't, I figured I always had room for it in the new apartment. It was more that I didn't want to look foolish—no, scratch that, desperate—in the eyes of Jeff and the other associates who'd been working on Delirium. Large law firms like Callahan Ross are like feudal kingdoms, where the number of knights you control reveals the size of your castle. While far from power hungry, I still had no desire to embarrass myself in front of the troops.

In the meantime I had other clients, clients who all had one thing in common—they expected to have their phone calls returned. As I worked my way through a three-day backlog of messages, I found myself glad to be diverted by other matters. I was also glad that Bill Delius and Mark Millman were busy at the COMDEX show at McCormack Place since it kept them from calling to ask what I was doing to resurrect negotiations with Icon. Under the circumstances I wasn't sure I wanted to tell them.

I don't know what made me think that Gabriel Hurt

would call. The telephone was hardly his métier, but nonetheless every time Cheryl buzzed to tell me I had a call, I felt a small jolt of adrenaline followed by the inevitable letdown of disappointment. It was just chance that I thought to check my e-mail. Usually I left it to Cheryl to sort through the interoffice spam, but Cheryl had another interview, so I logged on and gave it a cursory scroll.

The message from Hurt was very cool. When I clicked it open, a character that I recognized from the Dark Invaders pinball game appeared on the screen, walked forward, and knelt before me, beckoning with a graceful gesture of his hand. Unlike the figure illuminated on the back panel of the game, this warrior was three dimensional and astonishingly real. Behind him loomed an enormous iron gate whose intricately wrought arch spelled out the word ENTER.

Clicking my way through it, I was treated to a performance by three brightly clothed computer-generated figures from the game, doing impossible handsprings and acrobatics. Finally they scampered off, and a herald in rich medieval garb took their place and blew a fanfare. Lowering his horn, he unfurled a parchment scroll, which he seemed to turn for me to read. Written in Gothic script and beautifully illuminated in the margins, Gabriel Hurt's message thanked me for my gift and invited me "and my seconds from Delirium" for a Dark Invader tournament at the Four Seasons "commencing at nine o'clock this evening." I whooped my way down the hall to Jeff Tannenbaum's office to tell him about our summons from the king. Delighted, I told him that he needed to figure out a way to get in touch with Delius and Millman right away, even if it meant going down to McCormack Place with a bullhorn. Rolling his eyes, Jeff punched up the numbers he had for the two men on his computer Rolodex, but before he dialed, he fished a single sheet of paper from the in-tray on his desk and handed it to me.

"What's this?" I demanded, scanning the sheet on which were the names and addresses of what looked like three different bars.

"The only places within city limits that still have a working Dark Invaders game," he replied. "Their machines aren't in the same kind of cherry condition as the one we sent Hurt, but I figured they'd do for you."

"For me what?" I demanded.

"For you to practice."

Three hours and seventeen dollars in quarters and all I had to show for it was a matching set of blisters on my thumbs from working the flippers on the Dark Invaders machine at Mother's, the yuppie watering hole on Division. If that wasn't bad enough, my head ached from tracking the quicksilver ball and my ears rang from the game's incessant mechanical chirping. The only consolation was that I was billing the time to the Delirium file, which meant that if and when we made the deal with Icon, Gabriel Hurt would wind up paying for my crash course in his favorite game.

Unfortunately, I still wasn't any good. I suspected that pinball, like an appreciation of the Three Stooges, was one of those exclusively Y-chromosome activities. Not that it mattered. Tonight's "tournament" was like being invited to join in a pickup game of hoops with Michael Jordan. You went in knowing that you were going to get killed.

While I was busy dropping quarters at Mother's, Jeff managed to track down Bill Delius, who was attending the COMDEX engineering banquet. According to Jeff, Delius was so excited by the news that he practically

hyperventilated. I planned on using the drive from
COMDEX to the Four Seasons to deliver a little seminar
on the importance of keeping cool and the hidden costs
of gushing.

Like Soldier Field and the Field Museum of Natural
History, McCormack Place was one of those landmarks I
passed by every day but seldom visited. Yet in the years
since I'd first moved to Hyde Park, I'd watched the city's
convention center spread and mutate like a fungus. From
a simple, albeit gigantic rectangle of smoked glass and
steel, it now squatted on both sides of Lake Shore Drive.
With completion of the latest, most ambitious phase of
construction, it now resembled not so much a public
building as a space station, self-contained and turned
inward on itself against an inhospitable environment.
Futuristic walkways connected the far-flung buildings,
while the exhibition halls were linked by a catacomb of
underground service passages. When I thought about it, I
realized that the building was the nightmare stuff of
childhood, the kind of place one might venture into and
yet never emerge from alive.

Millman was supposedly having dinner downtown
with a group of Japanese businessmen and therefore un-
reachable. I had no way of knowing if this was true. I suspected that Delius wanted to have Gabriel Hurt all to
himself. As far as I was concerned, it was probably better
that way. As when dealing with two-year-olds, I found
that it was easier to handle the Delirium partners one at
a time.

But when I pulled into the service drive on the west
side of the building, there was no sign of Bill Delius.
Wretchedly certain that he was panicking in front of
a distant door in some other part of the building, I
punched in the number of his cell phone. But before I
could press SEND, I spotted him in the shadows. He was

sitting on the edge of a waist-high concrete planter. He was mopping at his brow with a handkerchief.

"Oh, no," I groaned. Even from a distance I could see that he looked drunk. The couple of times I'd had dinner with them I'd noticed that Millman was a hard drinker of the old school, but I'd thought Delius didn't drink alcohol at all. Obviously I'd been mistaken.

I got out of the car and crossed the concrete plaza toward him, wondering how on earth I was going to get him sobered up in time, when it occurred to me that instead of being drunk, he'd probably been mugged. The area south of the Loop around McCormack Place was the current hotbed of gentrification, but it was also still gang turf. That was the reason that conventioneers were funneled in and out of only a handful of entrances. It was also why the long lines of cars and unwieldy crowds sent convention veterans scrambling for alternate exits.

"Hey, Bill," I said when I got close to him. "Are you okay?"

"Oh, Kate, it's you," he said. He sounded startled to find me there. As usual, he was dressed entirely in black. Indeed, every time I'd seen him, Bill Delius had been wearing exactly the same thing: black trousers, a black single-pocket T-shirt, and a black blazer. Even his shoes were invariably the same. When I'd asked him about it, he explained that whenever he found something that he liked, he stuck with it. As for his shoes, there was something of a story behind them. He'd initially bought the black canvas slip-ons because they were comfortable and cheap. But when he learned that Sears was planning to discontinue the style, he'd used the several thousand dollars he'd made as a graduate student—by selling his solution to Rubik's Cube through a small ad in *The New York Times*—to buy every pair in his size that the retailer still had in stock. Shyly he'd confided that he had enough pairs left to last the rest of his life, with one pair set aside to be buried in.

As Bill Delius rose unsteadily to his feet he tried to stuff his handkerchief back into his pocket, but he kept on missing.

"Are you okay?" I inquired.

"Sure. Fine."

"You don't look so fine."

"I'm okay, really. Something I ate at dinner didn't agree with me, that's all," he complained. "I'm usually pretty strict about what I'll eat, but tonight I was so excited, I'm afraid I threw caution to the wind."

I was tempted to tell him that whatever he'd washed it down with probably hadn't helped, but I held my tongue and helped him to his feet, taking him by the elbow and gently steering him in the direction of my car.

As we passed under the streetlight I couldn't help but notice that his skin was not just pale, but a pasty shade of green—one that I'd had an opportunity to see quite a bit of in college, usually right before the one afflicted tossed their dinner. I slowed my pace, hoping that if he was going to throw up, he'd do it before he got into my car.

We were almost to the door when he lunged for me. At first I thought it was an attempt at ardor, only clumsier and more blatant than the guys who'd hit on me while I played the pinball machine at Mother's. But as soon as I got a clear look at his face, pouring sweat and in a rictus of agony, I realized that what was happening was infinitely worse. As if to confirm my worst fears, Bill Delius suddenly staggered as if he'd been struck in the chest, let out a feral cry of agony, and then collapsed to the pavement like a dropped marionette.

Even before he hit the sidewalk I began calculating the alternatives: the distance to the ballroom where the com-

puter wizards were still dining and the likelihood that
there was a physician among them; the time it would
take for an ambulance to respond to a 911 call; the
chance of the paramedics finding us amid the hundreds
of doors to the sprawling convention center; and, of
course, the probability of my being able to keep him alive
using CPR until they did.

I knew a little bit about heart attacks. While I was still
their chief legal counsel, Stephen's company had been
seeking FDA approval for a portable defibrillation device, the equivalent of jumper cables for the heart, designed to be used in situations just like this one. While I
wished desperately that I had one now, the information
gleaned from that time all came back to me with startling
clarity. I knew that CPR alone would not restart his
heart. The only way to save him was to get him to the
hospital.

To this day I don't know how I managed to get Delius
into the car. Even though he was thin, he was well over
six feet and he was dead weight. It took all my strength
to just drag him the few steps to the car and shovel him
into the front seat. Within ten seconds of shutting the
passenger door behind him, I was on my way to Prescott
Memorial Hospital with the gas pedal to the floor,
putting the limits of British engineering to the test.

I dialed 911 from my car phone, weaving wildly
through the late-night traffic, struggling to make myself
understood to the police dispatcher through my agitation. Passing Soldier Field, I caught sight of flashing
lights in my rearview mirror and slammed my hands
against the steering wheel in frustration, thinking the police meant to pull me over. It took me a couple of seconds
and the dispatcher's reassurance to realize that the patrol
car was there to hasten, not hinder, our progress to the
trauma center.

When I pulled up beneath the bright lights of the emergency room entrance, the trauma team was already assembled and waiting like the pit crew at an Indy race. Even before I came to a stop, they swarmed the passenger side and had Delius out of the car and onto a gurney. I got out of the car and watched the rapid grace and military precision with which every person went about their job. The whole transition—from car to gurney to hospital— happened so fast that it wasn't until the automatic doors had closed behind them that I realized that it was my roommate, Claudia, who was on the other end of the stethoscope pressed against Bill Delius's chest.

On the street, Prescott Memorial Hospital is called the Knife and Gun Club—something I hadn't known until Claudia told me. It wasn't the kind of thing they put in the glossy brochures they send out when they're looking for donations. It's also a piece of information that I've never felt the need to pass along to my mother. Her vision of Prescott Memorial was of a sunlit clinic where crippled children learned to walk again. While I understood that it was in no one's best interest to disillusion her, passing through the double doors to the emergency room I found myself wondering how she'd managed to believe the fiction all these years.

Tonight the waiting room was filled with the usual badnews ER crowd. Babies cried, drunks complained, and the air was filled with clashing odors characteristic to all hospitals: the salt smell of blood and the acid stench of vomit mingled with cleaning solution and the unmistakable scent of fear. A young woman in black fishnet stockings and a miniskirt so short it seemed to come up to her throat leaned against the wall holding a clump of bloody gauze to a laceration on her head. In an adjacent hallway a couple of drunks were sleeping it off on gurneys. I looked around to get my bearings and realized that compared to my office at Callahan Ross, my roommate went off to work every day into the Black Hole of Calcutta.

I felt at loose ends and wasn't quite sure what to do. I knew that I should probably try to call the Icon suite at the Four Seasons, but I couldn't bring myself to do it. I was still trying to convince myself to pick up the phone when the mechanical doors to the business end of the ER whooshed open and a young man in the short white coat of an intern hurried over to me. He looked barely old enough to shave.

"Were you the one who brought in the coronary arrest?" he demanded without preamble.

"Mr. Delius? Yes. I brought him in," I stammered, alarmed by the raw urgency in his manner.

"Then you'd better come with me," he instructed. "The doctor has some questions."

I opened my mouth to say that I hoped that I would be able to answer them, but by the time my mouth began to form the words I was already looking at his back, retreating through the doors that separated the waiting area from the treatment rooms. I hurried up and followed him into the first room—trauma one—a bad sign. This was Claudia's kingdom, the room they held open for the most serious injuries, the place where they kept all the heavy-duty equipment pumped and primed and ready to go.

Nothing had prepared me for the tumult—the bleeps of monitors, the scrape of gurney wheels, and the shouts of the medical personnel that formed an indecipherable cacophony. Through the open doorway I could see that the small room was jammed with people, all focused with a terrifying sense of urgency on the inert form of Bill Delius.

"Does he have a history of heart disease?" demanded the intern who'd come to fetch me.

"I don't know."

"Diabetes?"

"I don't know, I don't think so," I stammered.

"What medications is he currently taking?"

From over his shoulder I could hear Claudia asking for the defibrillator paddles as matter-of-factly as if she were asking a dinner companion to pass the salt. Even though we've all seen it reenacted so many times on television that it's practically become a cliché, there's nothing hackneyed about the actual drama of watching somebody try to jump-start the human heart. Even the intern paused in his questions at the sound of my roommate's voice, suddenly commanding and adrenalized, warning everyone to clear.

Bill Delius went asystole after the second attempt. His heart no longer had enough electrical life in it to even squiggle uselessly. The face that stared up at the ceiling was that of a dead man. Claudia straightened up and took a step back from the gurney, her eye catching mine for the first time.

"A friend?" she demanded.

"A client," I answered, feeling ridiculous.

Claudia blinked and then turned to the nurse standing at her side. "Thoracotomy tray, please," she said. "I'm going to open his chest, perform internal cardiac massage, compress his aorta, and see if we can't get some blood going to his head until cardiac surgery gets here."

"Sounds good to me," replied the nurse calmly.

"I'm afraid you're going to have to leave now," announced the intern, taking me by the arm as Claudia picked up the scalpel.

"She can stay," said my roommate, never taking her eyes off Delius. "Just make sure you stay out of the way."

She turned to the intern. "Come here and give me a hand. I'm going to crack his chest. I'll intubate, seven-point-five tube. Call respiratory therapy. Six units, type and cross match. Convert that eighteen-gauge to an eight French. Fluid wide open. Begin with O-negative blood as soon as it arrives."

Claudia bent over my client's lifeless face and opened his mouth with her gloved hand. She began snaking the bright light of the laryngoscope down his throat. Once she had the breathing tube in place, she stepped back and listened with her stethoscope for a moment.

"Two minutes," announced the nurse who'd been with Delius from the minute we arrived at the emergency entrance. It felt as if I'd already been there a year. I wondered how long it had been since the heart attack first hit. How long had I stood on the sidewalk debating with myself what to do? How long had the drive to the hospital taken? Two minutes? Ten?

I reminded myself that the heart is a resilient muscle, but I thought of Mrs. Lapinsky and how that in itself is a double-edged sword. Even if Claudia managed to get it restarted, how much time was left before brain damage turned Bill Delius into a lump of flesh, stripped of the feelings, insights, and ambitions that made him who he is?

"Two minutes, fifteen seconds," exhorted the CPR nurse.

Claudia reached for the scalpel, and I turned my head away, worried that Delius would feel the incision and wondering what kind of person could just cut through someone's flesh like that. Any moment I expected Bill Delius to buck from the table, to scream, to protest. But some part of me knew that Claudia wouldn't even be trying this if he weren't for all intents and purposes dead already. By the time I got up the nerve to look, Claudia had already cut through the skin.

"Spreader, please," she said. Despite the stakes her manner was not just calm, but unfailingly polite. I watched fascinated, like a secret onlooker at a satanic tea party. The spreader resembled a reverse vise, which she turned and pushed until she'd managed to open a small space in the wall of Bill Delius's chest, just wide enough for her to slip her hand through.

I stared, transfixed, as she eased her gloved hand into the opening.

"What was he doing when he collapsed?" my roommate asked. It took several seconds to register that she was talking to me.

"He was walking to my car. He'd just come from some kind of business banquet," I added idiotically. My voice sounded artificial from the strain.

"Three minutes, thirty seconds," the CPR nurse bleated.

"Pupils?" asked my roommate, her eyes closed in concentration.

"Still fixed and dilated," responded the respiratory therapist.

For a moment the whole room seemed to hold its breath, all eyes fixed on Claudia. Then, on my roommate's face, through the armor of her concentration, I saw the faintest glimmer of a smile.

"We have a rhythm," the nurse declared without emotion as the heart monitor began to chirp.

"Pupils?" inquired Claudia again.

"Responsive," the respiratory therapist reported. "Equal and responsive to light."

"Cardiac surgery is ready and waiting, Dr. Stein," someone called.

Suddenly Claudia looked down, as if surprised to

find that her hand was still inside the patient's chest. She pulled it out and quickly arranged moist towels over the wound. Then she stood back and watched as the nurses wheeled Bill Delius down the corridor to the operating room.

It wasn't until after they were already gone that I found myself worrying that Gavin McDermott might be the surgeon standing by, ready to receive him.

CHAPTER

6

"Thank you," Claudia called to no one in particular as the room emptied out. In a matter of seconds we were alone, but everywhere we looked, there was the detritus of calamity. The floor was littered with blood-soaked gauze and discarded packages from which tubes and needles had been ripped. I couldn't help but wonder, just for a second, how it could be possible to figure out the cost of what I'd just witnessed.

I turned and looked with new eyes at the petite figure of my roommate. I used to think that the demands of my profession—the endless workweeks and demanding travel schedule—set me apart from other people. But now I realized that my situation was nothing compared to Claudia's. How did you go to work knowing that your job was to look death in the face and stare it down? How did you put your hand inside another person's chest and hold their heart and then go home and have anything that resembled a normal life?

I knew eventually I would have to ask her, but not today. Instead I said, "Is he going to be okay?"

"We'll know better when we get him upstairs and open up his chest," she replied, automatically stripping off her bloody gloves. "A lot depends on where the clot is and how much damage was already done to the heart muscle. All we can do down here is try to give him a chance in the operating room." She picked up her stethoscope from the top of an adjacent rolling cart and slung it automatically around her neck. "So you say this guy's one of your clients?"

"You know the computer thing I'm working on?" I replied somewhat incoherently. "He's the engineer who invented the new input engine. Delirium is his company. I had just picked him up at McCormack Place. We were supposed to be going to a meeting," I said, feeling like I was relating events that had happened in another lifetime.

"Well, it's a good thing you were in the neighborhood," said Claudia. "With a massive MI like that, normally you'd give the patient a fifty-fifty chance at best."

I was about to ask her if she still thought those were Bill Delius's chances, when the nurse I recognized as having done CPR popped her head in the doorway.

"They just called down from OR three," she told Claudia. "Dr. Laffer wants to know if you're available to assist or if they should page Dr. Jacobs."

"Tell them I'm on my way," replied Claudia.

"It was cool to watch you work," I said, knowing that she was in a hurry, but not wanting to let the moment pass without saying it. "Thanks for letting me stay."

"Even you have to admit it," she grinned as she headed for the door. "I have the coolest job in the world."

I wandered back out into the waiting room and dug through my purse for my cell phone and asked the mobile operator to connect me to the Four Seasons. While I waited for her to find the number I checked my watch. I had no idea what time it was and was surprised to find that it was nearly ten o'clock. I remembered Claudia talking about how time stood still in the trauma room, and now I understood.

The operator at the Four Seasons regretted to inform me that she was under strict instructions to put no calls through to Mr. Hurt or any of the other Icon people's rooms. Apparently they were having some sort of party and did not wish to be disturbed. I did everything I could think of to persuade her to make an exception, short of bursting into tears—though at this point I probably could have managed that without too much trouble— but to no avail. The closest I was going to get to Gabriel Hurt that night was the hotel's voice mail.

I left a message that was long on apologies and short on detail. I had no idea if Bill Delius was going to survive the night, and even though it was my job, I couldn't begin to think about what impact this turn of events might have on any possible deal. Instead I dug through my Day Runner for Mark Millman's home number and tried to figure out what I was going to say.

I was so wrapped up in what I was doing that I didn't notice Claudia's ex-boyfriend, Carlos, until he'd plopped down into the seat beside me.

"Hi, Kate, how're ya doin'?" he asked, throwing his arm around my shoulder, the very picture of fraternal concern. Instinctively, I got to my feet, anxious to put some distance between us.

Carlos was an attractive, well-put-together man with a shock of thick black hair, a little boy's smile, and just enough mischief in his eyes to let you know that he knew just how much fun you could have being bad. With his chest muscles rippling through the dark fabric of the Chicago Fire Department T-shirt that the paramedics all wore, I had no trouble understanding what Claudia had found so attractive about him. She certainly wasn't the first woman who'd been fooled by him, and she surely wasn't going to be the last.

"I'm fine," I said. "How's your wife? Has she had the baby yet?"

"She sure did," he grinned. "A beautiful baby girl. We named her Gloria, after my mom."

"Congratulations," I replied with a brittle smile. "I'll be sure to tell Claudia. I'm sure you'll understand if she doesn't offer you her congratulations herself."

"Why's she still so sore at me?" he asked, with a hurt expression with which I'm sure his wife was highly familiar. Hell, for a split second *I* found myself wondering whether to spank him or give him a lollipop. "I didn't mean for her to get her feelings hurt—"

"I don't think you get it," I replied. "Claudia's not the kind of girl you snack with. If she wants to sleep with married men, she has her pick of doctors."

"So what you're saying is that she was slumming when she went out with me," he replied, getting angrily to his feet in order to get in my face.

"What I'm saying is that she thought you were telling her the truth when you told her that you were single," I said in a voice loud enough to compete with the TV playing in the corner. "What I'm also saying is that if you don't want to find yourself in court slapped with a restraining order, you'd better stop calling our house and pestering Claudia. And if you take one step closer to me, I'm going to scream like hell for Security. When Claudia told you it was over between you, she meant that if she never sees your lying face again, it's too soon. Have I made myself clear?"

Two old ladies and a hooker who looked like she'd been hit by a car burst into applause, and Carlos's face turned deep red. I couldn't tell whether it was from embarrassment or anger, and I was in no mood to find out.

But as I turned to walk away he grabbed hold of my upper arm, squeezing it so hard I knew there'd be a bruise.

"You tell your roommate from me," he whispered, his voice little more than an angry hiss, "that we had a good thing going, the two of us. You tell her that I know what she needs and I'm the one to give it to her." He dropped his voice even lower still. "You tell her that it's *never* over until *I* say it's over."

I used my cell phone to call Mark Millman from a relatively quiet corner of the waiting room. Luckily I caught him at home just as he was getting ready for bed. I couldn't think of how to soften the blow, so I just told him what had happened. From the silence on the other end of the line I could tell that I had just handed him the worst news of his life.

If you didn't count his ex-wife, Bill Delius had no family, certainly not in town, so Millman said he'd come. While I waited for him to make it down to the hospital I killed time by pacing the floor. Was Carlos just an angry guy? And now that he was mad, was he more or less likely to take it out on Claudia after the dressing down I'd given him that night?

Mark Millman pushed through the emergency room doors, looking for all the world like a heart attack waiting to happen. Pasty faced and out of breath, he pulled at his tie as if it might help him get more air. Without even looking for me, he made a beeline for the triage nurse and loudly demanded that he be allowed to see Bill Delius. I caught him by the elbow and steered him away long enough to explain that Bill was still in surgery and to fill him in on the little I knew about his treatment. Then I said good night. Mark was Delius's partner. I was just the hired help, a stranger who just happened to be there when the big one hit. The image of Claudia's hand thrust deep inside Bill Delius's chest suddenly pulsed across my brain. I'd already been witness to more than I had a right to.

As I made my way through the parking lot it occurred to me that although I'd long considered the hospital a fixture in my life, this was the first chance I'd had to *really* see it. Suddenly my lunchtime conversation with Joan Bornstein seemed much less abstract. What, I wondered, would be different when it became HCC–Prescott Memorial? Would someone like Claudia still be waiting at the door?

As I got into the car I slid a CD into the slot and watched it disappear. The sound of Elvis Costello's smoky voice filled the car and soothed me like a drug. I wondered what Claudia was listening to right now as she helped Carl Laffer cut through Bill Delius's chest. Puccini, perhaps. Laffer was an opera buff who liked to sing along with the tenor on the tape and encouraged the rest of his team to do the same. There were some nurses he reportedly wouldn't work with solely because they couldn't carry a tune. Luckily, Claudia was a gifted soprano, who reported that singing made the backbreaking labor of cardiac surgery pass more quickly. For my part I was just grateful that it wasn't Gavin McDermott now holding Bill Delius's heart in his hands.

When I got home Leo once again waited out front until I had gotten past the dead bolts and was safely inside. Apparently there'd been another break-in the night before, prompting a repeat of his offer to lend me his dog, as well as other, vaguely paternal warnings. I told him that I was grateful for his concern, but I was so tired that I honestly didn't care if someone broke in, just as long as the burglar was careful not to wake me up.

I let myself into the dark apartment, practically swaying on my feet from exhaustion. Even before I switched on the light, I saw that there were five messages on the answering machine. For a woman with almost no personal life, this was not a good sign. I flipped through the mail as the tape rewound, dropping credit-card come-ons and promises of long-distance savings unopened into the garbage can.

The first four calls were from my mother. Made at various intervals throughout the evening, they ranged in tone from irritated condescension to outright pique. These were followed by a short message from Elliott Abelman explaining that the defense had rested and the judge had called for closing arguments the next day. His exile to Springfield was drawing to a close.

Normally the messages from my mother would have sent me into an orbit of distress, but tonight I was immune from her displeasure. Instead, I reveled in the sound of Elliott's voice and felt my heart quicken at the prospect of seeing him again. I'd spent the last three years trying to figure out my feelings for the man, and for the first time, my heart spoke clearly. Tonight I'd seen blood and pain and glimpsed the capricious fates that hold us in their hands. Perhaps, I thought to myself, perhaps we're meant to accept love when it's given.

The next morning I slept through my alarm and woke up with the sun pouring in through the blinds turning the dust in the room into dancing glitters of light. I rolled over, wrapped in the familiar softness of one of Russell's old T-shirts, my body still heavy with sleep, and looked at the clock. It took a while for the numbers to penetrate the thickness in my brain. I couldn't believe that it was after nine o'clock.

I groaned and wondered whether seppuku was an option. Then I remembered Bill Delius and dragged myself to my feet, padding barefoot to the telephone in the front hall to page Claudia. Since we'd started getting hang-up calls, we'd unplugged all the phones in the back part of the apartment to avoid being woken up. By the time I'd made my way to the phone in the front hall, the soles of my feet were covered with dust. Now that both of us knew we would be moving, we'd stopped even talking about cleaning.

The message light was blinking again. Apparently I'd slept through another call. I hit the rewind button and waited, steeling myself for the worst. When I heard Claudia's voice on the tape, I actually held my breath.

"Hi, Kate, it's me," began my roommate, her voice thick with fatigue. "It's . . . let me see . . . it's four-thirty in the morning, and I thought you'd want to know that your client ended up with a double bypass, but it looks like we're going to be putting his name down in the 'save' column. You might want to stop in and see him in the next day or so and judge our handiwork for yourself. You might also want to tell him about the crack trauma team that saved his ass. At any other hospital they would have called him DOA the minute they wheeled him in the door." Even on the tape I could hear the piercing tones of her beeper going off again. "Uh-oh, they're playing my song. Got to go," she said, followed by another beep, this one from the answering machine signaling the end of her call.

I pushed the rewind button and listened to the message again, feeling a sudden lightness that was much more than relief. It had been so long since I'd last felt it that it took me a minute to put a name to the emotion. It was joy.

Joy, pure and simple. A delight in life. As I stood there in my underwear and old T-shirt, it struck me like a revelation. This was how it was supposed to turn out. Not Russell, wracked with pain and wasting away before my eyes, but Claudia reaching into Bill Delius's chest and dragging him back from the brink. If that was possible, there could be little else beyond our reach. Bill Delius had cheated death. By comparison, how hard could landing a deal with Icon be?

When the phone rang, it made me jump. I picked it up, hoping it was Cheryl or Claudia or maybe Mark Millman reporting on Bill's progress. Naturally it was my mother.

"What on earth are you still doing at home?" she demanded without preamble. "Are you ill? Where have you been? I've been making myself frantic trying to reach you, and that secretary of yours is absolutely worthless. She claimed to have no idea at all of what you're up to."

"And good morning to you, too, Mother," I sighed wearily.

"I have no time for chitchat," she replied, choosing for once to ignore my sarcasm. "I'm leaving for the club, and you have to get downtown for a meeting."

"What meeting?"

"I've arranged for you to meet with the people from HCC at ten."

I looked at my watch. "But that's in twenty-seven minutes," I protested. "I was at the hospital until late last night. One of my clients had a heart attack. I just got up. I'm not even dressed yet."

"Then I suggest you'd better hurry," she cut in, impervious to my excuses. "It's all set up. You're meeting at HCC's law firm. It's somewhere down there on LaSalle Street—McAdden, Kripps, and some Jewish name. I've written it down somewhere. . . ."

"McAdden, Kripps, and Steinbach," I replied as I rubbed the dirt on the bottom of my foot off onto the side of my leg. "I know where their offices are. What I want to know is what I'm supposed to be talking to them about."

"You're the big-time corporate lawyer. I thought I'd leave those details up to you."

"So what did you tell them?"

"What do you mean?"

"What reason did you give them for my wanting to meet with them?"

"I just explained to them that you're the attorney for the family," replied my mother brightly. "That and the fact that we are planning to sue them."

CHAPTER

7

The offices of McAdden, Kripps, and Steinbach were in one of the newer buildings in the financial district, a black marble edifice so sleek and forbidding that it had been inevitably dubbed the Darth Vader building by the denizens of LaSalle Street. I'm sure HCC's lawyers didn't mind—as a matter of fact, they probably liked it. McAdden Kripps attorneys were more upstart than Ivy League, and they had a well-earned reputation for playing both tough and dirty. What that meant in Callahan Ross terms was that while we were busy looking down our noses at them, they were thinking up new ways to kick our ass.

I got downtown in record time. I figured if I kept up this kind of driving, it was only going to be a matter of time before traffic cops went around with my picture taped to their dashboards and the auto-safety people put a bounty on my head. After handing the parking-lot attendant a twenty, I narrowly escaped being hit by two taxis and a bicycle messenger as I darted across Monroe and arrived breathless in the lobby. I crossed the expanse of marble at an uncivilized sprint and managed to find the appropriate bank of elevators to take me to the thirty-sixth floor on only the second try.

Riding up alone, I tried to catch my breath. I also

silently cursed my mother as I felt the thin silk of my blouse, soaked with sweat, clinging unpleasantly to my back. No doubt she was just arriving cool and collected at the club.

The elevator doors opened directly into the firm's reception area, a stark expanse of white marble punctuated by an outcropping of low-slung chairs of such modern design that I suspected it would take a gymnast to get in and out of them without injury. At the far end sat an elegant black woman wearing a telephone headset behind a massive wraparound desk that looked like it had been lifted from the bridge of the Starship Enterprise. I gave her my name and politely ignored her suggestion that I have a seat.

I didn't have long to wait. A female associate, so fresh faced she couldn't have been more than a year or two out of law school, appeared almost immediately to take me back to the meeting. Shining with self-assurance, she wore a suit with a skirt so short it would have immediately sent half the partners at Callahan Ross into apoplexy. As we made our way back through the brightly lit corridors lined with secretarial cubicles, she explained that Mr. Packman was on a very tight schedule and would be able to give me only ten minutes. It took a conscious effort to keep surprise from breaking my stride. I don't know what it was that I was expecting from this sit-down with HCC, but it certainly wasn't a personal tête-à-tête with HCC's chief executive officer.

My first instinct was to be furious with my mother. If she was really serious about quashing the deal with HCC, how could she even think about sending me into a meeting with its CEO completely unprepared? It struck me as yet one more indication that my mother had no idea of how things worked outside the constricted sliver of her country-club world.

In spite of myself I felt my heart quicken. Just the fact that Packman was in town spoke volumes about the relative importance of Prescott Memorial to HCC, and there was enough of Everett Prescott in me that I relished the opportunity to size up a potential adversary. That still didn't mean I was convinced that fighting HCC was a good idea, but there was no doubt that seeing the trauma team in action firsthand had made the discussion much less abstract.

Disconcertingly my escort stopped dead in front of a blank wall at the end of the corridor. At the push of a button, the wall turned out to be a hidden panel. Even I had to concede that it was a nice touch, a way to knock adversaries off balance before they even made it through the door.

The panel opened silently to reveal a long, narrow conference room dominated by a massive table milled from a single, enormous piece of black marble polished until it shone like patent leather. At the far end sat Gerald Packman—alone. Behind him hung an enormous painting that looked like a bucket of crimson paint had been hurled at a white canvas. The top of the table was completely empty except for a single glass of water and a small clock of the kind used to time moves in chess competition.

I knew little more about Packman beyond what Joan Bornstein had told me. There were only snippets about him in the newspaper clippings about HCC my mother had sent over. Neither had prepared me for the sheer force of the personality of the man himself. He was a big man in his early forties with the bearing of an athlete and the manicured hands of an investment banker. Well groomed beyond the boardroom standard, he exuded confidence from every pore. It was no wonder he'd set his sights beyond fried chicken.

"You have ten minutes," he said, reaching forward to press the switch on top of the clock that set the hands moving.

"Then perhaps you should spend it telling me why I shouldn't do everything in my power to keep you from buying Prescott Memorial Hospital," I said matter-of-factly. I'd seen all kinds of outrageous behavior in my time. Packman's gimmick with the chess clock may have been original, but I wasn't that impressed.

"It would only be a waste of both of our time," he replied. "Our purchase of Prescott Memorial Hospital is a done deal. The board of trustees has voted and the letter of intent has been signed. My lawyers tell me that it's a lock."

"I'm sure they also tell you what a great guy you are," I pointed out, surprised by his unwillingness to even pay lip service to diplomacy, "but that doesn't necessarily make it true."

"You're a very rude young lady," he said. It was a statement of fact.

I looked pointedly at the clock. "And you think you're more important than you are."

Packman leaned back in his chair, unmoved, and pressed his steepled fingers to his lips, focusing his gaze on me like a high-priced shrink.

"I didn't get to where I am today without being a pretty fair judge of people. I'm going to venture a wild guess and say your mother put you up to this," he observed.

"I'm here representing the interests of the people whose donations built the hospital you seem to think you're buying."

"In that case, let me offer you some advice."

"What's that?"

"Just let it go."

"What?"

"Walk away."

"Why would I want to do that?"

"Because it's in your family's best interests."

"I hardly think you're in the best position to judge what is or is not in the best interests of my family."

"I wouldn't be so sure about that if I were you."

"What's that supposed to mean?"

"Your family enjoys quite a reputation in this town—like the Kennedys but without all the scandals. I can only assume you'd want to keep it that way."

"Is that some sort of threat?"

"No, just a statement of fact. It would be extremely unpleasant for your family to have the details of the hospital's operations dragged out into the light of public scrutiny."

"More painful than seeing the institution that we have spent millions of dollars supporting being used to squeeze profits out of sick people?" I demanded, wondering what on earth Uncle Edwin had been up to that had given Gerald Packman not only the ammunition, but the sense of impunity to use it.

"Let's just say that Prescott Memorial's operations have gone unscrutinized for far too long. As you can imagine, I've had quite a bit of experience with so-called charitable institutions. More often than not they are ruled by ego and riddled with financial irregularities. When we come in, we invariably uncover a shocking lack of professional oversight and controls, problems that have been left to fester for years."

"So naturally you expect to find those same kind of problems at Prescott Memorial."

"Let's just say I wouldn't want anybody to be printing the hospital's postoperative mortality statistics in the newspaper right now."

"Is that so?" I observed blandly. Inside, my heart practically leapt from my chest. From everything Claudia had told me, I assumed that knowledge of the problem with postsurgical deaths was confined to the hospital. If so, how had Packman found out about it?

"In the real world the drive to make a profit forces companies to solve problems. In hospitals like Prescott Memorial, they just get swept under the rug. In my experience that's never a good thing."

"That's one of the things I wanted to ask you about," I said, eager for the opportunity to shift the conversation over to my agenda.

"What's that?"

"Your experience. I understand that prior to starting HCC you worked primarily in the fast-food and convenience-market industries. I was wondering exactly what it is about those endeavors that prepared you to run a health care company?"

"I know you intend the question as an insult, but I actually look forward to answering it. For your information the similarities between the two industries are actually quite striking."

"Really? In what ways?"

"Right before HCC bought its first hospital, I spent an entire day just hanging around in the emergency room, observing what kinds of things went on, and you know what struck me immediately? How similar it was to a fast-food franchise. People showed up in a hurry and went up to the counter to tell the person on the other side what they wanted. Not only that, but the measures of customer satisfaction were exactly the same: speed, courtesy, cleanliness, and convenience."

"No doubt you're right," I said coldly. "But there is one significant difference."

"What is that?"

"When the kid at the drive-through window screws up your order, you don't die."

I was on my feet and already out the door by the time I heard the timer go off.

I don't think it was any one thing that made me change my mind. Perhaps it was that I had seen the difference that one doctor in one hospital can make, or the fact that I'd seen how the ripples from that life can move through the world. Or maybe it was just the stunt with the chess clock, but whatever it was, I walked out of the Darth Vader building certain that Gerald Packman for all his audacity was simply wrong.

The night before at Prescott Memorial Claudia hadn't served up a Happy Meal. She'd saved a life. Trauma care wasn't a product line. It was a battle against death fought hand to hand. I suspected that Claudia would be amused by my reaction—a lawyer blown away by what she does not understand. But in my heart I also knew that she would agree with my conclusions. Gerald Packman had to be stopped.

I marveled at how light the traffic was this time of day, especially heading out of the city. I couldn't remember the last time I'd been out of the office on a weekday morning. It felt strange to see that there was a whole world beyond LaSalle Street, people going about their business and enjoying the day.

As I made my way down the familiar tree-lined drive toward the stately Tudor clubhouse, I tried to remember the last time I'd been here. Not that it mattered. The whole point of places like the Lake Forest Country Club was that nothing in them ever changes. No doubt my great-grandfather had driven past these very same elms on his way to play cards with his friends and boast about the hospital he planned on building.

I pulled up under the big green awning, handed my keys to the valet, and made my way up the carpeted steps to the club's main entrance. As I pushed through the heavy oak doors I could almost feel time slowing down. As I made my way to the ladies' card room the grand-father clock in the hall marked out the seconds like a miser doling coins from his purse. This was a place where people came to pass the time, not cram as much as they possibly could into every billable sixth of an hour.

As such, it was probably an anachronism, though one that managed to be embraced by succeeding generations. Comfortable and serene, it was governed by a set of ar-chaic rules set out in an oft-consulted volume the size of a small-town phone book. There were regulations cov-ering all forms of behavior. There were elaborate dress codes for both sexes and every situation, including a strictly enforced white rule for tennis that meant that members looked like they were batting the ball around in their underwear. There were separate dining rooms for men and women at the lunch hour and a men's-only grill at dinner where cigar smoking was permitted. Women were allowed on the golf course only during certain hours of the day in order to give the men who presumably worked downtown preference in the afternoons.

I sighed and turned the corner into the ladies' card room, a pink and white trellised space done up as a sort of gazebo. Today it was filled with so many women that it looked like a fire sale at Chanel. They were all sitting at tables of four, filling in the hours until lunch by taking a bridge lesson. They chatted and peered at their cards while a forbidding woman who sounded like a high-class dog trainer trilled out incomprehensible instructions about tricks and trumps.

I scanned the room and tried to pick out my mother. One thing that I'd never been able to understand is the singular energy with which these rich women simultaneously copied and competed with each other until they managed to transform themselves into a veritable army of well-dressed clones. No wonder their husbands were forever giving them expensive necklaces, I thought to myself savagely. Like dog collars, they're the only way to tell them apart.

I finally spotted her at a table near the front and made my way awkwardly through the room, bumping into chairs, stumbling over handbags, and offering whispered apologies.

"What on earth are you doing here, Kate?" demanded Mother in an irritated whisper once I finally reached her table.

"Since when do I need a reason to drop in and see my own mother?" I replied, unable to resist. One look at her face was enough to tell me that she did not appreciate the joke. "I need to speak to you about something," I continued. "It should only take a minute."

"Can't it wait?" she demanded. "We're in the middle of playing out a hand."

I rose to my feet from my tableside crouch. "That's all right," I said. "I'm heading back to my office. You can reach me there whenever you find time in your busy schedule."

I made it as far as the hallway outside of the men's grill before my mother finally caught up to me. I could tell that she was furious.

"Do you mind telling me what you think you're doing barging in and embarrassing me in front of my friends like that?" she demanded.

"You know, it was a nice day and I just felt like taking

a ride to the suburbs," I shot back. "Why do you think I came out here?"

Mother stared back at me uncomprehendingly.

"Why don't you let me give you a hint? I came straight from my meeting with HCC."

"Oh, that's right, I'd forgotten all about that," said Mother as if I'd just brought to mind an overlooked hair-dressing appointment. "How did it go?"

"Gerald Packman gave me ten minutes of his time," I continued.

"And?"

"And you were absolutely right about HCC. We have to stop them from buying the hospital." Mother stared at me over the tops of her reading glasses, no doubt rendered speechless by the fact that this was the first time I'd told her she was right about anything since I was six years old. "That's the reason I drove all the way out here today," I pressed, "to see whether you were serious about stopping the sale of the hospital or if you'd just gotten your feathers ruffled by HCC."

"How dare you even suggest that I didn't mean what I said?" declared my mother, stung.

"And how dare you insist that I drop everything else that I'm doing to deal with HCC, while you can't be bothered to interrupt a hand of bridge?" I snapped.

For a minute we just stood there glaring at each other. I doubted it was a picture anyone would want to put on a Mother's Day card.

"How do you propose to stop them?" inquired my mother finally.

"First of all, it's not me, it's us. I need you to be clear on that up front. There is no possible way to do this without a commitment from you."

"Then tell me, how do you propose we do it?"

For a minute I wondered if I was out of my mind. Then

I took a deep breath. "Let's start by getting a few things out on the table so that we're sure we understand each other. The first thing you have to realize is that if we do this, it isn't going to be like anything you've ever done before. HCC is a big company and they have a tremendous amount riding on this transaction. I guarantee they're not going to back away from it without a big, ugly fight—the kind of fight you can't win between bridge and lunch."

"There's no need to be insulting about it," said Mother. "You've made your point."

"Good, because if we commit to doing this, being insulted is going to be the easy part. HCC is not only aggressive, but they're used to winning. I'm willing to take them on because I think what they're doing is wrong and there has to be a way to use the law to stop them. But that still doesn't mean we're going to be able to beat them without an all-out fight, and I can't do that alone. You're the one who's going to have to marshal the political support, you're the one who's going to have to get into the media spotlight and put the weight of your social position behind this thing."

"You make it sound as if doing this wasn't my idea in the first place," protested my mother, "and I resent the suggestion that I'm not serious about seeing it through."

"Serious enough to use your connections?" I demanded. "Serious enough to risk not only finding yourself bearing the brunt of unfavorable publicity, but also seeing lies and rumors about you, your family, and friends in print? Are you serious enough about beating HCC to ask favors of people you normally wouldn't even think of entertaining in your woodshed?"

"I am prepared to do whatever it takes to preserve Prescott Memorial Hospital as a nonprofit institution," declared my mother firmly. "The question now is, are you?"

CHAPTER
8

As soon as I got back to the office I proceeded to launch my own personal jihad against HCC. Of course, not everyone in my little universe was necessarily delighted by this development. For a second I actually thought Cheryl was going to kill me. With final exams approaching and a Day Runner already crammed with job interviews, the last thing she needed was for me to start tilting at windmills. Even so, she took down in her own peculiar brand of shorthand the long list of things I needed her to do, and when I was finished, she stomped off in search of Sherman Whitehead, muttering something under her breath about misery loving company. I had no doubt she was already counting the days until she had a secretary of her own to push around.

Sherman showed up a few minutes later, bobbing and shuffling in the doorway his usual Saint Vitus' dance of nerdy ticks. At Callahan Ross, Sherman was considered a special breed of pariah. Having been deemed NPM (not partnership material) on account of his profound and terminal geekiness, he had confirmed everyone's fears by refusing to have the good sense to shuffle off, tail between his legs, to a smaller firm. Instead, he appeared content to stay on at Callahan Ross indefinitely, relegated to the

purgatorial role of "counsel." The sad part was that he
was not only brighter but more able than most of the
partners put together. However, I was one of the few
people who could get past the dandruff and greasy hair
to see it.

As I outlined the situation with Prescott Memorial and
HCC, Sherman honed in on the key issues before I even
had a chance to articulate them. Inside of five minutes he
outlined his plan to hunt down any legal precedent that
could potentially be used to block or, at the very least,
delay the sale. He also promised to dig up any other rele-
vant information about HCC: for example, the outcome
of any other attempted purchase of a charity hospital or
whether in the company's six-year history they'd ever
been sued.

What I didn't tell Sherman was that these efforts merely
constituted a backup plan. With three out of five trustees
voting in favor of the sale, the easiest way to thwart
HCC wasn't going to be to sue them, but simply to convince one of the trustees to change their vote. I even had
my candidate for "most likely to be swayed" picked out.
By the time Sherman departed for the library, Cheryl was
already on the phone trying to set up an appointment for
me to see Prescott Memorial's chief of surgery, the famous Dr. Gavin McDermott.

In the meantime I put in a call to Denise Dempsey.
Denise was one of the city's top PR specialists. Highly
professional and extremely well connected, she also made
no secret of the fact that she preferred social rather than
business issues. The rap against her was that in her heart
of heart she was antibusiness. In short, she was perfect.

I spent a little over a half an hour on the phone with
Denise, selling her on the idea of stopping HCC and explaining what I was trying to do. When I was done, she
offered up a thumbnail sketch of a public relations battle

plan. Listening to her, I had the fleeting sense that all of this just might work. Then I reminded myself that plausibility and persuasiveness were the PR expert's stock in trade.

It wasn't until we got down to talking about money that I started getting nervous. I must confess that I was shocked to learn that Denise charged even more an hour than I did—likability obviously being in much shorter supply than legal acumen. I wondered what Mother had been thinking when she said that she would do whatever it took to fight HCC. Well, I thought to myself as I said good-bye to Denise, I was definitely giving her the chance to put her money where her mouth was.

For the rest of the afternoon things pretty much went downhill—particularly when it came to Delirium. First I called the hospital to find out how Bill Delius was doing, but all they would tell me was that he was still in the cardiac intensive care unit and listed in stable condition. Then I tried to get in touch with Claudia, only to be told by the page operator that my roommate was seeing clinic patients all afternoon and was taking only emergency calls. To make matters even worse, I was convinced that Mark Millman was deliberately avoiding me. I left messages at every number I had for him, but my only reward was a profound and persistent silence.

Gabriel Hurt and everyone else from Icon were equally uncommunicative. In between calls to people who were not there, were on the other line, or whose cell phones were switched off, I checked my e-mail at ever shortening intervals, going so far as to read the day's list of firm birthdays and a memo outlining the partnership's policy on personal use of frequent-flyer miles. Jeff Tannenbaum, the associate who'd carried the heaviest load on Delirium, stopped in for an update and ended up moping around my office because I felt too guilty to tell him to get lost.

His yearly review was coming up, and his name was going to be considered for partnership. Closing the deal with Icon would have clinched the matter for him. While he didn't say it, I knew what he was thinking. It was easy for me, a partner with fuck-you money in the bank, to ride out the ups and downs of a difficult transaction, but it was Jeff's future on the line as much as it was Delirium's. Hunched inconsolably at the end of my couch, his presence was a physical reminder that I should be spending my energy getting talks with Icon back on track instead of letting myself be drawn into a futile and self-indulgent pissing contest with HCC.

By four o'clock I was more than happy to get out of the office in order to go see Gavin McDermott who had grudgingly agreed to squeeze me in between patients at his office at the Northwestern Memorial medical center. Like the other physicians at Prescott Memorial, McDermott conducted the bulk of his practice elsewhere, devoting only a handful of days a month to charitable cases. In addition to a faculty appointment at the Northwestern University Medical School, he was also a partner in a lucrative North Shore surgical practice whose patients and their problems were light-years away from those he treated at Prescott Memorial.

According to Claudia, Gavin McDermott, like the other private-practice surgeons who rotated through the hospital, saw their time there as a chance to practice real medicine uncomplicated by the intrusion of insurers' restrictions and the demands of operating a practice. Instead, they relished the opportunity to revisit the things that attracted them to medicine in the first place—the challenges of surgery and the chance to be a healer as opposed to a service provider.

I don't know what I expected when I got to Dr. McDermott's office, but it certainly wasn't to wait on a vinyl couch surrounded by people in bandages and surgical drains. While I realized that doctors delight in making lawyers wait—it is part of the petty friction played out between antagonistic professions—I hadn't expected to be treated this way by McDermott.

For one thing, Prescott Memorial's chief of surgery was a personal friend of my parents, who had endowed his teaching chair at Northwestern. Not only that, but his latest wife was a girlhood friend of mine. His marriage to Patsy placed us both within the claustrophobic confines of the same social circle. Even if he was a relative newcomer, Gavin knew as well as anybody how the game was played.

From Claudia, I was also well aware that McDermott was a man whose every action was the product of deliberation. While most OR personnel tied their face masks in quick bows, McDermott knotted his a half beat quicker and then broke it with a snap when he was done. Instead of wearing the paper booties everyone else wore to protect their shoes from blood, McDermott wore one of three identical pairs of dark red clogs, silicone treated and thus washable. If I was being made to wait, it was for a reason.

Eventually a nurse called my name and reverently ushered me into the great man's office. Under the circumstances I felt lucky that at least I wasn't being shown into an examining room and told to get undressed. The fact that McDermott was on the phone and didn't even look up when I entered merely reinforced my suspicions.

Prescott Memorial's chief of surgery was a theatrically handsome man in his late forties, though he looked a full decade younger. Tan and fit, even after a Chicago winter, it was only since his marriage to Patsy that his dark hair had turned the corner toward gray. His hair was one of his many affectations. He wore it combed straight back from his high forehead like the more pretentious variety of orchestra conductor. He had a beak of a nose, prominent and thin, and piercing blue eyes that I'm sure his patients thought of as all-knowing. But what was really remarkable about him were his hands—slim, expressive, and with sensitive fingers that seemed to measure everything they touched.

As I waited I listened to him describe in great detail the various ways that an elderly woman's bladder might be surgically enlarged. I couldn't help but wonder if he would have been half as rude if he knew that I was aware of how many patients he'd lost recently. As the conversation dragged on about the poor woman's bladder, I cast my eyes around the room. It was not a warm place. Diplomas and awards covered the walls. Duke, Indiana University, Columbia Presbyterian, and the University of Chicago had all contributed to Gavin McDermott's education, while a constellation of other institutions including the American College of Surgeons, the American Medical Association, and Prescott Memorial Hospital had all conferred awards on him. There were no family photos, no handmade tributes from grateful patients, no mementos of hobbies or outside interests.

The scary part was that in some ways his office was almost the duplicate of mine. Patient charts replaced case files, but there were Post-it notes everywhere, and a small tape recorder for dictation lay close at hand. Outside the window there was no view to speak of, just the red brick facade of another medical center building. The only objects approaching decoration were a series of plastic anatomical models lined up along the front edge of his desk to be used as visual aids for explaining procedures to patients.

As McDermott droned on I became increasingly restless. Almost without thinking, I picked one of the models up and turned it over in my hand. Automatically, I gave it a little toss, subconsciously registering its weight. Propelled as much by McDermott's arrogance as by my own boredom, I reached for a second model.

When I was in college, some guy at a party bet one of his buddies that he could teach anybody, no matter how inebriated, how to juggle. While I'm a little fuzzy on the details, I am a living testament to the efficacy of his teaching methods. Of course, when my mother said that every woman should be able to do some kind of handiwork, she was talking about needlepoint, not juggling. On the other hand, I doubted it would have had the same impact if I'd whipped my embroidery thread out of my bag as it did when I got a plastic set of tonsils, a sinus, and the cochlea circling each other neatly in the air.

McDermott hung up the receiver and looked at me with something very close to astonishment.

"I didn't know you could juggle," he observed.

"And I didn't know you could make someone's bladder bigger," I replied, catching the body parts one by one and carefully setting them back down on his desk.

"So, what are you still doing in the city this late on a Friday afternoon?" he demanded, no doubt forgetting that unlike my parents, I didn't live in the suburbs. "I thought that by now all the lawyers were out on the golf course."

"Oh, there are one or two of us still at work at this late hour," I replied with a smile. "We take turns staying at the office as a public service. We want to make sure there are enough tee times available for all the doctors who want them."

"Touché. I take it you've been sent to twist my arm about Prescott Memorial."

"I hadn't thought of that. I'd certainly be willing to give it a try if you thought that giving it a twist would work. Are you a righty or a lefty?"

"A lefty. But I'm afraid it's going to take more than brute force, no matter how prettily applied, to get me to change my mind."

"I was hoping that moral suasion and an appeal to your higher nature would do the trick."

"What's that?"

"I'm serious, Gavin. I want to know why you think it's a good idea to sell Prescott Memorial to a for-profit chain like HCC."

"Maybe I think it's best to just take the money when it's offered," he answered simply. "Who knows if we'll ever get offered this kind of money again? In my opinion it's a simple and straightforward business decision."

"In my experience very few business decisions are either simple or straightforward," I countered.

"Well, as far as I'm concerned, this one is. The handwriting's on the wall, Kate. It's either HCC or somebody else. Places like Prescott Memorial are dinosaurs, an aging facility at the mercy of a bunch of ignorant millionaires—no offense."

"None taken," I replied dryly. "But I confess I am curious how you arrived at this sudden revelation."

"Marrying Patsy was a big part of it. Seeing that whole crowd up close made me think about how truly vulnerable the hospital is."

"To be perfectly honest, I hadn't thought of it as vulnerable at all," I replied, "not until you voted to sell it to HCC."

"That's not what I meant. Have you ever thought of what would happen if your parents got divorced, or your

Uncle Edwin decided to use his money to set up retirement homes for aging hookers?"

"And what if there's a cure for cancer, or an asteroid hits Chicago?" I countered. "You can play the game of what-if forever and make it come out however you want. It doesn't mean anything."

"That's easy for you to say. What do you know about the day-to-day workings of the hospital beyond writing checks and going to parties?"

I was tempted to tell him that I knew he liked to work only with pretty nurses and his operating room profanity had earned him the nickname Dr. McDamnit, but I knew it would do little to advance my case.

"Medicine has changed in the last couple of years. It's hardly the same profession as when I first started out. Back then, I spent my time in the operating room. Now I spend it in here, arguing on the phone with insurance companies. Pretty soon we'll be doing operations in the parking lot and telling patients to bring their own bandages."

"What does any of this have to do with selling Prescott Memorial?" I demanded.

"It has to do with making choices while we still can," explained McDermott. "With every succeeding generation, the money that has traditionally been used to support the hospital gets split more ways. Talk to Kyle Massius about the kind of begging we have to do. Remember Megan Fredericks? Her parents have been supporting pediatric services in this hospital ever since she had encephalitis when she was ten. But now they're dead, and she wants to put that money into her art gallery."

"That's only one example."

"You want some more?" he countered savagely. "I'll give you some more. What about your cousin Cameron? He's been in and out of Betty Ford so many times that when he checks out, they don't even bother to change his sheets. Do you think we should count on his continued support? Or what about your sister Beth?"

"Beth is still in college."

"From what your mother tells me, she's majoring in becoming a crazy lesbian."

"Being crazy and a lesbian have nothing to do with one another," I pointed out.

"No, but being a lesbian and tormenting your mother do. What do you think Beth will do when she realizes that all she has to do on her twenty-first birthday to really make your parents angry is to give her money to Gays for Peace instead of Prescott Memorial?"

The electronic squeal of a beeper cut me off before I had a chance to reply. I watched McDermott's eyes drop automatically to one of the three clipped to the pocket of his white coat, and waited for him to continue. Instead, he was on his feet in an instant, patting his pockets for his keys.

"We'll have to continue this another time," he said in an urgent voice. From the look on his face, I could tell that mentally he was already out the door.

The people who worked late on Friday nights at Callahan Ross were a hardcore group. I may have joked with McDermott about doctors and lawyers on the golf course, but even the most workaholic attorneys at Callahan Ross usually went home to their families on Friday nights. Not having a family to go home to, I ordered a roasted red pepper and chèvre sandwich on focaccia bread from a restaurant whose evening business consisted of delivering overpriced meals to lawyers. For the price of the sandwich I could have rented an apartment in Iowa.

While I waited for dinner to arrive I wandered into the

library to check on Sherman. I found him in his favorite cubicle, tie loosened, sleeves rolled up. It looked like he was settling in for a long weekend. His usual dinner sat beside the computer screen. As far as I could tell, he had the same thing every night: a container of boysenberry yogurt, a Slim Jim, and a Snickers bar, all from the firm vending machines. At Callahan Ross a minor obsessive-compulsive disorder was practically a job requirement.

Walking back to my office, I lingered for a couple of minutes among the stacks of calf-bound volumes, slipping one or two from the shelves at random and breathing in their musty fragrance. For some reason it made me feel sad to think that nowadays these books were only there for show. Thanks to men like Gabriel Hurt, legal decisions were now entered into computer databases almost as soon as they were handed down, while search engines like Lexis steered the way through the virtual stacks. Progress might be inevitable, but I didn't think I'd ever get over my love of books.

When my sandwich came, I inhaled it greedily. I was so hungry I even ate the pickle. But I still didn't feel like settling down to work. Instead I dragged the boom box out of the bottom drawer of my credenza and plugged it in. Then I kicked off my shoes and pulled all the hairpins out of my French twist and literally let my hair down. Then I chose *Best o' Boingo* from the stash I kept in my bottom drawer, slipped the CD into the machine, and cranked up the volume.

I am without a doubt the absolute worst dancer in the known universe. Not only am I completely uncoordinated, but I lack any semblance of rhythm or grace. With a partner, things can really get ugly. I cannot tell my right from my left, and for some reason I insist on leading. Russell was the only person able to endure it more than once which is one of the reasons I married him.

Even so, I love to dance. As long as I am alone, I am utterly unselfconscious. I lose myself in the music, and by the time I get back to my desk, I feel not just happy, but reenergized. "Dead Man's Party" in and of itself is usually good for at least two more hours' worth of work.

I was prancing around my office probably looking like a chicken in mid-seizure when I suddenly realized that I was not alone. Stopping in midstrut, I turned and found myself face-to-face with a nondescript little man whose salt-and-pepper beard and perfectly round tortoiseshell glasses made him more recognizable than any movie star.

"How did you get in here?" I blurted to Gabriel Hurt ungraciously, my heart pounding furiously from the combination of dancing and fright.

"The security guard downstairs told me where to find you," he explained mildly.

"He's supposed to call before letting visitors up after hours," I pointed out, still struggling to regain my composure. I did my best to pull my hair away from my face and tuck my silk blouse back into the waistband of my skirt. When I looked down, I realized that my big toe was protruding comically from a hole in my black stockings, which had a massive run directly up the front.

"I guess he was willing to make an exception in my case," Hurt apologized. Even under the circumstances I found his tone of modest understatement endearing. "I told him you had sent me a gift and I wanted to surprise you by coming up and thanking you personally."

"You're welcome," I replied somewhat incoherently.

"I see you're a fan of Danny Elfman's music," he observed, cocking his head to one side quizzically as I lunged for the CD player and hit the PAUSE button. "Too bad he mostly writes soundtracks nowadays."

There was a stillness in Hurt's demeanor that worked as an effective counterpoint to the power he wielded in the world. Dressed in wrinkled chinos and a nondescript polo shirt, he stood perfectly still, his sneakered feet together and his hands clasped in front of his thighs. When he spoke, he was in the habit of keeping his voice soft and his speech slow, like a patient naturalist trying to approach a skittish animal.

"Would you like to sit down?" I asked, scrabbling for my shoes with one hand while gesturing toward the visitors' chairs with the other.

"Thank you," said Hurt proceeding to sit as deliberately as he'd stood. "I really did come to thank you for the game. I know it's hopelessly low tech, but it really is fun to play and it brings back such wonderful memories of my youth." For a minute I wondered if he was joking. Hurt's oft-cited age was thirty-one. But then again, he was the old man of an industry that used to joke that time progressed in dog years, but had now changed to hamster years.

"I'm glad you liked the gift. I was afraid you'd think it was presumptuous of me to send it."

"It was," he remarked. "But I like it anyway." He glanced around my office pointedly, adding, "In my world everything is so new, how we do things hasn't had time yet to develop into protocol. Besides, it showed initiative. Sometimes the person who wins the prize is the one who wants it more."

"And?"

"And sometimes it isn't."

"Is that why you canceled at the last minute instead of coming to the Wednesday meeting? Have you decided you don't want what Delirium is offering badly enough?"

"You're also direct," he said. "I like that, too. Let's just say that I was approached by another group that has developed an input driver very similar to Delirium's. I

wanted to have a chance to see it before I began negotiating with you in earnest."

If the three days' worth of wrangling that had preceded the aborted meeting with Gabriel Hurt had only
been a warm-up, I wasn't sure I wanted to experience the
real thing.

"So which one do you think is better?" I asked, figuring if I was going to get bad news, I might as well get it
over with.

"*Better* is such an interesting word when it's applied to
new technology," mused Hurt. With his white shirt and
his hands neatly folded in his lap, he looked for all the
world like a schoolboy reciting a lesson. "The natural response would be, 'better' than what? Or 'better' for what
application? Of course, what complicates the whole
question is the fact that a new technology is an evolv-
ing continuum. Comparing them is like comparing two
rivers. At any given point one river may seem far superior to any given point on the other, but how can it be
possible to compare the two rivers as a whole?"

"I don't know," I replied, feeling out of my depth in
this Yoda-like discussion. "How do you decide anything?
Economists talk about weighing different bundles of
goods. Businessmen use cost-benefit analysis. . . ."

"Oh, my way is much simpler than that," announced
Hurt.

"What way is that?"

"I simply choose the best person to solve the
problem."

"Meaning?"

"The input driver Delirium has today is not the same
one that Icon will put on the market in a year or eighteen
months. Between the prototype and the marketplace lie a
thousand different problems—some small, some large,
some of them unforeseen and others unforeseeable. The

question then becomes one of choosing who will do a better job of solving those problems."

"So how do you decide that?"

"I need to sit down with Bill Delius."

"He's in the hospital for observation," I replied instinctively, withholding the truth as much from the negotiator's habit of hoarding information as uncertainty over how best to proceed.

"No rush," said Hurt, getting neatly to his feet. "I'm in town until Monday. Get in touch with me anytime between now and then and we'll set something up."

As I drove home I mentally kicked myself for having lied to Gabriel Hurt. Well, I hadn't exactly lied, but failing to mention a client's double bypass had to at least fall into the category of dishonesty by omission. I tried telling myself that, like Gabriel Hurt, my job was to keep my options open. But at the same time I couldn't shake the feeling that the road I was on inevitably led to disaster.

I'd started out the day delighted that Bill Delius was still alive, but was ending it disgusted that he wasn't well enough to sit down and take a meeting with Gabriel Hurt. By the time I pulled up to the curb in front of my apartment, I was so thoroughly disgusted with myself that even Leo's cheerful banter couldn't improve my state of mind. I just wanted to pour myself a big Scotch, take a long hot bath, and crawl into bed.

But as soon as I walked in the front door, I knew that something was terribly wrong. Claudia's shoes were lying inside the door exactly where she'd kicked them off, their laces soaked with blood. The lights were on, but there were no sounds of movement or music in the apartment. I stood for a long time in the front hall and listened before I heard anything at all, and even then I couldn't be really sure.

Claudia and I had known each other for a long time, and we had been through a lot together. She'd held my head as I lay weeping through the desolate months that followed Russell's death. I'd listened as she whispered her secret fears about succeeding in a profession filled with men who wanted nothing more than to see her fail. I had seen her stumble home, drunk with fatigue and emotionally battered. I'd seen her on mornings after she'd been up all night stitching up people who'd been hacked to pieces by hatred; nights when she'd had to strip to the skin because everything she wore—right down to her underwear—was soaked in a dead man's blood; nights when she'd held dead children in her arms knowing that they'd been killed by their parent's hand.

But in all that time, I don't think I'd ever heard her cry.

CHAPTER

9

I know it must seem strange that it took me so long to decide what to do. Claudia was my closest friend, but she was also someone whose character had been forged in the crucible of the operating room. The better part of me hesitated because I didn't know if she would want me to see her cry, while the less admirable part of me held back from fear. Twenty-four hours ago I'd seen her slide her hand inside Bill Delius's dead chest and with perfect calm squeeze life back into his heart. What was it that was devastating enough to have reduced her to tears?

The only thing I could think of was that something terrible must have happened to one of her parents and I made my way down the hall toward her bedroom. Like all the others in the building, the apartment that I shared with Claudia was laid out railroad style. The living room and dining room, both palatially proportioned, sat at the front of the apartment, their grand windows facing the street. The other rooms all branched off a central hallway whose resemblance to the passageway of a railroad car had given the floor plan its name.

Our bedrooms were directly across from each other at the back end of the apartment. Architecturally they were mirror images of each other. They were big rooms with dingy windows encased in burglar grilles that looked out onto the narrow alleys that ran between all the buildings on the block. Each had its own drafty fireplace and an adjoining private bath with a deep, claw-footed tub that, like all the rest of the fixtures, dated back to the twenties.

But in every other way our rooms were completely opposite. For one thing, mine was decorated almost exclusively with dirty clothes. Stephen used to say that whenever he looked at it, he knew exactly what Saks would look like if it were ever leveled by a tornado. In contrast, Claudia's room, like her life, was arranged with the precision of a naval cadet. Of course, I liked to think that the rigors of her schedule gave her an unfair advantage. Years of wearing nothing but surgical scrubs had not only winnowed her wardrobe down to two manageable categories—socks and underwear—but left the hospital responsible for her laundry, while I had no choice but to dress like a grownup.

I knocked softly on her door and waited. When it comes to personal relationships, I believe in taking people at their word. Unlike my mother, when someone says they don't want to talk about something, I change the subject. Not only that, but when told to go away, I leave. I'm not sure why so many people find this bewildering.

Claudia's voice, hoarse from crying, bid me to come in. Inside, the room was dark, the only illumination coming from the desk lamp in the far corner of the room. But even through the darkness I could see that she hadn't changed out of the day's blood-splattered scrubs. She had also been crying for a long time.

"Is everything okay?" I asked quietly, setting myself gingerly onto the corner of her bed.

She shook her head in reply, still struggling to muster the composure to speak.

"Has something happened? Are your parents okay?" I pressed.

Hugging her knees to her chest, Claudia forced herself to take a couple of deep breaths. "My parents are fine," she answered finally, managing something that was meant to be a smile. "I'm afraid it's me that's the mess."

"Why? What's wrong?"

"I lost a patient today."

"Another patient?" I demanded reflexively. On some level every lawyer is a prosecutor, even against their better judgment. "Another respiratory arrest?"

"Not another patient," replied Claudia, the words bitter in her mouth. "*My* patient. My very first patient."

"What do you mean?" I demanded. Even though they were often more highly skilled than their counterparts in private practice, the surgeons in Claudia's training program were not technically responsible for their patients' care. As physicians in training, they were required to work under the direct supervision of one of the senior physicians on the medical staff. In practice, of course, the opposite was more often the case. At Prescott Memorial it was the fellows, working trauma full-time, who were considered at the top of their game. It was the rare attending physician who challenged their instincts or interjected themselves in the management of patient care.

"It doesn't make one fucking bit of difference who the surgeon of record was," Claudia declared miserably. "I was the surgeon who did the case. I'm the one who is ultimately responsible. McDermott never even set foot in the operating room."

"It was McDermott's patient?" I asked, the first inkling of bad things beginning to stir at the base of my brain.

"I told you it doesn't matter whose name was on the bottom of the chart. I was the one who operated on her, and I was the one who killed her."

"What was her name?" I demanded, instinctively taking the interrogator's tack of starting with simple questions and easy answers.

"Camille Estrada," said Claudia, as if even uttering the name was painful. "She arrived in the ER day before yesterday complaining of abdominal pain. They sent her up to OB-GYN, where Farah Davies had a look at her and admitted her with a tentative diagnosis of endometrial adhesions. While she was on the OB-GYN service they worked her up. When her abdominal ultrasound revealed cholelithiasis, Farah referred her to Gavin, who scheduled her for surgery."

"Would you mind telling me what happened again, but this time in English?"

"Instead of female trouble, she had gallstones," replied my roommate. "That's what was causing the pain in her belly. I'm surprised Farah Davis didn't suspect gallstones right off the bat. Farah is usually an excellent diagnostician, and Mrs. Estrada fit the perfect four-F profile."

"Meaning she was exempt from the draft?"

"No. Meaning she was fair in terms of her coloring, fat, forty, and fecund, i.e., she's had children. For some reason most gallstone patients fit that profile. So anyway, she was on the schedule for a laparoscopic cholecystectomy this morning—that's a relatively new procedure for removing the gallbladder. You make a small incision and go in with a scope, kind of like playing a video game, but the small incision means that patients have less pain and heal faster."

"So why didn't McDermott do the procedure?"

"In the middle of the night last night Mrs. Estrada started complaining of pain in her abdomen and began running a fever. The resident ordered a lab workup, and the results came back with an elevated white-blood-cell count, so, not knowing his ass from a hole in the ground, he called me. I just assumed that she was experiencing a flare-up of her cholecystitis and told him to bump her off the OR schedule until the inflammation calmed down."

"Is that normal?"

"Absolutely. I figured we'd watch her for a day or two and see if she got any better. If she didn't, we'd have to send her home and wait for the acute attack to pass before rescheduling her surgery."

"So did things get better for her?"

"No, they just got worse. Instead of subsiding, the pain started to localize, which means that it not only became sharper but it seemed to move. But what really caught my attention was that it didn't move to the right upper quadrant, which is where the gallbladder is, but to the right lower quadrant of the abdomen."

"Meaning?"

"Meaning that the whole thing was turning into a mess. The abdomen doesn't always give you pain directly above the diseased organ. Not only that, but by that time I'd been awake and on my feet for thirty-six hours straight. I wasn't sure I could find a gallbladder if someone dropped one in my lap with a label on it. Besides, Mrs. Estrada was not my problem. She was assigned to the surgical service, not trauma. The only reason I got called to see her in the first place was because the resident was scared shitless of McDermott and wanted someone to back him up in case he needed to cover his sorry ass."

"So what did you do?"

"Not much. I wrote orders for something for her pain and went and hid in the on-call room to see if I could catch some sleep before morning rounds."

"And?"

"And the minute my head hit the pillow the fucking resident was shaking me again. Mrs. Estrada was being a pain in the ass. Not only was she refusing to take her medication, but she was screaming blue murder that *this* wasn't her gallbladder, *this* pain was different. The resident begged, the nurses begged, please, go and see this woman and make her shut up.

"So I dragged my ass out of bed and went to see Mrs. Estrada, and *damn* if my examination doesn't show exquisite tenderness in the lower right quadrant."

"Meaning?"

"Appendicitis."

"You're kidding."

"Nope. Just because you're paranoid doesn't mean you don't have enemies."

"So what did you do?"

"I started her on antibiotics, gave her some pain medication, which she took like a lamb, and left a message with McDermott's service that his six A.M. cholecystectomy was now an appendectomy. Then I went back to bed.

"The next thing I know, the resident is waking me up again. Apparently Mrs. Estrada's appendix was heating up, and he wanted to know what he should do. I got out of bed, letting him know in no uncertain terms what I thought about his prospects for making it as a surgeon if he didn't hurry up and start growing a spine. Then I told him to alert the OR coordinator, page anesthesiology, and go scrub. In the meantime I paged McDermott and went to see Mrs. Estrada to see how she was doing for myself and get her signature on the surgical consent forms."

"How did she seem?"

"In a fair bit of pain and a little freaked out. She kept

on repeating that she couldn't believe this was happening to her."

"Why would she say that?"

"Probably because she was in the hospital for one operation and was about to have another, that and the fact that the pain meds were making her goofy. I patted her on the hand, told her that she couldn't have picked a better place for her appendix to go bad on her, and ordered the nurses to get her up to the OR stat."

"So what happened to McDermott? Did her appendix rupture before he made it to the hospital?"

"Nope. He was scrubbed and ready to go when she got there. The only problem was that the OR coordinator called at the same time to say that Farah Davis was in OR four and needed a pair of hands stat. Apparently she had a patient with a uterine rupture and she couldn't control the bleeding. She was asking for an assist from McDermott."

"What did he do?"

"He had them page me to surgery and when I got there told me to get scrubbed and remove Mrs. Estrada's appendix."

"So what did you do?"

"I took out Mrs. Estrada's appendix."

"How did it go?"

"Piece of cake. Believe me, it's a lot harder to give a good haircut than it is to take out an appendix. After I finished the appendectomy, I took a minute to irrigate her abdomen and check out her gallbladder since I was in the neighborhood."

"How did you do that?" I asked, not sure that I wanted to know.

"All I did was slide a couple of fingers into the incision and move them toward the liver and gallbladder, gently pressing the liver with one hand to bring the gallbladder into reach."

"And what did you find?"

"Nothing. That was the weird part. I didn't feel anything at all. No stones."

"So then what?"

"I closed her up and sent her to recovery."

"Any complications?"

"None. I've just spent the last three hours going over and over every step of the procedure in my mind. Other than the fact that I didn't find gallstones, there was nothing remarkable about it. The whole procedure couldn't have taken more than twenty minutes from scalpel to suture."

"Did you tell McDermott about not finding the gallstones?"

"Yeah. He told me it was no big deal. I guess sometimes the stones are so small that you can't feel them. Not only that, but the tiny ones can actually cause more trouble than the big ones. He also made some crack about my knowing more about gunshots than gallbladders."

"I thought you said the stones showed up on ultrasound," I pointed out.

"You're right, but that wouldn't necessarily mean that you'd be able to feel them with your finger. Still, I must confess it bothered me, so I looked at the films when I pulled her chart. I've got to tell you this woman had *stones*—I mean, we're talking cherry pits."

"So when did you bring it up again with McDermott?"

"The next time McDermott and I had words, Mrs. Estrada was already dead. She coded around four o'clock this afternoon. She'd already been moved out of recovery into a regular room. The floor nurse went in to check her vitals and found her in full arrest."

"Were you there?"

"No, I was busy checking your Mr. Delius out of CCU. But as soon as I got the page, I was out of there like a bat on speed. Not that it made any difference. By the time I got to her room, there was nothing left for me to do except pronounce her and break the news to the family."

"How did they take it?"

"About as well as can be expected, which is to say pretty terrible. The husband kept on asking me how something like this could have happened, and I didn't have any answers for him."

"Was her death like the others?"

"You mean the other postsurgical deaths? Only in that I have no more idea of what caused it than anyone has about any of the others."

"What did McDermott have to say?"

"Oh, McDermott said plenty," replied Claudia, barely suppressing a shudder. "They had to page him at his office at Northwestern, and he was still ballistic by the time he got to Prescott Memorial. I was in the hall talking to one of the nurses on the floor where it happened, and he just shot out of the elevator and tore into me. We actually drew a crowd. Patients even came out of their rooms to see what was going on. I have never felt so humiliated in my entire life."

Having been on the receiving end of more than one unfair tirade, I knew just how devastating they could be.

"Did he say anything of substance?"

"You mean besides the fact that he thought I was incompetent and incapable of performing even the most basic procedure without him holding my hand?" she reported, the lash of the chief of surgery's words still fresh. "I guess you could say that he did. He told me that if he had anything to say about it, I could consider my career over."

"You know he didn't mean that."

"Oh, please, I haven't even told you the worst part."

"Which is?"

"Mrs. Estrada's husband overheard the whole thing. He was still in her room collecting her things. He heard every single word."

"Did you talk to him?"

"I tried, but he said that under the circumstances he thought it best if all our communications went through our lawyers."

"But won't the autopsy show what killed her?" I asked, wanting desperately to reassure her.

"Normally when a patient dies in the hospital after surgery, they don't do a post. They just assume that the death was caused by whatever underlying disease prompted the surgery."

"But I thought you said you couldn't feel any gallstones."

"I couldn't, but there's no question her appendix was inflamed, and I performed an appendectomy. Under those circumstances you'd expect McDermott to sign the death certificate, no questions asked."

"Will he?"

"Not now. Mrs. Estrada's family has requested an autopsy."

"Well then, it's out of your hands. Now it's up to the medical examiner to find the answers."

"The medical examiner isn't going to be doing the autopsy. I'm sure they've hired an independent forensic pathologist."

"I didn't know there was such a thing."

"Are you kidding? There's even a mobile service. They call themselves 1-800-Autopsy. They show up in a black van and do the post on your loved one, parked in your driveway."

"Remind me to add that to my list of signs that the apocalypse is near."

"For me, I'm afraid it's nearer than you'd think. I have to appear before the morbidity and mortality board on Monday."

"What's that?"

"The M&M conference? It's a confidential, closed-door review board that's supposed to catch and correct physician error. Every hospital has one, but the proceedings are secret. You aren't even allowed to take notes. They can be pretty brutal."

"Have you ever been asked to appear before one before?"

"No, but I sat in on them as a resident."

"What about McDermott? Doesn't he share responsibility for all of this?"

"Oh, sure. He'll hang his head and say he's sorry for letting me do the procedure solo, and they'll give him a rap across the knuckles and tell him not to do it again. Then they'll hang me out to dry."

"Won't McDermott stand up for you?"

"Why on earth would he do that when it's in his best interest to crucify me? Don't you see? Up until now, every single respiratory-arrest death has been his patient."

"So was this one," I pointed out.

"But he never even set foot in the operating room. Not only that, but I looked at her chart. He never so much as ordered medication. I mean, unless the pathologist determines at autopsy that Mrs. Estrada died from having her abdomen palpated, then he's off the hook."

"And he gives up his title of Dr. Death," I mused.

"Absolutely. Up until this afternoon, everybody's been whispering about him. Has he lost his touch? His luck? His nerve? Could he be drinking? Dipping into the old pharmacy cupboard? But on Mrs. Estrada he's clean, which means he has everything to gain from nailing it on me."

"Who else knew that you were the one who operated on Mrs. Estrada?" I asked, suddenly seized by a truly terrible thought.

"The resident who assisted, the scrub nurse, and the anesthesiologist. Maybe the OR coordinator if she ever lifted her nose out of her romance novel."

"Anybody else?"

"No. Not unless McDermott happened to mention it to somebody."

"Would he?"

"Probably not. Technically what he did by letting me do the case wasn't kosher. He wouldn't want to advertise it. But I still have no idea what you're getting at."

"Don't you see? Ever since you've been at Prescott Memorial, the hospital has been losing patients, all from respiratory arrest following routine surgery, all Gavin McDermott's patients. No one can figure out why. Now, all of a sudden, Mrs. Estrada dies the same way after you operate on her."

"I'm still not getting it."

"To everybody but Gavin McDermott and the handful of people who were actually in the operating room with you, Mrs. Estrada wasn't your patient, she was Gavin McDermott's. What if those deaths weren't caused by something that happened in the operating room? What if it was something that happened after?"

"You mean like an infection or a bad drug interaction? Believe me, Kate, the first thing they did was rule those things out," protested my roommate.

"What I'm suggesting is much worse," I said slowly. "I think somebody is going around Prescott Memorial Hospital killing off Gavin McDermott's patients."

CHAPTER
10

That night I slept so badly that it almost didn't feel like rest but rather just an inferior form of waking. Claudia and I had stayed up until the small hours of the morning discussing what she'd dubbed my angel-of-death theory. It's true that talking about something can make it seem real. By the time I finally went to bed, I found myself fearing for the helpless patients at Prescott Memorial.

Usually I'm not prone to flights of fancy, but Claudia had had no trouble coming up with any number of ways to keep an already weakened patient just recovering from surgery from taking their next breath. She ticked them off on her fingers—everything from a pillow over the face to an overdose of morphine, all unlikely to be suspected or detected, especially in the absence of an autopsy.

But what I found really chilling was the matter-of-fact way that Claudia had accepted the idea of the deaths being caused deliberately. Claudia went to work every day in a world where mothers set fire to their children and fathers raped their daughters. To her, the idea that someone was wandering the halls of Prescott Memorial killing off patients hadn't seemed far-fetched. Indeed, murders of this kind were not uncommon. Exhausted caregivers, burned-out nurses, and the occasional psychopath had all been known to systematically help patients into the great unknown.

However, how any of this was related to Mrs. Estrada—much less the other deaths at Prescott Memorial—was pure conjecture. Claudia had no idea whether the bodies of any of the other patients who'd died had been autopsied, much less what the results had shown. She also couldn't say whether Mrs. Estrada and the other patients had anything in common other than the fact that they were patients of McDermott. When I asked her whether the hospital had conducted any kind of inquiry into the other deaths, she'd replied that as a mere trauma fellow, she would be the last to know and suggested that I talk to the chief of staff, Carl Laffer.

But when I woke up the next morning, talking to Laffer—at least about patient deaths—was the last thing on my mind. Indeed, in the light of a new day my entire discussion with Claudia seemed absurd—the product of my desire to offer an explanation that would exonerate Claudia from responsibility for Mrs. Estrada's death and Claudia's eagerness to embrace it.

As I made my way to the kitchen to start the coffee I stopped long enough to peek into Claudia's room, but she'd already left for the hospital. As I went about the business of getting ready for my day I found myself wishing her a quiet shift. It had taken a fair amount of courage for Claudia to just go into work. By now there wasn't a dietary or maintenance worker at Prescott Memorial Hospital who hadn't heard about yesterday's tongue-lashing from Dr. McDermott.

Saturday-morning traffic was light going downtown, and the lakefront was already filling up with people who were out enjoying the beautiful day. I wondered what it would be like to wake up and have a whole weekend to myself. To get up and look out the window at the weather and then sit on the sunporch sipping coffee and considering the alternatives—a leisurely run by the lake, window shopping, reading a novel in the park . . . It was an agreeable fantasy, like daydreaming about being a ballerina. In my line of work, Saturday was a workday, distinguished from the rest of the week only by the facts that the phone didn't ring quite so much and I didn't have to put on stockings and high heels.

When I arrived at Callahan Ross, I found Sherman in the library in exactly the same place I'd left him the night before, only this time with his face pressed to the keyboard, fast asleep. I shook him by the shoulder and told him to meet me in my office. Then I sent out for coffee. Sherman and the coffee arrived at the same time, and we got right down to work.

It took us most of the morning to draft our complaint against Health Care Corporation. Legally we both knew that it was something of a stretch. Our claim was based on a dubious precedent that Sherman had unearthed involving the sale of a nursing home owned by the Catholic Church to a for-profit chain. While the decision itself supported our argument, the facts of the two situations were hardly identical. However, at this point we didn't have time to come up with something better.

Neither Sherman nor I thought our claim would stand up under judicial scrutiny, but with a little luck it might be enough to buy us a thirty-day injunction delaying the sale, which would give us time to come up with something better. Besides, all my instincts told me that time was on our side. I still had no idea why HCC wanted to move so fast, but whatever their reasons, there was a good chance that any delay would work to our advantage. Sherman, who had a weakness for football analogies, referred to this as our Hail Mary strategy.

Mark Millman called just as I was about to take the first bite of my lunch. "Polish interruptus," quipped Cheryl, who'd stopped at Gold Coast Dogs on her way from Loyola. The business half of Delirium was calling from his cell phone in the lobby of the building to say that he was on his way up. He did not sound pleased.

I sighed and wrapped my lunch back up and handed it to Cheryl, who departed along with Sherman, leaving the scent of melted cheddar and jalapeños in their wake. I didn't know what to expect from Millman, so I braced myself for the worst. It wasn't a wasted effort.

Mark Millman looked like a man who'd spent the night on a ledge threatening to jump. His shirt was grimy around the collar and saddlebagged with sweat. There was an unhealthy flush to his complexion, and unless he'd been substituting Absolut for Aqua Velva, it seemed a fair guess to say that he'd been hitting the bottle pretty hard.

"Hello, Mark," I said, waving him into a chair. "You're an awfully hard man to get ahold of."

"I've been busy."

"At COMDEX?"

"Uh-huh. I've been hanging out at the Icon hospitality suite. They have the best booze. Not only that, but I figure it's all I'm going to get out of that asshole Hurt so I might as well get as much of it as I can."

I punched the button on the intercom and asked Cheryl to bring us in some fresh coffee, not that I thought it would actually help. Years of watching my father had taught me all the signs. Millman had been drinking for so long that he didn't seem overtly drunk, but whatever you wanted to call his current state, it was a far cry from sober.

"Why don't you let me get somebody to drive you home," I suggested.

"Home? I can't go home. That bitch threw me out."

"Your wife threw you out?" I asked, feeling a little foggy on the details of Millman's personal life.

"She put all my stuff in trash bags and left them out on the driveway. She told me she never wanted to see me again."

"Why would she do that?"

"She's my second wife," he confided, dropping his voice conspiratorially. "First wives marry you for better or for worse, but with second wives it's for better or better. The minute she heard about what had happened to Bill, she started stuffing my shirts into Hefty bags."

"Why? What does Bill have to do with her throwing you out?"

"After the house it was the last straw."

"The house?"

"I put the house up as collateral for that bridge loan, you remember. That pissed her off pretty good. But when she heard Hurt didn't show and that Bill had a heart attack, that did it."

"You mean you used your house as collateral to borrow the money that you put into Delirium?" I said, wanting to make sure I was getting it right.

"Yeah. The two hundred grand we needed for the bridge loan. I was tapped out on all my other sources, and with Icon in the game it seemed like a safe bet. Now . . ." He pulled an imaginary lever and made a flushing sound.

Cheryl arrived with the coffee. I waited until after she'd poured us each a cup before asking her to call Jeff Tannenbaum and tell him to get himself down to the office. They don't teach you anything about drying out drunks and preventing nervous breakdowns in law school, but that doesn't mean that they shouldn't.

Somehow Cheryl managed to get me out of the office in time for my appointment at the hairdresser. The fact that she threatened violence undoubtedly helped. Shortly after I dumped Stephen, in a moment of weakness I agreed to let my mother make an appointment for Christopher to do my hair. It wasn't that I didn't like Christopher—far from it. My mother's hairdresser was not only charming but extremely talented. But I felt more comfortable in a board room than a beauty shop, and I did my best to avoid them by leaving my hair unshorn and favoring an unfashionable French twist.

Christopher's salon was in an elegant converted brownstone on Oak Street that catered to the designer-handbag set. They even had valet parking. Christopher was waiting for me at the door. He bent at the waist to theatrically kiss my hand (as if he'd really been born in Hungary instead of Des Moines) and announced that he was going to make me AGAP. When I asked the shampoo girl what that meant, she explained that the initials stood for "as gorgeous as possible." In my case that meant full makeup and an "up do," a complicated, upswept hairstyle that made me look like Audrey Hepburn on steroids.

I emerged from the salon wondering why anyone would ever want to do this to themselves on a regular basis, much less pay a small fortune for the privilege. I was also worried sick about Mark Millman and having cold feet about taking Elliott to the Founders Ball. Three months ago, nervous about the prospect of attending my first Founders Ball in years without Stephen Azorini on my arm, it had seemed like a good idea. Now I wasn't so sure.

It wasn't just that strong men had been known to crumble under my mother's astringent scrutiny, or that by inflicting the Founders Ball on Elliott, I was, in effect, presenting him with everything that I chafed at in my life in one large, unpalatable lump. Part of me was terrified that once he got a good hard look at where I came from and what was expected of me, he would do the only sensible thing and bolt.

Stephen Azorini had moved easily through my parents' world, effortlessly making up for whatever deficiencies he'd had in background with his intelligence and spectacular good looks. It also helped that Stephen actually liked it. With Elliott it wasn't just that I was worried that he would be cut less slack. I was also afraid that he would trip up socially, and that after all my years of declaring that those things didn't matter to me, I would think less of him—and myself—for it. After all, hair shirts have a way of becoming terribly uncomfortable when the time comes to actually put them on.

As I got dressed I felt all the nervousness and expectation of prom night compounded by more adult concerns. Even without Elliott this was destined to be an emotionally complex evening. After all, those of us who knew about the pending sale of the hospital were in the awkward position of raising funds for an institution whose charitable status had exactly seven more days to run.

Not only that, but Gavin McDermott was sure to be there. I did not relish the prospect of making small talk with the man who'd not only done his best to publicly humiliate one of the people I cared about most in the world, but had unfairly accused her of incompetence and threatened to end her career, as well. As I stepped into my high heels I considered pouring myself a Scotch but decided against it. This was probably going to be one of those nights that was best faced dead sober.

* * *

They were tearing up the street in front of our apartment. It was part of the city's perpetual losing campaign against potholes, and it made parking on Hyde Park Boulevard—normally difficult—now next to impossible. Choosing to ignore everything my mother had ever taught me about dating etiquette, I told Elliott I would wait for him out front.

It was not yet quite dark, and I instantly regretted my decision. I felt terribly conspicuous as I stood clutching my Judith Leiber evening bag on the busy city street. My mother had picked my dress, an off-the-shoulder gown of russet-colored satin with a fitted bodice that contrasted with a skirt so dramatically voluminous it could have easily accommodated a bustle. Over it I wore a gauzy, satin-edged shawl that was the fashion equivalent of a fig leaf, useless against the evening chill but meant to keep me from feeling naked.

I must confess I was completely unprepared for the effect my outfit had on people. Young men honked their horns, and old women who got off the bus stopped to tell me that I looked beautiful. A little girl, walking with her mother, asked shyly if she could touch the fabric of my skirt, and a pair of college kids asked if I wouldn't mind twirling around because they just wanted to see the skirt move. By the time Elliott pulled up to the curb, I must confess I felt a little bit like Cinderella—enchanted and transformed.

"You look beautiful," said Elliott, hopping out of the car to hold the car door open for me. I clambered into the passenger side of the Jeep, pulling masses and masses of shimmering rust-colored satin in behind me. As he slid behind the wheel he flashed me a grin so big and gorgeous that it set my stomach doing flip-flops. "Thanks for not making me come in to meet your father," he quipped.

"You're welcome," I replied, as we pulled away from the curb. "However, I have news for you. The requisite paternal inquisition is still to come."

"I've had some experience with fathers," Elliott confided easily. "All you do is call them sir and they're putty in your hands. It's your mother who scares the bejesus out of me."

"Be afraid," I said ominously. "Be very afraid."

As we drove north on Lake Shore Drive past the ever increasing number of boats that now dotted the harbor, I cast a surreptitious glance in Elliott's direction. I was rewarded by the sight of the familiar tousle of brown hair, the fluid assurance of his hand on the gearshift, and the realization that nothing between us had changed. I still wanted to sleep with him as badly as I had ever wanted anything.

The Founders Ball has always been held in the grand ballroom of the Drake. As we made the turn onto Walton, traffic thickened and slowed to a Saturday-night crawl. Up ahead I could see a phalanx of red-vested car parkers sprinting to relieve the black-tie crowd of their Lincolns and their Lexuses. It seemed strange to think that this was taking place on the same block as my new apartment. Granted, the block was enormous and the north side (with the exception of the back of the Drake) was entirely residential. Still, it was quite a contrast to Hyde Park, with its bodegas and its bus stops, its Nobel laureates and its poets of street violence.

As we inched our way toward the Drake, Elliott, who'd been chatting easily about the trial in Springfield, suddenly turned serious.

"There's something I've been meaning to ask you," he inquired, nervously eyeing the ornate portico of the Drake.

"What's that?" I asked.

"Can you get a beer at one of these things?"

Before I had time to decide if he was pulling my leg, the passenger door was pulled open and I was being welcomed to the Drake. I stepped out onto the red carpet that had been laid over the curb and pulled my skirt out after me. Then I waited demurely under the gilded awning while Elliott accepted the claim check for the car and came around to take my arm.

We went through the big brass doors together, up the stairs to the first landing, where a floral arrangement the size of a Volkswagen was meant to signal the fact that you had finally arrived. We crossed the burgundy carpet past the Palm Court and were about to ascend the second set of stairs that led to the ballroom when I stopped dead in my tracks.

"So how come you aren't wearing a rented tuxedo?" I demanded, marveling at how quickly the sensation of fine wool beneath my fingers had somehow formed itself into this question.

"So how come you're supposed to be so smart and you didn't realize I was giving you a hard time?" he countered.

I looked at him for a moment and reached up to ostensibly straighten the loops of his tie, which was not only perfectly straight, but hand-tied, as well.

"You look wonderful," I said, leaning forward to kiss him on the cheek.

"As wonderful as him?" inquired Elliott, chucking his head over my shoulder. I turned in time to catch sight of Stephen Azorini sweeping past with some kind of Nordic goddess on his arm. I didn't say anything. Instead I moved closer and kissed Elliott softly on the mouth.

"Better," I whispered in his ear, oblivious to the popping of flashbulbs all around us.

Elliott took my hand and didn't let go. I couldn't tell which one of us the gesture was meant to reassure, but I was grateful nonetheless. As we climbed the half flight of stairs up to the ballroom together I took a deep breath and felt a wave of something that felt suspiciously like contentment. After Russell died, I'd sleepwalked through the years, hiding inside a carapace of work and obligation. Lacking energy for anything else, I'd allowed my personal life to follow the path of least resistance, resuming my relationship with Stephen Azorini, avoiding complications, and doing only what was required.

But reaching the point where I was arriving at the Founders Ball on Elliott Abelman's arm had been anything but uncomplicated. As perverse as it may seem, I took this as a good sign. Not that I was going to get anything like a chance to enjoy it.

No sooner had we entered the ballroom than one of my mother's friends—I couldn't for the life of me remember which one, they all look alike—grabbed me by the elbow and told me in an urgent whisper that my mother was looking for me. It was a message that was repeated a dozen times by a dozen stylish matrons as Elliott and I made our way through the crowded room in search of my female parent.

The theme for this year's gala was "Starry Nights," and as if to illustrate the point, the entire interior of the ballroom had been draped in black velvet—the walls, the ceiling, and even the floor. Illuminating this artificial night were thousands and thousands of tiny white lights pushed through the fabric that covered the ceiling. The overall effect was beautiful and romantic. It was also an awful lot of trouble to go through for a charity that was about to disappear.

We found my parents in the center of the room. As always my mother looked beautiful. She wore a simple sheath of pewter-colored satin designed to complement an old-fashioned choker of diamonds and rubies that she wore only once a year to the Founders Ball. The necklace had originally belonged to her great-grandmother, a gift from her husband, the man who'd given the city Prescott Memorial Hospital.

My father was at her side, looking handsome in his genial, silver-haired way, and no doubt already half in the bag. That my father was an alcoholic was something that I hadn't consciously considered until college. That was when I realized that other people's fathers didn't start their day with an eye-opener at breakfast and switch to gin and tonics at noon. Of course, it was hard for me to be too critical. After all, my father was sweet even if he was ineffectual, and I was pretty sure that if I were married to my mother, I'd want to be drunk most of the time, too.

Whether it was a form of familial telepathy or just from having been so often at the receiving end of her temper, I could tell even from a distance that my mother was furious. All I could do was pray that it wasn't at me.

As promised, when introduced, Elliott shook my father's hand and called him sir. Father, as Elliott had predicted, seemed pleased. Mother, whose scrutiny of Elliott I'd been actively dreading for months, seemed to take barely any notice of him. Instead her attention was focused, laserlike, on a handsome figure across the room.

"Can you believe he'd even have the gall?" she demanded. "The nerve of that man showing up here!"

I followed her gaze, fully expecting to see Stephen Azorini and Miss Norway. Instead, I was surprised to see Gerald Packman, the CEO of HCC, warmly shaking hands with the mayor and his wife.

"I should call security and have them escort him out," she fumed.

"I don't think that would be a good idea," I countered, secretly worried that she might actually do it. The trouble with Mother was that she was like the little girl in the Mother Goose rhyme, the one with the little curl. When she was good, she was very, very good; but when she was bad, she was horrid. The plain fact was that Mother was capable of almost anything when she was angry.

"Then I want you to go over there and find out what he's doing here."

"Mother," I protested, "anyone who buys a ticket can come. His money is as good as anyone else's. Ten to one he's here as someone's guest."

"Well, that doesn't mean I have to be in the same room with him," she huffed, and taking my father by the arm, promptly marched out, leaving Elliott and me speechless.

"And to think that I was afraid tonight was going to be boring," declared Elliott finally. "Is this what all these things are like—cocktails and intrigue?"

"Oh, no," I deadpanned. "Later there'll be dancing."

CHAPTER

11

I couldn't help admiring the way that Gerald Packman worked the room. Patting the chairman of Chicago's largest bank on the back and trading quips with Paul Riskoff, the real estate magnate, he moved with ease among the city's rich and powerful, like a candidate for public office who knows he already has the election in the bag. While I didn't share my mother's sense of outrage, there was something disturbing about his presence here tonight, something that said as much about the man and his nerve as his gimmick with the chess clock.

Knowing private detectives to be an inquisitive bunch, I pulled Elliott aside and treated him to a whispered, rapid-fire account of what was going on between Prescott Memorial and HCC. When I'd finished, Elliott placed his hands gently on my shoulders, looked deeply into my eyes, and told me that I was completely out of my mind to get involved. I was about to agree with him when I felt a strange arm around my waist. Turning toward its owner, I found myself face-to-face with Gavin McDermott and his wife, Patsy.

I'd known—and envied—Patsy ever since I was in the second grade. Athletic and adventurous, she'd gotten into trouble with impunity and even as she'd gotten older seemed to personify the adjective *saucy*.

In Patsy I suspected McDermott had finally met his match. A world-class distance runner in college, upon graduation she'd traded the challenges of elite athletic competition for the more visceral thrills of mountaineering. She'd set her sights on ascending all seven of the world's most arduous peaks, and she'd been steadily making progress achieving her goal. While I couldn't remember how many she had left to climb, I was fairly certain that I was in the presence of the only woman in the room who'd been to the top of Everest and back.

Patsy had had as many husbands as McDermott had had wives, and enough money of her own to not be impressed by a surgeon's salary—not a bad thing considering the things I'd heard about McDermott's weakness for nurses. It was Patsy who'd dragged him over, propelled as much by curiosity about Elliott as her eagerness to boast about her recent ascent of Kilimanjaro. If Gavin remembered he'd run out on our meeting the day before, he certainly didn't acknowledge it. I wasn't bothered by the lack of apology. After the way he'd treated Claudia, no show of manners would ever redeem him in my eyes.

I made introductions all around, my irritation compounded by the fact that McDermott still had his arm draped around my middle. Surgeons, I knew from Claudia, are literally a "touchy" bunch, inured to the physical boundaries by which most people conduct themselves and used to experiencing the world by touch. On the other hand, female lawyers almost universally object to being embraced by middle-aged men with whom they are vaguely acquainted and coincidentally mad at.

"So how do you and Kate know each other?" asked

Patsy after she'd given us a brief account of her experiences in Tanzania.

"I'm a private investigator," replied Elliott. "I met Kate a couple of years ago when she hired me to do some work for her."

"I should probably get your number in case Gavin starts getting any ideas."

"He looks absolutely trustworthy to me," replied Elliott, with a pointed look at Gavin McDermott's hand, which was still around my waist.

"Who says Gavin is trustworthy?" demanded a striking woman with a mane of honey-colored hair that cascaded down her bare back.

"Have you met Dr. Farah Davies, Prescott Memorial's inestimable chief of obstetrics and gynecology?" inquired Gavin, stepping aside to make room for her to join our circle.

Dr. Davies was definitely a presence. Tall and athletically thin, she carried herself with the same brand of physical confidence I recognized in Patsy. She was dressed in a strapless gown that might have been a Vera Wang and carried a simple Kate Spade satin evening bag to which she'd clipped her pager. Her hair was an amazing amber mane of twisted ringlets that was no hairdresser's creation. Her makeup, dramatic but expertly applied, somehow served to draw her intelligence into sharper focus rather than diminish the forcefulness of her personality. The fact that her eyes were different colors—one brown, the other blue—merely reinforced the contradiction. It also made it hard to look at anything else. I wondered how long you had to know her before you got over the incongruity of it.

"You know, I think we may have met before," remarked Elliott as he took her hand in his, "but for the life of me I can't think where."

"I'm sorry I can't help you—" Dr. Davies smiled warmly. "—but I see so many people that when I run into someone in a different context, I have the hardest time placing them."

"Ten to one he isn't a patient," McDermott chortled as he traded his empty champagne glass for another from a passing waiter's proffered tray.

"Thanks for the tip, professor," replied Farah dryly. "I don't know how any of us would ever manage to get along without you."

At this, McDermott's face darkened dangerously, and his wife laid a restraining hand on his arm.

"You might want to ask yourself that same question the next time one of your patients starts bleeding out on you," he snapped.

Farah Davies cast her mismatched eyes heavenward as if entreating the lord for patience. "Don't even think of trying to lay what happened to your patient at my door," she warned. "All I needed was an extra pair of hands. I could just as easily have asked one of the fellows to scrub in. The trouble with you prima donnas is that you always think you're rushing in to save the day, but when things go wrong, you look for someone else to blame."

"And the trouble with you gynecologists is that you think that just because they let you have a scalpel, you know how to use it."

I work in an arena filled with blunt talk and big egos, but not like this. The tension between the two physicians sang like a high-voltage wire. Good manners dictated that someone change the subject, but good breeding aside, I had absolutely no interest in making things easier for McDermott. Besides, I was enjoying seeing him pick a fight with someone who was in a position to fight back.

"Children, children," admonished Carl Laffer, stepping in to spoil the fun, "let's save these petty disagreements for the operating room where there are plenty of sharp instruments at hand."

Carl Laffer was a very tall man who had played basketball in college. In spite of his gray hair and bifocals, he still maintained the look of a center about him, one that had retired and become a particularly good-natured coach. He was the hospital's white-haired elder spokesman, a pragmatist inside the operating room and out. He was genial and endlessly diplomatic, and his appointment as chief of staff had required him to tap into deep personal reserves of goodwill. While long on responsibility and short on remuneration, the chief of staff post at Prescott Memorial was considered one of the most prestigious in the country. Both Farah Davies and Gavin McDermott had lobbied furiously for the appointment, fomenting divisiveness among the medical staff that had taken Laffer the better part of the last year to repair.

Through Claudia over the years, I had come to see the unromantic side of medicine. While few patients pause to consider it, there are more good physicians in every subspecialty of medicine than good positions. Competition is intense and promotions are often based on considerations other than ability. In medicine, like any other high-stakes profession, personal animosities can infest professional relationships and ruin careers—something that Claudia's recent run-in with McDermott had brought sharply into focus.

I had long suspected that the same traits that drove people to excel in highly competitive professions like law or medicine—relentless perfectionism, intolerance of failure, and almost manic compulsion—were the ones that also made them assholes. I remembered asking Claudia about the surgeons she'd worked with at Prescott Memorial. She told me that if she'd had to pick, Carl Laffer was her favorite to scrub with, but if she were the one on the operating table, she'd choose Gavin McDermott every time. Of course, that was before his patients had started inexplicably going into respiratory arrest.

A white-gloved waiter sounded the gong for dinner, and like two fighters sparring in the ring, Gavin McDermott and Farah Davies separated as if on cue. Elliott and I let the tide of partygoers slowly carry us in to dinner. I was in no hurry. As soon as we sat down, we would be trapped at the family table through dessert. I was also reluctant to bump into Stephen on the way into the dining room.

"I don't think those two like each other much," I whispered to Elliott, meaning Drs. Davies and McDermott. "I wonder if perhaps there isn't some sort of history there. After all, McDermott has a reputation as a womanizer, and Farah Davies looks like someone who's turned a few heads in her time."

"I know, that's why it bugs me that I can't remember where I've met her before."

"I'm going to have to ask Claudia if Farah Davies and McDermott were ever an item."

"How does Claudia know them?"

"She's doing her six-month rotation through Prescott Memorial's trauma unit. McDermott works trauma there one day a week."

"That's funny. He doesn't seem like the type to spend his time digging bullets out of junkies."

"Shhhh," I whispered in his ear. "In this group we prefer to refer to them as the deserving poor."

We eventually made it to our table, which was at the very front of the room at the foot of the dais. Under my mother's watchful eye I dutifully took Elliott full circle around the table, introducing him to the various Prescotts and Millhollands in attendance. Except for their bank balances, they weren't exactly an impressive lot. Besides my mother and father, there was my idiotic cousin Hermione and her husband, Lamont, who'd both been members of a cult in college and who to this day maintained an aura of otherworldliness that I suspected of having been pharmacologically induced. Next to them was Hermione's mother, an acid-tongued harridan whose nickname was, of all things, Bubbles. Her husband, Art, whose claim to be hard of hearing I never believed but nonetheless understood, sat mutely at her side concentrating on his salad. Uncle Edwin and his latest bride, a beauty queen from Tennessee with a gravity-defying cumulus of blond hair and even more improbable breasts, rounded out the party.

Fortunately we were spared from the necessity of making small talk by the proximity of the band. Elliott gave my hand a reassuring squeeze under the table, and I found myself desperately wishing that the evening would just be over. After waiting for three years to get Elliott into my bed, the thought of waiting three more hours suddenly seemed interminable.

When the band stopped playing, Kyle Massius, the president of the hospital, climbed the stairs to the podium to introduce my mother. Like everyone else I grew up with, I had a hard time taking Kyle seriously as an adult. No matter what his accomplishments, in my eyes he would forever remain the skinny smart-ass kid who always got us all into trouble. The fact that he now stood up, straight faced, and sang my mother's praises after stabbing her in the back by voting to sell the hospital did little to improve my assessment.

When he was through being insincere, my mother rose to her feet and ascended to the podium. Every year since I could remember, my mother had risen to make her customary welcoming speech. As a child it used to astonish me how hard she worked to prepare these few banal sentences of thanks and welcome. It wasn't until I was older that I understood how few opportunities the women of her generation had to stand in the spotlight and how greatly they were cherished.

But tonight there was the glint of something dangerous in her eyes as she took her place behind the podium, her great-grandmother's necklace glittering at her throat. She paused for a moment, looking out over the hundreds of faces, nearly every one belonging to someone she knew personally and who had shelled out a thousand dollars a couple to be there.

"An event of this magnitude is made possible by the work of many, many people," she began. "Every year the members of the Prescott Memorial Hospital Auxiliary's steering committee work for the entire year to plan the event you are enjoying this evening, an event that I might add raises more than a half a million dollars to provide health care for the most needy citizens of Chicago.

"While many of you may not be aware of this, there is another annual tradition associated with the Founders Ball. Every year on the Monday morning following the gala, next year's steering committee hosts a luncheon at the Saddle and Cycle Club to thank the committee members who worked so hard to make this night possible." The partygoers paused in the middle of their salads to offer up their hearty applause. Mother waited until they'd finished before she continued.

"Thank you," she said. "It is in this way, with only one day in which to rest and put their feet up, that the tireless members of the Prescott Memorial Auxiliary go about their business of raising the funds necessary to support the charitable work of this unique and world-class hospital.

"When my grandfather, Everett Prescott, founded

Prescott Memorial, it was with the idea of helping those less fortunate than ourselves. His friends took up his call to do the same, and his children and their children followed in his example. For four generations these families embraced the object of his generosity. Thus, supporting the hospital became more than an obligation, it became a tradition, one that has grown from those few founding families to include many, many members of the community, including all the wonderful people who are here tonight.

"But tonight I'm afraid Prescott Memorial Hospital takes your money under false pretenses," my mother declared. The room fell silent, and she paused to let what she had just said sink in.

"Oh, no," I thought to myself, thinking of her signature at the bottom of the confidentiality agreement with HCC and yet powerless to do anything to prevent what I knew was coming next.

"Last Thursday the board of trustees of Prescott Memorial Hospital voted to sell it to a company called Health Care Corporation." Small gasps of surprise went up around the room, and Mother again waited until they had subsided.

Her eye searched the crowd until she found Gerald Packman. Now she spoke to him directly. "If Health Care Corporation is successful in its bid to acquire the hospital, not only will these traditions end, but every penny that is raised here tonight, along with the millions of dollars in charitable contributions that have been raised in years past, will go to line the pockets of a for-profit corporation. That is why this year's steering committee and I have just voted to refund to you all contributions made this evening.

"But, please, let's not let such a sad turn of events put a damper on the lovely evening so many people have worked so hard for. My husband and I have just written a personal check to cover the cost of this evening's meal, and I hope that you all will continue to enjoy the evening as our guests."

Of all the possible scenarios that I'd imagined for how this evening would turn out, none came even close to the reality of that night. Like the moment of terrible quiet that follows an accident, as soon as she made her announcement, the entire ballroom seemed to stand still. For a full minute nothing out of the ordinary happened.

Mother folded up the small piece of paper she'd consulted when she spoke, and made her way down off the dais. But the usually bored society reporters who'd come for the open bar expecting to write fluff were still sober enough to recognize a story when it fell out of nowhere and hit them in the head. By the time Mother set her foot atop the bottom step, they were sprinting for the phones.

Not surprisingly, Elliott was the first person to grasp the implications of what was happening. While Gerald Packman gaped and the medical staff buzzed, I remained glued to my seat by my own sense of incredulity. But Elliott was already on his feet and at my mother's side, whispering in her ear as he walked her back to the table for her purse. As he bent his head to hers I saw her nod, her eyes wide with understanding, as he led her firmly by the arm.

As she bent to get her bag he collected me with his eyes, and I rose and made my way to my father's side.

"Come on, we're going," I whispered to him urgently. Startled, he did not protest, but drained his glass and heaved himself to his feet.

We followed behind Elliott, who laid a protective arm across my mother's shoulders and steered her through the room, firmly but politely moving her through the press of people rising from their chairs to besiege her with questions and congratulations.

As soon as we'd cleared the door, I led the way, picking up the pace as we ducked down the half flight of stairs past the elevators that led not toward the Walton side of the hotel where the main entrance lay but, like Alice down the rabbit hole, to the now darkened arcade of chichi shops that ran along the Michigan Avenue side past the Cape Cod Room to the seldom used entrance on East Lake Shore Drive.

Compared to the crush of Walton this was a quiet residential street, an urban backwater with neither shops nor businesses, buffered by a small park and the deeper quiet of the lake. Of course, it was only a matter of time before some enterprising reporter realized that there was more than one way out of the Drake. We fled like the Romanovs, as fast as our evening clothes allowed, along the row of elegant apartments until we reached the haven of the lighted portico at the end of the block.

"Evenin', Ms. Millholland," said Danny the doorman, touching his cap as he swung the big glass door open to admit us. "And a good evenin' to you, Mr. and Mrs. Millholland," he continued, his good-natured face splitting with a grin of pleasure at the sight of my parents.

I breathed a sigh of relief, realizing that in Danny we had a solid ally. Danny's father had been doorman when my parents lived in the building. When I was a little girl, Danny was a lanky teenager, always willing to carry packages and run errands to pick up pocket money.

"It's so nice to see you again," beamed my mother, as serenely as if she'd just dropped in for a chat. "How's your family? Is Michael still in the navy?"

"Yes, ma'am. He's stationed in the North Sea, off the coast of Scotland. He went back to see my gran' just this past Christmas. He'll be so pleased to hear that you asked about him."

"And your father and mother? Are they still well?"

"Yes, ma'am, though now that they've retired and moved out to Arizona, we don't get to see them nearly as much as we'd like."

Elliott and I both stood staring at my mother as if she was out of her mind. Without consulting a soul, she'd decided to violate the terms of the confidentiality agreement with HCC by dropping the bombshell of the year in front of a half a dozen reporters. Now, with the press on her tail, she was standing in the lobby of her old building catching up on family gossip with the doorman. I seriously considered strangling her.

"Well, Danny," she continued calmly, finally getting to the matter at hand, "we seem to have run into a little trouble with some reporters who are following us. Do you think you could be good enough to call us a taxi without drawing too much attention?"

"You just leave that to me, ma'am," he replied, growing half a foot at the thought of being of service in such an emergency. "You just stay right here and out of sight."

We waited together in the awkward silence of the lobby, avoiding each other's gaze. Outside we heard the shrill sound of Danny's whistle summoning a cab, though we waited until the doorman reported that the coast was clear before hustling my parents out and shoveling them into the cab. At the last minute Elliott thrust his cell phone into my mother's hand.

"Don't answer your regular line at home," he instructed. "Let your answering machine pick it up, or better yet, let it ring. I guarantee the only people who'll be calling will be reporters. I'll give Kate the number, and she'll call you on this line."

My mother, who never did anything I told her without an argument, took the phone. As the cab pulled away from the curb we spotted a group of middle-aged men in raincoats who'd just turned the corner from Michigan Avenue at a labored jog. Elliott grabbed me by the hand and pulled me back into the shadow of the garage entrance to the adjacent apartment and enveloped me in a passionate embrace. Despite the circumstances I felt my body soften against his, the current crisis momentarily forgotten. I don't know how long we lingered there until finally, reluctantly, he pulled away.

"Are you sure they've gone?" I whispered breathlessly. "Perhaps we should wait a little while longer?"

"You know very well we both have work to do."

"This was going to be the part of the evening when I invited you upstairs to see my new apartment."

"At least I got a chance to meet your doorman. I think you should wait in there with him while I go and get the car. I've got to get some of my people out to your parents' house, or they'll have reporters coming in through the doggie door."

I sighed and reached into my evening bag for my cell phone.

"You know what the funniest part of all of this is?" I asked as he turned to head back toward the Drake.

"What?"

"I think my mother likes you."

As Elliott disappeared into the darkness I punched in the number Denise Dempsey had given me. I felt guilty enough about handing her the biggest public relations nightmare of her career without adding to it by having her hear about it on the news. Denise picked up on the first ring. From the noises in the background it sounded like she was at a restaurant. It must have been one nearby, because we agreed to meet at her office in ten minutes.

I punched the END button and wondered what my mother had been thinking when she decided to go ahead and ruin my life. No doubt she'd claim that her only thought had been to do the right thing, but that was like saying that you'd invited the Ringling Bros. and Barnum & Bailey circus to your cocktail party because you knew they'd be entertaining. It was going to end up being a bigger circus than she could have possibly imagined.

Elliott dropped me in front of Denise's building, a glass-and-steel skyscraper nestled in the crook of the Chicago River, and gave me a decidedly unchaste kiss good night.

"I'll call you tomorrow from Springfield," he said.

I stood on the deserted sidewalk, the thin fabric of my wrap useless in the chill, and found myself blinking back tears of disappointment.

"Get a grip on yourself, Millholland," I told myself out loud and grimly made my way inside.

Mother's announcement led the eleven o'clock news on all three networks. We watched them simultaneously on the bank of television sets mounted on the wall of the conference room where Denise and I had set up our command center. With videotape unavailable, the networks settled for photos of my parents taken earlier that evening as they'd greeted arriving guests.

However, there was live footage of Kyle Massius. The president of Prescott Memorial Hospital had apparently decided to give an impromptu press conference in front of the Palm Court fountain. Sweating under the klieg lights, he'd read a hastily prepared and overly shrill press release. In it he'd declared that Astrid Millholland had no authority to refund any of the money that had already been donated to the hospital. The fact that there was live footage of Kyle Massius versus the grainy still of my parents seemed to lend credence to his point of view.

Mother's initial reaction to all of this was a tirade of indignation delivered through the squawk box of Denise's speakerphone. She honestly couldn't believe why she was being blamed for all of the fuss. After all, it was HCC who was clearly at fault. Denise did her best to talk her around to a more realistic point of view, eventually getting her to commit to our battle plan. By then Elliott's people had arrived at my parents' house and, having chased a reporter from Channel Eight out of the garbage, had secured the property.

I crossed the bridge of midnight not wrapped in Elliott's passionate embrace, but at the office of the public relations firm. I didn't know if Elliott had joined his security chief at my parents' house, but wherever he was, I hoped he was thinking longingly of me. As the clock struck twelve it occurred to me that all my Cinderella premonitions had come true. The only difference was that instead of my coach turning back into a pumpkin and my dress reverting to rags, I was the one who underwent the transformation—changing from an aspiring princess yearning for romance back into a stressed-out corporate attorney fielding calls from reporters on a headset phone as I paced back and forth along the floor of the conference room, barefoot and in my evening gown.

CHAPTER
12

I woke up to a quiet apartment with no sign that Claudia had come home during the night. A check of the answering machine yielded seventeen calls: three from reporters, thirteen hang-ups, and one message from Elliott. While the message from Elliott was worth listening to twice just to savor the longing in his voice, it was the hang-up calls that captured my attention. Not only were there more of them than we'd ever gotten before, but for the first time they'd come while Claudia was at the hospital. It made me wonder whether yesterday had been on her regular call schedule or if she'd agreed to cover for somebody at the last minute.

In honor of it being Sunday I decided to dress casually—at least for me—blue jeans worn soft as a second skin, an old Ralph Lauren blazer bought back in the days when he still just designed clothes, and a plain white cotton shirt. I had a long day of work ahead of me, and I wanted to at least be comfortable. Besides, I'd already used up too much energy on my hair. After all of Christopher's teasing and spraying I'd crawled from my bed looking like Frankenstein's bride. It had taken a stiff brush and a strong arm to get things back to normal.

Once I was dressed, I called Leo to have him bring me

my car. Luckily I managed to catch him before he and
Angel left for church, which meant that I was treated to a
glimpse of Leo in his Sunday best. When he stepped out
of the Jag in his double-breasted suit with a matching fe-
dora hat, it occurred to me that the gangsters in Capone's
day hadn't dressed much differently—except for the fact
that Leo's entire outfit, from shoes to chapeau, was mus-
tard yellow. As I got behind the wheel I slipped him a
twenty for the collection plate.

"I'll make sure they say a prayer for you," he said with
a slow grin.

"Good," I replied. "Today I'm going to need it."

Making my way north, I stopped and had breakfast
at the University Club with a sober and repentant Mark
Millman. Of the two of them it was Jeff Tannenbaum
who looked the worse for the wear and gratefully seized
the opportunity of my presence to go home. From the
look on his face, I could tell he'd found baby-sitting
Millman a less-than-congenial assignment. I didn't blame
him. Making sure the client stayed away from the bottle
wasn't what people went to law school for.

Upstairs in the dining room only a handful of tables
were taken. The University Club was so far from exclu-
sive that it was sometimes referred to snidely as the
Ubiquitous Club, which was probably why I liked it. But
except for the athletic facilities, on weekends it was
pretty much deserted. Only a smattering of the guest
rooms were occupied, mostly by members temporarily
on the outs with their wives.

We were ushered to a table by the window that overlooked Buckingham Fountain, which had just recently
been turned on for the season. Millman still looked a
little green around the gills, a condition I knew was unlikely to be improved by the University Club's indifferent

kitchen. Serves him right, I thought to myself savagely. Cheryl had sent him over some fresh duds—a navy blazer and khaki pants from Brooks Brothers—clothes that if we didn't manage to make a deal with Icon, I'd end up paying for out of my own pocket. After we ordered, I asked Millman about Delius. I was glad to hear that he and Jeff had gone to Prescott Memorial to look in on him the night before. I'm sure it was just how Jeff had planned on spending his Saturday night.

"I still can't believe that of the two of us, it was Bill who had the heart attack," declared his partner, shaking his head over his coffee cup. "Look at me. I'm forty pounds overweight—at least—eat red meat, drink like a fish, and haven't seen the inside of a gym in the last ten years except to watch my six-year-old play basketball. So who gets it in the chest? Professor wheat germ of the Nordic Track. Go figure."

"So how's he doing?"

"They've got him hooked up to so much electronic equipment I bet he can pick up the Cubs game without an antenna."

"Is he awake? Is he talking at all?"

"When we were there, all he did was moan," said Millman. "I don't think he even knew we were there. But I did talk to one of the doctors, and he told me that his recovery was progressing normally and he's going to end up being fine."

"Did he say when?" I asked, knowing that I must sound callous. The arrival of our eggs, served on chargers of antique silver and predictably cold, delayed his answer.

"Why? Does it matter?" asked Millman miserably.

"Gabriel Hurt came to see me Friday night." I raised my hand up, signaling that he should let me finish. "He's still interested in making a deal for the input driver, but he wants to sit down face-to-face with Delius."

"Shit!" exclaimed Millman under his breath as he slammed his hand on the edge of the table, making the silverware jump. "I can't believe it!"

"I'm afraid you can't swear in this club," I informed him calmly, helping myself to a sip of my coffee. "Better keep that in mind when I tell you the rest of it. Apparently, Hurt's also been talking to another group that's developed a similar product."

"Whatever the other guys are willing to give him, we'll give him double," he said without a moment's hesitation. With his partner in the hospital, unable to make the case for maintaining control, all Millman could see were dollar signs.

"I'm afraid that's not the issue," I replied. "Icon's going to drive a hard bargain no matter what. I'm sure they'll wring the same concessions out of whomever they decide to go with."

"Then what are they interested in?"

"People."

"We're talking about a computer system," Millman shot back.

"Not entirely," I ventured. "I don't know the first thing about this other group—"

"There's only one other company it could be, and they're a bunch of snot-nosed kids from Seattle who don't know their asses from—"

"Don't tell me," I said as I wrote down Elliott's office phone number for him. "Tell him."

"Who's he?"

"A private investigator. He has people who will find out everything there is to know about these guys in

Seattle. In the meantime I need to know who Delius has working with him on the input driver."

"Nobody really, just a bunch of kids. He picks his top students and lets them work on the project in exchange for credit as an independent study."

"Is there any student in particular who stands out? Anybody who's been with him a long time?"

"There's this kid Felix, or maybe it's Fernando, who's been his research assistant for a couple of years . . . ," Millman offered uncertainly.

"Then I need you to find this young man whose name begins with *F* and tell him that I need to see him right away."

I spent the rest of the day holed up at my parents' house with Denise and her public relations minions planning Mother's assault against HCC, while security guards patrolled the perimeter and kept the minicams at bay. I had to admit that I found the whole thing interesting. Besides her usual staff, Denise had brought along the public relations equivalent of a SWAT team: a video coach, a "content" specialist, and a wraithlike young man dressed from head to toe in black who was in charge of hair and wardrobe.

Like the theater inherent in the courtroom or at the negotiating table, the battle for public opinion was an effort to influence the point of view of others. However, in this case, the stage was not only much bigger, but the rules were much less clearly defined. Instead of constructing arguments and interpreting precedent, Denise was trying to influence events by creating the appearance of being right. It didn't take long to figure out that *appearance* was the operative word.

While my father retreated to the library with his bottle of gin and whatever sporting event was on television,

Denise and the video coach set up operations in the music room. Having never seen my mother so much as take a suggestion from anybody, much less an order, I stood at the ready to smooth ruffled feathers, but to my surprise there weren't any. Mother was an apt pupil, intelligent and intent on getting it right on the first try. She was also indefatigable, keeping at it until she was polished and perfect on every conceivable issue relating to Prescott Memorial, nonprofit medical care, and the future of charitable institutions in Chicago.

Of all the people in the room, I was the most impressed.

The next morning Mother and I were at the courthouse early. The time had come to file our suit against HCC. We were not alone. Callahan Ross employed four full-time docket clerks whose job it was to file documents and keep track of court appearances. The most senior of them, Libbert Pinto, a barrel-chested man with elaborately brilliantined hair, walked ahead of us at a decorous distance. The truth is I was a stranger to the courthouse and didn't have the first idea of where to go to file a complaint. Indeed, my presence and more importantly that of my mother had less to do with administrative necessity than with the TV cameras waiting for us on the other side of Daley Plaza.

The paperwork took only a minute, and by the time we were done, the news crews had finished setting up. One look at them clustered together expectantly and I had to fight the urge to bolt, but Mother fixed her most winning smile on her face and prepared to face her inquisitors. Even I had to admit that she was nothing short of amazing.

Coached by Denise, Mother distilled our reasons for wanting to block the sale of Prescott Memorial Hospital into snappy sound bites, which she dispensed with the poise of a professional. Without any sense of irony, Denise had convinced Mother to sell our legal challenge as a David versus Goliath story with the small and determined Prescotts and Millhollands pitting themselves against an unfeeling and monolithic corporation. This struck me as so preposterous that I was worried about keeping a straight face, but just as Denise had predicted, the reporters ate it up.

When her PR handlers signaled that it was time for Mother to move on to her schedule of print interviews, I was grateful. Even the horror show of a day that I was facing seemed preferable to a daylong grin fest with the press—and that was even taking into account the fact that my first call of the day was at the hospital.

It always amazes me how quickly the prosperity of the business district gives way to something else. Five blocks from where the young Turks of the financial markets juggle buy and sell orders from Japan and worry about making the payments on their Ferraris, families live from welfare check to welfare check from one generation to the next. There were no Starbucks on these street corners, no Armani-clad strivers, just empty bottles and swirling trash and the hard, cold reality of the street.

Traffic thinned out as soon as I shook clear of the Loop. Everybody who had someplace to go was heading in the other direction, trying to get to work on time. I turned west on Sixteenth Street, heading over the railroad yards toward Canal. In the daytime the neighborhood surrounding Prescott Memorial looked even shabbier than at night. Fast-food wrappers blew through the streets carried by the breeze while the asphalt glittered with shards of broken glass.

I parked in the lot closest to the main building and said a silent prayer for my car. My grandfather had always envisioned his hospital as an oasis, a place of beauty as well as healing. Now the eaves sagged on the stately red brick buildings, the lawn was trampled, and the sidewalks were cracked. Still, compared to what lay around it, the hospital campus looked like Lourdes.

I decided to see Bill Delius first. I was also hoping that I might bump into Claudia. Something about the hang-up calls was still nagging at me, and I wanted to ask her about her weekend schedule. I also wanted to wish her luck in today's morbidity and mortality conference.

But when I arrived on the postsurgical floor, there was another doctor sitting at the nurses' station. When I asked, he told me that a construction worker had just been helicoptered in from the work site where he'd fallen, impaling himself on a ten-foot length of steel pipe. My roommate would be in the operating room for the foreseeable future.

I found Bill Delius easily enough. He may have been only a semi-impoverished college professor, but by the standards of Prescott Memorial, the fact that he had health insurance made him a wealthy man. He had one of the private rooms reserved for paying patients down at the end of the hall. I knocked softly, not wanting to disturb him if he was resting. Receiving no reply, I stuck my head in cautiously for a peek.

He looked terrible, though I don't know what else I expected. After all, they'd opened him up from stem to stern and even harvested veins from his legs to graft onto the vessels leading to his heart. According to Claudia, even though the procedure is common, it's one of the most invasive—and for the surgeon, exhausting—in the medical repertoire. When they're done, they still have to connect the two sides of the breastbone with steel wires, and just sewing everything back up can take two surgeons working together for hours.

Looking closely, I thought Delius seemed more out of

it than asleep. The drugs that poured in through the IV line to control his blood pressure, his heart rate, and his pain also caused a backlash of interactions and side effects. As I eased myself into the visitor's chair it occurred to me just how vulnerable he was lying there unconscious and alone. I thought of Mrs. Estrada and the other patients who had died, and wondered if they had been on this floor.

Bill Delius wasn't dying—at least not while I was in the room—but unfortunately he wasn't doing anything else either. Seeing him hooked to monitors and with tubes running in and out of his body, I felt all my Monday-morning bravado drain away. I'd known what Bill Delius had wanted before his heart attack, but everything had changed in those terrible seconds on the sidewalk outside of McCormack Place. Did I have any idea of what he would want now? And who the hell did I think I was, going to bat in his place with Mark Millman and whatever graduate student he managed to get ahold of?

I looked down at Bill Delius's sallow face, the oxygen cannula taped to his nose, but as hard as I looked, I saw no answers there.

I found Kyle Massius in his corner office in the hospital's administrative wing. He did not look at all happy to see me.

"I really should call security and have you thrown out," said the man I'd dunked in the pool every summer when we were still kids.

"I'd love to see you try," I countered easily, settling into a chair. After all, it's hard to be intimidated by somebody once you've seen them with French fries stuck up their nose. In an earlier generation Kyle would have been considered the classic second son. Clever and ambitious, he'd been raised to privilege and then pushed out to

make a living when his father left his mother and squan-
dered all his money on a twenty-two-year-old soap opera
star. With an interest in science but a talent for business,
he'd gotten his degree in hospital administration and
used his family connections to land his job at Prescott
Memorial.

"Do you have any idea how much trouble your mother
is going to end up causing for herself with this crusade of
hers?" he demanded, running his hand through what was
left of his hair and giving me what I'm sure he thought of
as a very pointed look over the top of his glasses.

"Trouble for herself or for you?" I countered. "What
did you really think would happen when you decided to
sell out this hospital? You know my mother. Did you
really think that the family would just genteelly step
aside while you dismantled everything that they've spent
four generations working to build?"

"That's got to be the first time the Prescott family has
found its name associated with that ugly four-letter word
work," Massius observed dryly.

"I don't know of many people who are putting in their
forty hours a week who have enough left over to endow
a place like this," I pointed out.

"For your information, *nobody* has what it takes to
endow a place like this anymore. When Everett Prescott
decided to dazzle his friends by founding a hospital, all
he needed to do was put up a big building and fill it with
beds. Now we have MRIs and joint-replacement surgery,
operating rooms that are filled with enough specialized
equipment to launch a space shuttle. Nobody can write a
check for all of that."

"Maybe no one person can," I countered, "but many
people pooling their resources can."

"But for how much longer? Do you have any idea how
deeply in debt we are already? Do you know how hard

it is for this hospital to keep constantly raising money? It's not just the Founders Ball, you know, it's the constant begging for people to remember us in their wills, the perpetual scraping to corporations, the competition with more trendy charities—AIDS, breast cancer, the homeless—everyone clawing for the same charitable dollar."

"You make it all sound so noble," I observed dryly.

"Oh, for Christ's sake, Kate. Will you get off your high horse? I've spent the last three years fighting a losing battle. Do you know how many patients we turn away for every one that we admit? Every year it just gets harder."

"And you honestly think that it will get easier once HCC takes over?"

"The community will be better served," declared Massius sanctimoniously. "Differently perhaps, but better."

"So who put you in charge of deciding what's in the best interest of the community?"

"Your mother, the woman who's so terribly in touch with the people. She did when she put me in charge of this hospital. Don't get me wrong, Kate. I understand that your family feels a certain proprietary interest, but a hospital is an institution that has to change and grow with the times. Just because you paid for it doesn't mean you can control it."

"We'll have to see about that," I said.

"Is that what you came here to tell me?"

"No. I came to get copies of all the correspondence between HCC and the hospital, as well as copies of the budgets for the last five years, and a copy of the charter."

"You don't want much, do you? What makes you think that you can just waltz in here and ask for all of that?"

"The fact that you're going to have to turn it over to

me anyway during discovery, so you might as well get it over with," I replied, pulling a copy of the lawsuit we'd just filed out of my briefcase and sliding it across his desk. "Consider yourself served."

"Well, isn't this just my lucky day," he declared bitterly, showing no sign of picking it up. "Two lawsuits in one day. It's too bad we had to close down our psychiatric unit because we didn't have the money. But who knows, maybe there's still a padded cell somewhere for me."

"Two lawsuits?" I inquired. "What's the other one?"

"Oh, you'll love this. The family of a woman who died last week from a botched appendectomy filed suit against the hospital this morning."

"When did she die?" I asked, fearing the worst.

"This past Friday."

"The family didn't spend much time thinking about it," I observed. Poor Claudia. I remembered her once telling me that emergency room docs get sued an average of once every four years, but to end up with a malpractice suit on your first patient was enough to drive a doctor into dermatology.

"They didn't need much time."

"Why is that?"

"She was perfectly healthy except for her appendix."

"How can you be so sure?" I demanded, remembering what Claudia had said about her having been scheduled for surgery to remove her gallbladder.

"I'm sure because I hired her. The woman's name was Camille Estrada, and she was a professional patient."

"What?"

"She was what they call an undercover patient, an employee of the consulting firm we use to evaluate our patient care. We've been having some problems on our surgical unit, so we had her admitted through the OB-

GYN service for some kind of vague abdominal problems, and Farah Davies dummied up a diagnosis that would require surgery."

"You mean she would have actually gone ahead and had an unnecessary operation?" I inquired incredulously.

"No, of course not. We wouldn't have let it go that far."

"So what about her appendicitis? Was that real?"

"Yes. It was just coincidence that it ruptured while she was working."

"So what happens now? I assume that whoever operated on her carried malpractice insurance."

"Unfortunately it's more complicated than that. It appears that it was a member of the house staff who actually performed the procedure. It's only a matter of time before the family finds out. They'll subpoena the records, or they'll depose the nurses. I'm telling you, Kate, our exposure on this is huge."

"I know you've been experiencing an unusual number of patient deaths," I said. "How can you be so sure that this isn't one of them?"

"Who told you that we were experiencing a high rate of anomalous deaths?" demanded Massius sharply.

"Gerald Packman," I replied. It was the truth.

"You listen to me, Kate," replied Massius with a note of real menace in his voice. "There is no way the hospital can survive the lawsuit and the publicity it would generate if a story like that gets out. The hospital's official position is that the attending surgeon behaved understandably but irresponsibly in leaving Mrs. Estrada in the care of an inexperienced resident in order to assist in what he perceived was a greater emergency. He had absolutely no way of knowing the fellow was incompetent and would botch the operation."

"So let me get this straight," I said. "You're saying

that no matter what other problems the hospital might have been experiencing on the surgical unit, problems that you deemed serious enough to justify hiring Mrs. Estrada to investigate, it was still the fellow's fault that the patient died?"

"What I'm saying, Kate, is that when you look at it from the point of view of the greater good of the hospital, the fellow is the only variable in the entire equation that's completely expendable."

CHAPTER

13

The telephone is the lawyer's scalpel and as I drove back to my office I wielded it as best I could to try and extricate my roommate from her perilous predicament. My first call was to the hospital operator to try and warn Claudia. She told me that Claudia was in surgery and unable to be paged. Suppressing my frustration, I asked her to connect me to Carl Laffer. I understood Claudia's reluctance to have her connection with me made public, but under the circumstances I felt justified in using any ammunition that came to hand, and there was no doubt that this was my best weapon. Unfortunately, not just Laffer but also McDermott were in the operating room and unavailable. I left messages for each of them before pushing the END button on my cell phone in disgust. The truth is I was not used to having so much of what was happening being completely outside of my control, and I didn't like it.

As I parked the car I found myself wondering when they were going to do the autopsy on Mrs. Estrada and what they were going to find. Had Claudia somehow actually made a mistake? Even the premier surgeons are just people doing the best job they can on any given day.

Over the course of a career every surgeon makes mistakes. But even if Claudia had made a mistake, the hospital and McDermott stood to take the blame in all but the most blatant cases of negligence. I remembered what Farah Davies had said about prima donnas like McDermott feeling the need to rush in and save the day. If all she'd needed was another pair of hands, then McDermott should have sent Claudia in to help Davies and done the appendectomy himself. Once again I found myself thinking about the strange chemistry between Davies and McDermott and wondered if there was something else that had prompted him to come rushing to her aid.

And what about the other deaths? How were they related to Mrs. Estrada? Claudia and I had talked long into the night about how someone could go about killing off patients, but we hadn't talked about why. Most cases that Claudia had heard about involved deranged individuals whose motives were beyond understanding. But would someone who was mentally unstable go about systematically killing off the patients of only one particular surgeon? Claudia had mentioned a well-known case where a surgeon had murdered the patients of a rival surgeon in order to drive him from the hospital. But there was no competition for patients at Prescott Memorial. Physicians there worked for the prestige of affiliation and a token salary. The whole thing made no sense.

When I arrived upstairs at Callahan Ross the receptionist informed me gravely that Skip Tillman, the firm's managing partner, wanted to see me right away. I suppressed a groan.

This wasn't exactly good news. Tillman's wife and my mother are best friends, which means that ever since my first day at Callahan Ross I have found myself with a bad case of in loco parentis. The worst part is that my peers routinely misconstrue his concern for interest, mistakenly assuming that he is my mentor. For some reason they think that what he doles out behind closed doors is guidance, whereas its much more likely to be disapproval.

I stopped by my own office only long enough to hand my briefcase to my secretary, who reiterated that Tillman wanted to see me.

"Why do you always have to make him mad?" Cheryl demanded rhetorically.

"I didn't make Skip mad," I pointed out, ramming loose bobby pins back into my hair. "I happen to know on good authority that he was born that way. Listen, I need you to do something for me while I'm upstairs visiting the spanking machine."

"You speak and I obey. Isn't that how it's supposed to work?"

"Page Claudia at Prescott Memorial every five minutes." I rattled off her pager number. "As soon as you get her on the phone, come and get me. I don't care if I'm still in with Tillman. I don't care if you have to break the door down. I absolutely, positively have to speak to her as soon as possible."

"Why? What's up?"

"I'll explain it all later. But it's really important. Call her every five minutes."

"Consider it done," replied my secretary. As I turned the corner and headed down the hall toward the stairs, she called out after me. "Do me a favor and try not to get fired. I still haven't finished paying off my last semester's tuition."

When I arrived at the double mahogany doors that led to Tillman's office, Doris, his secretary told me to go right in. She didn't smile, and the fact that he didn't keep me waiting boded no good. Tillman was very much a lawyer of the old school, a product of the time when men were men, women were scarce, and cocktails were lunch. His office was a shrine to that golden era, with its massive mahogany desk, beaded paneling, and antique globe depicting the vast borders of the British Empire. On the wall behind him hung his three Harvard diplomas—known within the firm as the holy trinity—B.A., M.Div., J.D.

"What on earth do you think you're doing?" Tillman demanded before I'd even crossed the threshold. He was a patrician prototype, white haired and perennially annoyed.

"I'm not sure I understand what you're talking about," I replied, settling into one of the leather club chairs opposite his desk and steeling myself for the inquisition.

"You know very well what I mean, this business with Prescott Memorial Hospital. Do you know who I just got off the telephone with?"

"I have no idea," I said.

"His Holiness Archbishop Greenville."

"How spiritually uplifting," I said, doing my best to sound sincere.

"Cut the crap, Kate. The archbishop is a very angry man."

"Is that allowed? I seem to remember something having to do with the meek inheriting the earth and turning the other cheek."

"It seems that the archdiocese has been negotiating with Health Care Corporation to contract out the administration of the church's hospital operations."

"You're kidding," I said. The Catholic Church was the single largest provider of health care in the city of Chicago. Joan Bornstein had been right about HCC and their motives. Not that it gave me any satisfaction. Instead it sent a chill down my spine and made me wonder what else I didn't know about HCC and their plans to take over the Chicago market.

"Of course, after your mother's stunt on Saturday night and now this frivolous lawsuit that you've filed, they're being forced to back away from the deal because they're afraid it will generate too much negative publicity."

"Good," I said, secretly amused by the thought of God's minions fretting over His PR.

"What do you mean, 'good'?" snapped Tillman. "Do I really need to remind you that this is a *corporate* law firm? Representing large companies like HCC is what we do. How do you think it makes us look when our clients turn on the television and see you and your mother pontificating against big business?"

"I hope what they see is a Callahan Ross attorney living up to her obligation to represent her client zealously—even when the client is her mother."

"The law as it is practiced at Callahan Ross is about money, power, and the pursuit of private good," Skip Tillman said, rising to his feet to signal that the interview was over. "If it's crusades you're interested in, I suggest you go to work for the ACLU."

When I got back to my office, I found Cheryl walking down the hall toward me.

"How did it go?" she asked. "Would you like me to see if I can find you a tourniquet to help stop the bleeding?"

"No thank you. I stand before you bloodied, but unbowed. Did you manage to get ahold of Claudia?"

"Not exactly."

"What does that mean?"

"It means that I never managed to reach her but she's here anyway."

"Here?"

"In your office. I was just on my way up to Tillman's to get you."

"Hold my calls," I said, the words feeling dry in my mouth.

I found Claudia on her feet, looking out the window at the windows of the office building across the street. She was still dressed in her scrubs, as incongruous as a Girl Scout uniform in the dark-suit, white-shirt environs of Callahan Ross.

"Hi, there," I said warily. "What brings you downtown?"

"I never thought I'd say this," said Claudia, turning to face me, her eyes bewildered, her arms stiff with rage. "But I think I need a lawyer."

CHAPTER
14

There is an aspect of the confessional in the practice of law, of confidences accepted and secrets kept. Even so, it seemed strange to be listening to Claudia in the bright light of day. I couldn't shake the feeling that this was a conversation better suited to our nighttime living room, not surrounded by the ramparts of files in the chill of my Callahan Ross office.

"The minute I walked through the door, I knew I was walking into an ambush," she said, pacing the floor, propelled by agitation and disbelief. "It was like I'd showed up at a lynching with a rope around my neck."

"What happened? Did they tell you about Mrs. Estrada?"

"You mean that she was a phony?" she demanded, her voice soft from shock. "That her gallbladder was a setup and that she'd been hired by the hospital?" She gave me a hard look. "Am I the only person who *didn't* know?"

"I only found out this morning. Kyle Massius told me. That's why I had Cheryl trying to page you. I wanted to warn you—"

"I went straight from the OR to the morbidity and mortality conference. I didn't have a chance to call and pick up my pages. I guess they just couldn't wait to rail-road me."

"Who's 'they'?"

"I'm not supposed to tell you anything about it, not even who was there. All M&M proceedings are supposed to be secret."

"Not between lawyer and client," I pointed out.

"And not when the people who are supposed to be educating you decide it's in their best interests to destroy you." Hearing this, I felt my heart drop. Massius hadn't been exaggerating when he'd said that Claudia was expendable.

"So who was there?" I asked.

"Carl Laffer, of course. As chief of staff he heads the panel. Raj Banerji, Cameron Strand, and Yoash Wiener were the other physicians. Then there was Sharon Ringle, the hospital's head of nursing services."

"What about McDermott?"

"Oh, McDermott was there all right. He was wriggling like hell trying to get off the hook, but he was there."

"Why? What was he saying?"

"Right off the bat he demanded to know why he'd been asked to appear before the panel. How could he be responsible if he never went anywhere near the patient?"

"I thought he was the one who was supposed to take out her gallbladder."

"Yes, but his decision was based on faked test results. He only examined her once, and that was only for thirty seconds."

"So what did the panel have to say about that?"

"Carl Laffer seemed determined not to let him off so easily. I've actually never seen him so mad."

"What was he mad about?"

"For one thing, the fact that McDermott left me to do the case. Laffer wanted to know why he didn't send me in to assist Farah Davies with her bleeder. He said I was a highly skilled surgeon who could handle anything. Then he threw the book at him for letting me do the procedure without supervision, as if that made any sense."

"And how did McDermott respond?"

"Oh, you know Gavin. He hemmed and hawed and acted injured. He knows that the hospital needs him more than he needs the hospital. In the end he just said he was sorry and it was never going to happen again. I mean, what are they going to do? Revoke his privileges? It doesn't matter how furious Laffer is. They both know there's nothing he can do except yell."

"What about the other members of the panel?"

"Oh, I think everyone thoroughly enjoyed watching McDermott getting reamed. Who wouldn't want to see him forced to gag down his own medicine?"

"I mean what did they think about what happened?"

"The only thing anyone seemed able to agree on was that it had to have been my fault. They raked me over the coals for more than an hour asking me questions about the procedure. What kind of symptoms did she present with? What tests did we run? What kind of incision did I make? What kind of clamps did I use? On and on. Their questions took longer than the actual procedure. But it still doesn't change anything. Mrs. Estrada's dead and somehow it has to be because of something I did wrong."

"What about the other patients who died? McDermott's patients?"

"If I brought them up, it would be professional suicide," replied Claudia. "I could just imagine what they'd think if I told them about our theory about someone going around killing McDermott's patients. They'd slap me into a straitjacket and take me down to County. Face it, we have absolutely no evidence that anything of the kind is actually going on. It would just make me look like I was so desperate to cover up my mistakes that I'd stoop to saying anything."

"Did they tell you that her family has filed suit?" I asked.

Apparently they hadn't, because Claudia stopped her pacing and sank into the nearest chair and buried her face in her hands.

"I wouldn't get too comfortable if I were you," I said. "You and I have someone we need to see."

Joan Bornstein's office was ideally located for a medical-malpractice defense attorney. In the heart of the Gold Coast, it was a couple of blocks from the Northwestern medical center in a building that catered to physicians. Joan's firm had their office on the eleventh floor. Inside, the waiting room was decorated like a tasteful gynecologist's office in shades of peach and beige. There were comfortable chairs, an assortment of magazines, and classical music played through hidden speakers.

Having been tipped off by Cheryl about our imminent arrival, Joan was waiting for us at the door.

"You must be Dr. Stein," declared Joan, taking Claudia by the hand and drawing her past the receptionist and down the wide corridor that led to her office. "I've heard so much about you from Kate, it's nice to have a chance to finally meet you, even under these circumstances."

She ushered us into a spacious, sunlit office that commanded a stunning view of the lake. Out on the water the first sailboats of the season dotted the horizon with their bright spinnakers. It was a soothing view, not much different from the one from my new apartment, but a world away from the sunless canyon of LaSalle Street.

The interior of her office couldn't have been more dif-

ferent from the old-money insides of Callahan Ross. At
Callahan Ross the walls were white and there were rules
for everything, including how many chairs you could
have before you made partner (two) and how many personal photographs you were allowed to display (three).
Joan's office, on the other hand, was a dramatic expression of her personality. The walls were painted a deep
carnation pink, and the black leather couches were littered with faux leopard-skin pillows. Everywhere you
looked, there were pictures of Joan, her husband, and
their young son, including one displayed on the credenza
directly behind her desk that was apparently taken just
moments after Jared was born. It showed Joan, her hair
matted with sweat, beaming down at her new arrival,
both mother and child still swathed in surgical green.

As striking a contrast as it presented to the buttoned-
down conformity of Callahan Ross, I knew there was
more to it than Joan's flamboyant personality. Like an
attorney specializing in divorce, Joan's practice was a
highly intimate one. When a doctor was sued for malpractice, his or her personal competence and integrity
were called into question in the most fundamental
fashion. While my clients hid their shortcomings behind
the corporate veil, Joan's were being exposed to the most
humiliating type of personal scrutiny. Everything about
Joan's office said, this is who I am, trust me.

While I sipped coffee and enjoyed the view, Joan took
Claudia through the events leading up to Mrs. Estrada's
death, pausing frequently to ask questions and quietly
making notes.

"You did the right thing coming to me," concluded
Joan, laying down her pencil once Claudia had finished. I
suspected that she said it to everyone who brought their
problem to her door, but it was reassuring nonetheless.

For Claudia these were uncharted waters. After the security of being part of the medical staff, she now found herself cut adrift, an outsider. "Though I must confess I'm surprised they were so quick to cast you to the wolves, given your association with Kate's family."

"Nobody knows that Kate and I are friends," answered Claudia. "The last thing I wanted was for everybody to be whispering that the only reason I have my job is that I'm friends with the Prescotts and the Millhollands."

"Well, don't you think that it's maybe time they found out?" inquired Joan.

"I'm not so sure we're such an asset anymore," I pointed out. "In case you haven't heard, the family filed suit against HCC this morning, and as we speak, my mother is sucking up to every journalist who's ever asked her for an interview, in order to explain what a terrible mistake the hospital is making."

"In that case maybe you're right. I think we should start out by focusing on figuring out the best way to defend against these allegations of malpractice that have been leveled against you."

"Before we start, I have to ask you how much this is going to cost," Claudia said, swallowing hard. I knew that her salary, though adequate, was dwarfed by an Everest of debt owed to the government that had financed her education. While her surgical skills would eventually earn her a lavish income, her current net worth consisted of a nine-year-old Honda, an impressive collection of classic CDs, and the outstanding balance on an amazing number of student loans.

"Don't worry about that," I cut in. "Joan and I will work that out."

"You know I can't let you do that," Claudia protested.

"Listen," I said. "I'll make you a deal. When my appendix blows, I expect you to take it out and not send me a bill. Not only that, but I expect *all* the really good painkillers."

"Deal." Claudia laughed in spite of herself.

"Good," said Joan, rubbing her hands together. "I'm glad that's settled then."

"There's still something that Claudia hasn't told you about," I said. "Something you should know."

"What's that?" asked Joan.

"Mrs. Estrada isn't the first unexplained postsurgical death at Prescott Memorial," I said.

It took some prompting, but Joan finally managed to get Claudia to relate what she knew about McDermott's patients who had died and our theory about an angel of death being at work in the hospital.

"And you're saying that, like Mrs. Estrada, all the people who died were Dr. McDermott's patients?"

"Well, not necessarily to begin with. For example, Mrs. Estrada was originally Farah Davies's admission, but she was referred to Dr. McDermott when it was determined that she was a candidate for surgery."

"Farah Davies was the one who took that picture," remarked Joan offhandedly, indicating the picture on her credenza, the one of her immediately following the birth of her eldest. "Now, of the patients who died, how many were you directly involved with, as far as their care?"

"I don't know," replied Claudia. "Maybe one or two. Most of the deaths that occurred after I began my rotation weren't trauma patients. They were scheduled for routine procedures like tumor removal, bowel resection, stuff like that. I don't know about the ones before I came."

"So," mused Joan, the gears turning, "these deaths definitely began before you arrived to begin your fellowship?" I immediately saw what she was getting at. If she could establish that all the deaths were part of a pattern, a pattern that began before Claudia even arrived at the hospital, then the case against Claudia was substantially weakened.

"That's what I've heard," replied Claudia. "I remember after the first time we lost a patient, the nurses telling me that there had been at least two other similar deaths that had happened before."

"I hope you realize that McDermott and the hospital will do almost anything they can to keep us from raising the issue of these other deaths," said Joan, speaking more to me than to Claudia. "No doubt that will also make them eager to settle with Mrs. Estrada's family—anything to avoid seeing this matter go to trial."

"But if they're so desperate to keep us from showing that Mrs. Estrada's death was part of a pattern, won't that just make them all the more determined to blame it on me?"

"Yes. But it also gives you something terribly important."

"What's that?"

"The ability to help yourself," Joan Bornstein replied.

"How?" demanded Claudia, her face lighting up with something very much like hope.

"Your job is to find out as much as you possibly can about the other patients who died. Review their charts, talk to the nurses who took care of them."

"What for? What am I trying to find out?"

"You're looking for patterns. Any kind of similarities. Did they all die at the same time of day? During the same shift? What kinds of medications had they been receiving? What kinds of procedures had been performed? Anything that links them together."

"Patient records are confidential," Claudia reminded her.

"I know that and I'm not asking you to divulge any

information to me or anyone else," Joan was quick to assure her. "But there are no moral, ethical, or legal reasons why *you* can't go back and review patient records. We'll cross those other bridges when and if you find some sort of pattern in the charts."

"And what am I supposed to do in the meantime?" inquired Claudia. "How am I supposed to go into the hospital every day? Half the people I work with think I did something wrong that killed my patient, and the other half assume I'm being set up to take the fall for McDermott. Either way I'm going to be under the microscope."

"I know it's going to be hard," Joan assured her earnestly, "but now more than ever it's absolutely imperative that you go into the hospital every day you're scheduled and continue to do your work according to your usual high standards. You can't let yourself be coerced or co-opted into making it any easier for them to sabotage your career. It's all about showing them that you aren't about to roll over for them. To make them realize that if they want to take you down, they're going to have to fight you every inch of the way."

Claudia absorbed all of this with a kind of grim stoicism. From her face, I couldn't even begin to guess what she was thinking.

I prayed that my faith in Joan Bornstein, in whose hands Claudia's future now rested, was not misplaced. Of course, I was also furious at Gavin McDermott for having put her in a situation that put everything she'd worked so hard for, for so many years, at risk. I was disgusted by his calculation and his cowardice, not to mention his eagerness to offer her up as sacrificial victim.

But overriding all of this was a terrible sense of fear, fear not just for Claudia, but for myself. Sitting in Joan Bornstein's office with my old college roommate brought

home the fact that it is a small world filled with over-
lapping relationships and conflicting loyalties. The truth
is I didn't know what I would do if it came down to
choosing between saving my roommate's reputation or
that of Prescott Memorial Hospital.

CHAPTER

15

In a perfect world I would have not only driven Claudia home but also made her a cup of tea, chatting with her until she'd drunk it and drifted off to sleep. Having spent thirty-six hours at the hospital before being dragged in front of the M&M panel, my roommate was starting to resemble an ambulatory corpse. But today of all days I was acutely aware of the world's imperfections, and I had to settle for putting Claudia in a cab and sending her back to Hyde Park by herself.

As we were walking out of Joan's office her receptionist handed me a message from Cheryl. It said that Gabriel Hurt was returning to the West Coast earlier than expected. The only time he was now available to meet with Delirium was two o'clock at the Four Seasons. I looked at my watch. It was ten minutes to two. I hoped that the words *your secretary will coordinate* written on the message pad meant that Cheryl had managed to get in touch with Millman and that he and Bill Delius's graduate student were on their way.

As I watched Cheryl's taxi disappear from view I realized that I had ten minutes and the Four Seasons was nine blocks away. I suddenly felt exhausted, as if I'd lived half a dozen lifetimes since I'd stood beside my mother on the courthouse steps that morning. As I stepped out into the street to flag down another cab I tried to remind myself that this was what I lived for.

I had the driver drop me at the corner of Walton and Michigan. The entrance to the hotel is on Walton, but the street is one-way the wrong direction. At this time of day it could easily take ten minutes to just make it around the block. On foot, I made it to the Four Seasons breathless, but with two minutes to spare.

The actual lobby of the Four Seasons is on the fifth floor of the Magnificent Mile building. All that greeted guests on the street level was a smallish marble foyer with a security desk and a bellman's station. It was here that I found Millman pacing like an irritated jungle cat. Doing his best to stay out of his way was a scraggly youth with dirty blond hair pulled into a scrawny ponytail and what I'm sure he hoped passed for a goatee on his chin. He was dressed in a pair of enormous blue jeans, so wide they might have been wings, a rumpled plaid shirt, and a pair of much-worn black Converse high-tops.

I'm not normally the sort of person who likes to touch people in the course of conversation. I was raised believing that unless you're engaged to be married, a handshake is more than enough. But as soon as I spotted Millman, I cast repressed Waspdom to the winds and put my arm around his shoulder. The gesture was meant to reassure, but I was the one who was relieved when all I smelled were Altoids on his breath. Delius's computer prodigy might look like a dopey skateboard delinquent, but at least he hadn't driven Millman to drink. It was much too early to tell what effect he would end up having on me.

Millman introduced us. The young man's name was Floyd Wiznewski, and he looked so nervous that you'd think he was about to meet God, or the Lord High Executioner, or both. I put my arm around him, too.

"Listen," I said, as Millman pushed the button to summon the elevator. "Gabriel Hurt is a man just like anybody else. He chews his food. He gets wet when it rains. Don't let him scare you."

I looked at Floyd to see how he was taking this. He looked like he'd just swallowed a mouse.

The elevator stopped, and we stepped out into the lobby, opulent by any standards but all the more incongruous for being on the fifth floor. I didn't know anything about Floyd Wiznewski, but judging from his expression, I guessed he'd never been inside a four-hundred-dollar-a-night hotel before. I sent Millman to the desk to have them call up to Hurt's suite and did my best to keep Floyd from gaping.

"I went to see Bill Delius this morning," I said, walking Floyd slowly past the fountain and the indoor plantings of orchids toward the bank of elevators that whisked people silently between the fifth floor and the penthouse.

"How's he doing?" Floyd asked. Either he had some kind of weird speech impediment or all the moisture in his mouth had disappeared from nervousness.

"He seemed much better than the last time I saw him," I said truthfully, neglecting to add that the last time I'd seen him, he'd been clinically dead. "He was so relieved when I told him that you were going to be meeting with the Icon people," I continued, passing with a tiny blip of guilt into the realm of pure invention. "He told me that you'd been with him right from V1," I said, hoping I was getting the jargon right, "and that nobody understood how he coded things better than you did."

Floyd seemed to relax a little, or at the very least he seemed to be breathing.

"I assume you've seen *Star Wars*," I ventured,

knowing it was like asking a priest whether he'd ever heard of a book called the Bible. "Then maybe you'll remember that throughout the whole movie Luke Skywalker never seemed nervous. Now I'm sure that there are some George Lucas fans out there who'll tell you that it was because of the Force, that he knew what his destiny was and so he wasn't afraid. But I actually think the explanation was simpler than that."

"Of course it was the Force," protested Floyd, indignation overriding his nervousness. "That was the whole *point*."

"Maybe," I replied. "Or maybe it was that Luke knew from the first time that he saw the message from Princess Leia that the Rebel Alliance was no match for the Death Star. It was hopeless. It was the classic David-versus-Goliath situation. He wasn't afraid, because he had absolutely nothing to lose.

"Now I'm just a lawyer, not a Jedi master. I can't tell whether it's our destiny to make a deal with Icon and go on to greatness. But what I *can* tell with complete certainty, is that, at this point in time, we have absolutely nothing to lose by trying."

A butler was summoned to the hotel lobby; he had a special key to the elevator that would allow it to take us up to the penthouse. Millman muttered something about feeling like he was in a James Bond movie, but when the doors opened, we stepped over the threshold of what looked like a very well appointed college dormitory on the night before exams. Icon had apparently taken the entire floor. Kids no older than Floyd, and some who looked younger, padded around in their stocking feet, talking on cell phones and babbling about bugs and beta versions.

An acerbic-looking young man in a custom-made suit was waiting to receive us. I smothered my instinct to introduce myself and shake his hand. In Silicon Valley the rules of corporate behavior are the inverse of those in the rest of the universe. In the computer world, formality is the exception, and power rests with the least well dressed person in the room.

We were escorted into the penthouse living room, which looked like a room in my parents' house but with an even more spectacular view. With the city spread out in one direction and the lake in the other, it was easy to be distracted from the chaos going on all around us. Several people I recognized from the transaction team lounged around the room, either pecking at their laptops or with their cell phones glued to their ears. The wreckage of lunch was strewn over the coffee table. I eyed the cold shrimp as I scanned the room for signs of Gabriel Hurt. I spotted him in a distant corner of the room playing pinball.

We waited, awkward and ignored, in the center of the room. I thought about Gerald Packman and his chess clock and realized that in his own way Hurt was every bit as controlling.

"Well, hi there!" he announced genially once he'd finished his game and crossed the room to join us. "I'm trying to get back up to my old college score, but I must be getting old or something." We all laughed dutifully. "Where's Bill?" demanded Hurt.

"He wishes he could be here, believe me," I answered quickly. "Unfortunately he's still in the hospital. He's sent you Floyd Wiznewski in his place. Floyd's been working with Delius on the project from the very beginning."

"Pleased to meet you, Floyd," said Hurt, keeping his hands in his pockets and rocking back on his heels. He turned to the dark-suited man who'd met us at the elevator. "Darren, will you please take Mr. Millman to review the numbers with the guys from banking?"

The seeds of an objection formed themselves in my mind, but I deliberately ignored them. Icon held all the cards and called all the shots.

"Oh, good, there's Mindy!" exclaimed Hurt. "Mindy, this is Kate Millholland. She's the one who sent me the game."

"Cool," said Mindy, an athletic young woman whose white jeans and white T-shirt made her look like some sort of hip private nurse.

"Mindy, will you take Kate into the dining room and treat her to some of your famous Reiki?"

"No, thank you," I answered, thinking that I was being offered something to eat."

"No, no, I insist," said Hurt. "Consider it a thank-you for the game. Besides, you look like you could use it."

Mindy gave me the same beatific smile you see on the Moonies who accost you at the airport and invited me to follow her into the dining room.

"Just take your shoes off and lie down on the table," she said, pulling the curtains and dimming the lights. The table was covered with bed sheets and there was some kind of incense burning in little brass pots on top of the Sheraton sideboard.

"Excuse me?" I inquired with as much poise as I could muster, which frankly wasn't much.

"Don't worry," replied Mindy. "I'm only going to do your hands, feet, and head. There's no need to get undressed."

"And what exactly are you going to do to my hands, feet, and head?"

"Didn't Gabe tell you?" she asked, tipping her head back and laughing. "I'm his personal masseuse."

I considered for a moment. Then I sighed and hoisted myself up onto the table. In less than a minute, I found myself listening to Indian sitar music while Mindy pressed the various spots on my feet that she assured me were connected to my internal organs. There was also something about trying to visualize different colors that I didn't quite follow. Not that I was actually paying any attention. All I could do was keep thinking to myself that they didn't do this kind of thing in any other business.

By the time I left the Four Seasons, I felt much better, though I couldn't decide whether it was because Mindy had succeeded in releasing my toxins or because I had the draft copy of a deal term sheet in my hand. As the doorman held the door of the cab open for Millman and Wiznewski, who were heading to Morton's to celebrate, I realized that I hadn't even told Floyd that because Delius had given him shares in Delirium in lieu of a raise the past two years, he was about to become a millionaire. As they pulled away from the curb I decided it was okay to save it. He was already walking on air from having beaten Gabriel Hurt at pinball.

From elation to desperation in under three blocks— anyone who didn't like the ride should avoid transaction work. As I crossed Michigan at Chicago Avenue to get back to my car, something at the news kiosk caught my eye. From the front page of the afternoon's *Sun-Times*, a picture of my mother and me looked back at me. The headline was big enough to read from the corner: SOCIALITES BATTLE HOSPITAL GIANT. I could hardly wait to hear what Skip Tillman was going to say about this latest public service announcement for Callahan Ross from the women Millholland. I figured it might not be a bad time to start thinking about a new job—in Australia.

A quick phone call to Cheryl confirmed my worst fears. Not only was Tillman beating the drums for me, but my mother was on the warpath. According to Cheryl she was calling every couple of minutes. From what my secretary told me, it sounded like she was in the middle of a full-fledged nervous breakdown.

Driving back to the office, I tried to set that particular anxiety aside and called Jeff Tannenbaum with the good news about Icon. I felt entitled to have someone share in my sense of victory, if only for as long as it took for me to drive back into the Loop. Besides, there was a ton of document preparation that needed to be done and Tannenbaum was the one who was going to get stuck doing it.

By the time I got upstairs to my office, Cheryl was looking a bit shaken. My mother, the undisputed world champion of underling abuse, had clearly gotten to her. I asked her to bring me a cup of coffee and pulled out my emergency stash of M&M's as I settled down to wait for my mother to call.

It didn't take long. Cheryl hadn't exaggerated when she'd reported that my mother was on a three-minute schedule. But, if anything, Cheryl had played down the thermonuclear intensity of her anger. Perhaps she was afraid if I knew the kind of tantrum my mother was having, I wouldn't have come back to the office at all.

"Where have you been?" snapped Mother. "I've been trying to reach you for almost an hour."

"I was out of the office on another matter," I replied matter-of-factly. "Why have you been trying to reach me? Has something happened?"

"Has something happened?" she echoed sarcastically. "Has something happened? Not unless you count my complete and utter public mortification as 'something.' "

"Why don't you just tell me what happened," I suggested as I emptied the bag of M&M's on top of my desk and began sorting them by color.

"I was in the middle of doing my live interview with CNN. We were all set up in a lovely private dining room at the Ritz-Carlton, and I was talking to that very pretty girl, Suzanne or LuAnne or something like that, you know, the one with the dark hair and those startling periwinkle eyes? Well, it was all going along quite well . . ."

"Just tell me what happened."

"This horrible little man barged in and right on camera he thrust this nasty wad of papers into my hand."

"What kind of papers?"

"Legal papers. It turns out he was some kind of process server," she declared, sounding aghast. "I've been sued by HCC on national TV!"

I told myself that I should have seen it coming. If I'd been in HCC's place, it was exactly what I would have done—gone after my mother with both barrels for violating the confidentiality agreement. However, even I had to admit that suing her for $540 million in damages for derailing the company's negotiations with the archdiocese was a truly sharklike touch. Naturally my mother, who'd managed to live her entire life blissfully unaware of the evil that lawyers do to each other, was beside herself. Even so, she couldn't say I didn't warn her.

I decided that the time had come for us to start playing hardball. I buzzed Cheryl. I told her to call Abelman & Associates and set up a meeting with whichever senior investigator had time to see me right away. I figured I was entitled to as much in my role as would-be girlfriend.

In spite of my distress, or perhaps because of it, I felt a sense of relief when a few minutes later I pushed through the revolving doors of the Monadnock Building.

The Monadnock was a historic treasure. Once slated for the wrecking ball, the lovingly restored Victorian masterpiece was now the unofficial home of Chicago's defense bar. On any given afternoon celebrity defense lawyers and their equally well-known clients could be seen crossing the mosaic floor of the lobby on their way to see the judge.

I took the wrought-iron staircase up to the second floor and made my way down the narrow corridor to the smoked glass door whose Sam Spade lettering indicated that I'd reached the offices of Abelman & Associates. The small waiting room was empty, as usual. The sensitive nature of Elliott's business made it awkward for his clients to have to wait. I gave my name to the receptionist, a motherly woman in her fifties who I remember Elliott had said was a retired matron from the county jail. She beamed at me knowingly and ushered me back to Elliott's office, where the boss himself stood unexpectedly there to greet me.

"Are you okay?" he asked, giving me a long hug and then stepping back to hold me at arm's length long enough to give me an inquiring look.

"That depends on how you define *okay*," I said. "I've got all my teeth and my limbs are still attached, so I guess that's something. However, my love life is not progressing nearly as smoothly as I'd hoped, and several other parts of my life seem to be bumpy, as well."

Elliott bent his head and kissed me slowly, making a very satisfactory effort to remedy my first complaint. It was lovely while it lasted—all six seconds of it—until a young woman barged in with a stack of files and bumbled out again, embarrassed and stammering out apologies.

"We don't seem to be able to catch a break," sighed

Elliott as we pulled apart and drifted to our respective places. His desk was an antique deal table of well-worn oak with an old-fashioned wooden office chair to go along with it. Behind him was an antique telescope in perfect working condition, a gift from a grateful client.

"So what are you doing back in town?" I asked. "Did you get a summary judgment?"

"No. The judge is giving her instructions to the jury this afternoon, but Carlson thinks that the earliest we'll get a verdict is tomorrow afternoon. I was worried because I jobbed out that background investigation you needed on Cypress Computer, that outfit out of Seattle, and I wanted to check in and see how things are going. I know how important this computer thing is to you."

"As it turns out we don't need the information anymore," I said. "I'm sorry. The good news is we were able to make a deal without it. The even better news is that my client will be able to pay whatever bill you send them."

"That good?"

"That good. But I'm still sorry you made the trip for nothing."

"I had to come back anyway to get some work started for a new client. As soon as I finish up, I'll be heading back to Springfield to help keep the vigil."

Never having been a trial lawyer, I've never had to endure the suspended animation of waiting out the verdict. However, I'd heard enough from other people to understand the reasons the legal team needed to suffer through it together. For everyone who'd worked on the trial, the agony of waiting rendered even the simplest of tasks beyond their attention and made them unfit to be with normal people. I imagined them filling in the hours back at the Ramada pacing the halls and talking over the

CHAPTER
16

"Please tell me that you're kidding," I begged.

"What's the big deal? I get assignments from Denise all the time. She wants us to do a quick backgrounder on HCC."

"I understand, but it seems weird to think of you working for my mother," I sighed.

"In my experience it never hurts to have Mom on your side," Elliott pointed out with a sly grin that immediately brought to mind thoughts that would have made my mother blush.

"So what have you dug up?"

"I've had people working the phones since yesterday, talking to anybody who's had dealings with HCC. We started out targeting transactions that are similar to the one they're attempting with Prescott Memorial."

"So what have you found out? Anything?"

"Well, for one thing, there's no shortage of people eager to talk to us. Usually people are reluctant to spill their guts when they get a phone call from an investigator out of the blue, but apparently the people who've been burned by HCC are just panting to tell their stories. One of my people suggested that we bill the people she's talked to, charging them for a therapy hour."

"So who have you talked to?"

"Mostly doctors and hospital administrators. Like I said, the problem isn't getting these people to talk, it's getting them to shut up."

"So what are they saying?"

"Basically that HCC is a take-no-prisoners operation."

"There's no law against being ruthless," I reminded him.

"True. But there's ruthless and then there's breaking the rules."

"Any proof that HCC has done the latter?"

"Do you know what it says below Gerald Packman's picture in his high school yearbook?"

"Please tell me that you didn't actually check to find this out. . . . No, I take that back, tell me that you're not *billing* me for the time it took to find this out."

"Are we thorough or what?" he countered, smiling. "Under his picture it says, 'If you aren't cheating, you aren't trying.' "

"I don't think I want to live in a world where people are held accountable for what it says in their yearbooks. As I recall, I think I quoted some Warren Zevon lyrics. You know the one: Send lawyers, guns, and money. Dad get me out of this."

"It's just interesting in light of a common thread that seems to be popping up in a lot of these interviews."

"Which is?"

"People keep hinting that one of the reasons that HCC is always able to close their deals so quickly is that they have someone inside the target hospital feeding them information."

"What kind of information?" I demanded.

"What kind of information would you want if you were trying to take over a hospital?"

"Financial information, inside dope on the medical staff, like which docs are calling the shots and which ones are bringing in the bucks. I'd want to know about the physical assets, the property, buildings, and equipment, union contracts, relationships with suppliers, any formal referral contracts they have in place—"

"So who would have access to that kind of information?"

"Depends on the hospital, but it would be someone at the top, either a doctor or an administrator. Do you think there's any chance that they're pulling the same stunt in Chicago?"

"I have no way of knowing, but in my experience companies aren't that different from the people who run them. They tend to stick with what they know and what has worked for them in the past."

"Is there some way to find out for sure?"

"You know our motto. There's always a way to find out; all it takes is time and money."

"We don't have much time."

"Then it would help if we could narrow down the field. Who at Prescott Memorial is in a position to provide the kind of information we're talking about to HCC?"

"Not too many people. Most of the docs at Prescott Memorial are only there a couple of days a week. They're not involved in the running of the hospital per se. That puts Kyle Massius on the top of the list. He's the president of the hospital, and he'd not only have access to the information, he'd know most of it off the top of his head. The only trouble is that he's also made no secret of the fact that he's in favor of the sale."

"Why would that be a problem?"

"Because it makes him either incredibly altruistic or incredibly naive."

"Why is that?" Elliott prodded.

"One of the first things HCC will probably do if they

take over the hospital is fire him and bring in their own people."

"Not if he's already cut a deal with them. One of the things we keep hearing from people is that after HCC takes over, unexpected people wind up on top."

"Which is why everyone thinks the winners in the takeover were secretly working for HCC before the fact. I don't know. The whole thing sounds like a mixture of sour grapes and paranoia to me. Besides, what kind of incentives could HCC offer? Villas in Tuscany?"

"How about a cut of the profits? According to the company's annual report, and I quote, 'Aligning physicians through financial incentives is one of HCC's primary tools for medical efficacy.'"

"Meaning that the best way to get doctors to do what you want is to cut them in on a piece of the action. How big a piece do you think we're talking about?"

"I don't know, but apparently the dollar amounts are huge," Elliott replied. "According to one source there was a radiologist in Kansas City who actually did buy a villa in Tuscany after HCC took over."

"Yeah, but you couldn't even buy a cheeseburger with what Prescott Memorial makes a year. They lose money."

"I see your point."

"Unless whoever it is has made a deal for a piece of the bigger picture," I mused out loud. "It's pretty obvious that HCC is trying to make their move into a major metropolitan market and Chicago is it. I just found out they've approached the archdiocese about taking over the management of the city's Catholic hospitals. The good news is that my mother seems to have succeeded in derailing that. The bad news is that they've sued my mother, alleging millions of dollars in damages."

"But I still don't get why HCC is interested in Prescott Memorial."

"Because none of the physicians at Prescott Memorial are on staff full-time. They're all affiliated with other hospitals, and most hold medical school appointments, as well. Win the hearts and minds of the Prescott Memorial medical staff and you've got a foot in the door of every major hospital in the city."

"So who at Prescott Memorial besides Massius would be in the best position to help them do that?"

"When you think about it, it's still a pretty short list. There were only three trustees who voted for the sale: Carl Laffer, the hospital's chief of staff; Gavin McDermott, who's chief of surgery; and Kyle Massius."

Elliott jotted their names down on the legal pad in front of him. "Anybody else you can think of?"

I considered for a moment. "Farah Davies."

"You mean the woman we met the other night? The one with the hair and the eyes?"

"Yes. She's the head of obstetrics and gynecology at Prescott Memorial, as well as a professor at the University of Chicago medical school. I wouldn't be surprised if there wasn't some kind of history between her and McDermott. Not only that, but if I remember correctly, she was pretty steamed when she got passed over and Carl Laffer was named chief of staff at Prescott Memorial. There was even some talk about her filing suit for sex discrimination, but in the end she decided against it."

"I just wish I could remember where it is I know her from," sighed Elliott, shaking his head.

"Maybe she was one of your old girlfriends' gynecologist?" I offered helpfully.

"Very funny. What made her decide not to sue? She didn't exactly strike me as the type who'd run from a fight."

"They bought her off by making her head of OB-GYN."

"Interesting . . . ," mused Elliott.

"Why is that so interesting?"

"Because if someone bought her off once, then somebody else could buy her off again."

That night I stopped on my way home and picked up Thai food from the storefront across the street from the apartment. After I'd put her in a cab outside of Joan Bornstein's office, Claudia had gone home and tried to nap on the couch, only to be woken by yet another hang-up call. By the time I got there, her nerves were such a mess that I dragged out the bottle of Absolut we kept in the freezer for just such emergencies and poured her a healthy shot. After we'd knocked back a couple and helped ourselves to pad thai, the conversation turned to Carlos.

When I mentioned that I'd run into him at the hospital on the night of Bill Delius's heart attack, she confessed that he'd taken to hanging out in the ER even on the nights he wasn't working if she was on trauma call. Not only that but she'd found roses in her locker and love notes on the windshield of her car.

"Your locker in the on-call room?" I demanded. "Isn't that off limits to everyone but house staff?"

"Yes," agreed Claudia. "After it happened, I went to the head of security about it."

"What did he say?"

"He practically laughed me out of his office. There was no note left with the flowers, no way of proving that Carlos was the one who'd left them. I'm sure he was thinking that women should be thrilled to have someone leaving them notes and flowers. He told me to come back if Carlos threatened me."

"I'm sure you found that reassuring," I remarked as I refilled her glass. Claudia might be a ninety-eight-pound weakling, but she could drink like a stevedore.

"Absolutely," replied Claudia. "I can sleep so much better at night knowing that if Carlos decides to beat me up in the parking lot, I'll be able to go back to that jerk in security and tell him 'I told you so.' " She drained her glass. "You know, before this happened with Carlos, I used to be so smug. I'd see these women in the ER who'd been abused by their boyfriends, and I'd ask myself why they didn't just get out, or worse, why they got mixed up with these losers in the first place. I don't know what I was thinking. I guess I figured they showed up on the first date wearing a T-shirt that says, 'I beat women.' "

"So what are you going to do?"

"I was thinking of calling his wife, except that I'm afraid that if she says anything to him, he may end up taking it out on her . . . ." She groaned. "This whole thing is making me crazy. Half the time I think I'm being stalked, and the other half I think I'm just being paranoid."

"You're not being paranoid," I said. "There has to be somebody else you can go to. What about Dr. Laffer? Isn't he in charge of the fellowship program?"

"Yeah, but I hate to go to him after this whole thing with Mrs. Estrada. He's going to end up thinking that I'm some kind of wacko—killing patients, being stalked by married ex-boyfriends . . . ."

"I thought you said he stood up for you in the M&M conference. Besides, you're always telling me what a good guy he is."

"You're right," said Claudia. "That's the trouble with being stalked by a psycho. It actually does make you paranoid."

* * *

I couldn't speak for Claudia, but the next morning I was forced to confront the cruel reality that I wasn't getting any younger—or at least my head and stomach weren't. Of course, it didn't help that I had to be in court bright and early. We were scheduled to present our request for an injunction against the sale of the hospital to HCC at eight. While Tom Galloway, one of the firm's marquee litigators, was set to make the argument for our side, I still had to show up.

Even without a hangover I find the courthouse depressing: the hallways crammed with milling people, the tired cops and harried lawyers who seem less concerned with justice than with just keeping a large and imperfect system grinding forward. I chafed at the feeling of supplication that hung in the air, the asking and the arguing, the sense of being at the mercy of some black-robed functionary who'd more likely than not risen to the bench less for his legal acumen than his ability to suck up. Fortunately I didn't have anything of substance to do. All I had to do was sit at the counsel table, pretend to take notes, and if possible, avoid throwing up.

There were only the two of us at the plaintiff's table, with my mother sitting demurely in her St. John's knits behind us. In contrast, HCC had a phalanx of lawyers, who overflowed the seats and spilled a full three rows back. There were attorneys for Prescott Memorial as well as HCC, giving my mother and me the bitter satisfaction of knowing that we were paying, however indirectly, for the services of the people working against us. I spotted Kyle Massius among them, looking as though he fit right in there with the suits and the stiffs. My mother, sitting ramrod straight, fixed him with a look of diamond hardness.

Tom, I thought, did a magnificent job of presenting our request for an injunction delaying any sale of the hospital for an additional thirty days. But it made little impression on the judge, a phlegmy old man who I suspected of being a borderline narcoleptic. He ruled against us, seemingly without reflection. At least the lawyers for HCC had the decency to save their high fives for the hallway.

Even though I knew that being granted the injunction was a long shot, I was surprised by the extent of my disappointment. Ruefully I had to admit that while failure was one thing, failure in front of one's mother was quite another. The dry thanks she offered up for my doing my best did little to assuage my feelings of inadequacy and, even less explicably, guilt.

My disappointment was mitigated somewhat by the fact that Mother was clearly winning the public relations war. Unfortunately, whatever ink she garnered not only aided our fight against HCC, but also provided ammunition for their breach-of-confidentiality suit against her. While she might not be aware of it, with every interview she granted—and they were already waiting for her on the courthouse steps—Mother raised the stakes. We *had* to figure out some way to keep Prescott Memorial out of the clutches of HCC.

As soon as I got back to Callahan Ross I summoned Sherman Whitehead to my office and instructed him to draft a new complaint against HCC. The argument I outlined for him was based on the premise that their offer to buy Prescott Memorial was tainted by illegally obtained insider information. I was gambling that within the next four days Elliott would succeed in unearthing the name of the HCC mole in time for us to insert it into the complaint. However, I could tell from the look on Sherman's face that if anything, he thought that this one was an even longer shot than the first.

*   *   *

That night I was pleased to see the lights burning in the apartment window when I finally arrived home. I found Claudia sitting in the dining room with patient charts fanned out around her, making notes on her legal pad with the concentration of a monk copying a holy text.

"Are these charts from the patients who died?" I asked, appalled to think that each of the buff folders lying on the table represented a life lost.

"So far. The advantage of being a female doctor is you get a chance to get to know the nurses from the changing room. Once I asked, it was easy to come up with the names. Everyone remembers the ones who die, especially the nurses."

"Why's that, do you think?"

"To the surgeons, they're just another case. You know, the gallbladder in room four. We don't really have too much to do with them when they're awake, but for the nurses it's different. To them, the patients are actually people."

"So how's it going?"

"A lot slower than you'd think. It's hard to look for a pattern when you have no idea what you're looking for."

"Just take your time. It'll come to you."

"That's the problem. It's against the rules to remove patient charts from the hospital. If they found out I took them home, it's a firing offense."

"How would they find out?"

"They're signed out to me. All it would take is someone else coming around looking for them. That's why I have to get them back to the hospital as soon as I can."

"Why don't you photocopy them?"

"I thought of that. But there are literally thousands of pages. It would take me days."

"Then let me take them into the office. I'll have our duplicators do it. You'll have them tomorrow night. That way you can get the charts back to the hospital before anybody has a chance to miss them."

Claudia took off her glasses and laid them in front of her on the table, making her face look simultaneously unfinished and exposed. With her thumb and forefinger she massaged the bridge of her nose as wearily as an old man.

"Goddammit, I wish I worked someplace where if you screw up, a brick'll be out of place or there'll be a little ripple in the cement, but folks aren't going to die."

"I know it's something of an understatement, but you've had a bad couple of days," I reminded her.

"No, the more I think about it, I've had a bad couple of decades."

"Oh, come on—" I protested.

"No, no, listen to me. I've been giving this a lot of thought. How long have you known me?"

"Since freshman year."

"And when did you find out that I wanted to go into medicine?"

"Probably the first day I met you."

"You know why? Because I've known that I wanted to be a doctor from the time I was thirteen years old. Not only that, but from that time on I set out to do it in the most focused and rational way I could. In high school, college, medical school, choosing an internship—I never let anything or anybody stand in the way of what I wanted to do. My whole life was plotted and planned and aimed at getting this degree, getting this profession."

"Yes. And look what you've accomplished."

"I know. It makes me jealous."

"Jealous of what?"

"Jealous of medicine. I love it and I'm mad at it." She

sighed as she put her glasses back on. "There's a lot of talk among the nurses about surgeons being a bunch of superannuated adolescents. I'm starting to think that they're right. We all spent the years that most people use to learn how to be grownups learning to be surgeons. I used to tell myself that it was just a guy thing, you know, boys and their toys. But now I see that there are things I should have done, things I'm sorry I didn't have the courage to do."

"Like what?" I asked, conjuring up the image of Claudia with her hand inside Bill Delius's chest and wondering what on earth she'd be afraid of tackling.

"I should have taken a year off and gone to Europe when I had the chance when I was nineteen. I should have bought a Corvette when I couldn't afford it or had my heart broken by the captain of the football team. Hell, when I was in high school, I didn't even know they had a football team. I was always in the library studying. All the dumb little things that don't amount to a hill of beans, but give you a chance to make mistakes, to get to know what it's like to fail."

I saw her point. In the years since I'd begun practicing law, I'd gotten my lunch handed back to me on a fair number of occasions, but somehow having had practice falling on my ass as a teenager had made it easier. They say that good judgment is the product of experience, and experience is the product of bad judgment. But what happened when all you'd experienced was success?

"This thing with Mrs. Estrada has just wiped me out," confessed Claudia miserably. "The problem is that surgery is a catch-22. You couldn't do it if you didn't believe in yourself, believe in your abilities. You'd freeze up, you'd worry so much about the potential consequences of your mistakes that you'd end up making them. But you not only let it make you cocky, you even lie to yourself that it's not arrogance. Instead you say that you owe it to your patient to have complete confidence in your skill. You tell yourself that if you show doubt or hesitation, even for a second, then it affects the entire team and hurts the patient. You actually start believing that there's nothing you can't fix, nothing you can't cure. But do you want to know what the worst part is?"

"What?"

"Somebody has to die before you realize that you were wrong."

CHAPTER
17

The next morning I got up early hoping to catch Claudia before she left for the hospital. Even though I wasn't sure what I wanted to say, I knew that I needed to talk to her. I'd gone to bed feeling uneasy, overwhelmed by the sense that with both Claudia's and my worlds thrust into turmoil over Prescott Memorial, events were moving too fast to be understood. I had gone to bed with the nagging feeling that I was missing something central, something important.

But when I woke up, I realized that what was really worrying me was Carlos. Just the fact that Claudia, the least alarmist woman on the planet, had gone to Security about him spoke volumes about the magnitude of the threat. I was glad that she'd taken it seriously. Having spent the better part of the last four years in emergency rooms, Claudia knew firsthand that more women seek treatment for injuries caused by their husbands or boyfriends than from car accidents, robberies, and rapes combined. It seemed worse than ironic that a hospital security officer, of all people, would choose to do nothing about a female doctor clearly at risk.

But when I got up and went looking for her, Claudia had already gone. In her place in the dining room was the neatly packed carton that contained the Prescott Memorial files. Beside it, with a surgeon's customary economy of effort, was a one-word note in my roommate's draftsmanlike print. All it said was "thanks."

Disappointed, I went into the kitchen and made coffee. As I waited for the hot water to hiss and chug through the filter into the pot, I watched the changing of the guard. Outside the window, the street people and the scavengers roused themselves with the first light of the morning and got to their feet. They folded up their greasy blankets and moved on to the park or, if the police were already finished with their late-night sweeps, the relative warmth of the train station. No sooner had the last of them slipped from view than my neighbors began trickling from the building, clutching their commuter cups against the chill, unlocking the Club from their steering wheels, and heading off to work.

When the coffee had finished brewing, I poured myself a cup and made my way back down the long hall to my bedroom. I spent much longer than usual rooting through my closet trying to decide what to wear. As I pushed through dark suit after dark suit it seemed as if my entire wardrobe consisted of garments designed to either intimidate or impress. The only problem with that was that today what I wanted to do was persuade.

I settled on a gray wool suit with a blouse of pinkish silk, and in a radical departure—for me at least—I elected to wear my hair down. I brushed it carefully, pulling it back off my face with a velvet band. Then I forced myself to take my time with my makeup, extending my usually slapdash routine of mascara and lipstick with eye shadow and blush. So far my usual tactics had gotten me nowhere with the first two Prescott trustees. With only one more pitch ahead of me, it was time to try a different approach.

Cheryl had set up the meeting with Dr. Carl Laffer at

his medical school office, away from the distraction of patients and the emotionally charged ground of Prescott Memorial. Of all the members of the Prescott Memorial board, the hospital's chief of staff was the one with whom I was least well acquainted. He was also the one I'd heard the best things about. I thought about how he'd managed to diffuse the animosity that had crackled between McDermott and Farah Davis at the Founders Ball, and crossed my fingers. With any luck I was finally about to find myself face-to-face with a reasonable man.

Normally I avoid the freeway by force of habit. Before the Jaguar, I drove an ancient and unreliable Volvo that wheezed dangerously whenever I ventured above fifty and shuddered through every pothole. But today, almost without thinking, I found myself hopping on the interchange that would get me onto the Eisenhower Expressway, eager to avoid passing by McCormack Place, whose hulking presence now conjured up visceral memories of Bill Delius's heart attack.

Rush-Presbyterian-St. Luke's Medical Center is an amalgam of merged hospitals that were cobbled together during the last crisis in medical care. It lay directly west of downtown and encompassed the west-side VA and Cook County Hospital, home of the world's largest and busiest emergency department. Like Prescott Memorial to the south, it was a refuge and a lifeline for the city's poorest of the poor.

Rush-St. Luke's sprawling medical campus was confusing to all but the initiated, and enormously difficult to find your way around. Cheryl had drawn me a map and typed out instructions to Laffer's office. They were so detailed they read like directions for finding the Holy Grail. Once I'd parked the car, I did my best to follow them as I tried not to think about what would become of me once Cheryl graduated.

I navigated the endless string of white-coated corridors, eventually ending up at Carl Laffer's office almost as much by accident as design. Like McDermott, Dr. Laffer was talking on the phone when his secretary showed me in. But he not only hung up as soon as I was through the door, he also apologized, rising to his feet to bid me welcome and to take my hand in his mighty grip.

Laffer was a tall man, tall enough to make me feel short. If his altitude weren't enough of a tip-off—he was at least six inches over six feet—his office made no secret of his passion for basketball. The way that Laffer liked to tell it, if he had been a half a step faster, medicine would have lost a compassionate physician and the NBA would have gained a mediocre center. He was, according to Claudia, passionate about three things: opera, Hoosier basketball, and surgery—not necessarily in that order. I smiled and took my seat, wishing I'd had the time to bone up on Bobby Knight's biography. Claudia reported that Laffer believed that the Indiana University basketball coach was the greatest strategic thinker of the twentieth century. On second thought, maybe he wasn't as reasonable as I'd hoped.

"I'm sorry I wasn't able to make time to see you sooner," Laffer began, pushing aside a pile of patient charts eerily similar to the ones in the trunk of my car. "But between teaching, seeing patients, and my administrative duties at Prescott Memorial, my days get pretty full."

"I appreciate your making the time to see me at all," I replied. "It gives me the opportunity to thank you in person."

"For what?" he asked. From the look on his face I

knew that at least I wasn't going to have to juggle to get his attention.

"You saved my client's life Friday night."

"Your client?"

"A man by the name of Bill Delius who came into the emergency room with a heart attack." While I knew it violated my agreement with Claudia about keeping our friendship in the background, I told myself that circumstances had changed. Not only might Laffer listen more closely to what I had to say if he knew that Claudia and I were friends, but at this point it couldn't hurt Claudia for the hospital to know that she had friends in high places.

"So you're the lady lawyer Dr. Stein was talking about," he observed with a strange look of enlightenment. "As I recall, Claudia lectured me that I'd better save Mr. Delius or her roommate was going to sue us. I knew she lived with a lawyer, I just didn't know that the lawyer was you. So how do you two know each other?"

"We were roommates at Bryn Mawr," I explained. "We've been friends ever since."

"She's a gifted physician. Your client was lucky she was on trauma call the night his heart decided to act up. At any other hospital they probably would have pronounced him DOA."

"I know," I said. "That's one of the reasons I came to see you today."

"Oh?" he inquired warily, no doubt wondering if I'd come to pressure him to intercede on Claudia's behalf in the matter of Mrs. Estrada's death.

"I must confess that when my mother first asked me to help her stop the sale of Prescott Memorial, I had never given much thought to the hospital. Even when Claudia began her rotation and started telling me about her cases, I didn't really realize how unique it is as an institution and how important a job it does, not just in caring for patients but in training doctors."

Laffer looked surprised. "I thought all lawyers were pragmatists," he said.

"And I thought all doctors were altruists."

"It looks like we're both wrong." He chuckled dryly. "Medicine has changed. There isn't a lot of altruism left these days."

"Is that why you think the HCC deal is a good thing?"

"Good for whom? A hospital is a complex organization operating in a rapidly changing environment. Are we talking about what is best for the hospital? The patient? The doctor? As a physician, naturally I am committed to treating my patient to the very best of my ability. But what is my responsibility as chief of staff of the hospital? I cast my vote in favor of the sale because Gavin McDermott and Kyle Massius did a better job of convincing me that by selling to HCC we would keep Prescott Memorial in the business of serving the under-privileged. Your mother and her brother didn't have any concrete ideas except that we should keep on doing things as we've always done."

"What would make you change your mind?"

"Let's see—" Laffer chuckled, mischievously. "—how about a Learjet and season tickets for the Met?"

"I was thinking more in terms of a well-reasoned appeal to your better judgment, but maybe I could throw in a boxed set of Maria Callas CDs."

"I see you know all about my weakness for sopranos. What else has your roommate been telling you, I wonder?"

"She tells me that you're an able administrator and a good teacher," I replied truthfully. "She also told me that if you have a weakness, it's that you tend to think the best of everyone."

"Until proved otherwise."

"Then what if I told you that I could prove that HCC has no interest in continuing to serve Prescott Memorial's current patient population? That as soon as they take over, they plan on dismantling the residency and fellowship programs—"

"HCC has given us every assurance—" protested Dr. Laffer.

"In writing?" I demanded. "Anything that they can later be held to?" Laffer did not reply, and I knew from his silence that they had not. "Because even though I can't speak for the world of medicine, I can tell you for a fact that in the world of business, assurances are cheap, and as you very well know, providing high-quality medical care is expensive. HCC may be paying lip service to the idea of continuing the mission of Prescott Memorial, but do you know what kind of people we're really dealing with? In every market that HCC has moved into, they've attempted to control the number of patient beds by closing hospitals. If they succeed in making a move into Chicago, which hospital do you think they'll end up closing first?"

"It's as easy for you to say that as it is for Packman to make promises he doesn't intend to keep," pointed out Laffer.

"What if I can prove it?"

"Prove what? How can you prove what someone will or will not do in the future?"

"What if I can prove that Packman isn't playing by the rules? What if I can prove that he's cut a secret deal with someone on your staff—information now in exchange for a piece of the action later?"

"You have proof?"

"I can get it. All I want to know is yes or no. If I can prove that HCC has been dealing under the table, would you reconsider selling the hospital to them?"

Carl Laffer leveled his gray eyes at me. The expression on his face remained impassive. "You bring me hard evidence that HCC isn't playing by the rules or that they don't intend to keep their promises regarding continuing the work of the hospital," he said quietly, "and you have my word that I'll change my vote."

I stood on the sidewalk after my meeting with Carl Laffer, filled with hope and fear. Hope that I might be able to make enough of a case for HCC's perfidy that I would be able to convince Laffer to change his vote, and fear that I wouldn't be able to get the proof in time.

I also knew that there was very little that HCC wouldn't stoop to. From the suit they'd filed against my mother, I knew that HCC liked to play rough, and from what Elliott had told me, they didn't have any qualms about playing dirty. If they found out about what I was trying to do, what might they be willing to do to stop me? I was so preoccupied by the question that I didn't see Julia Gordon until I practically ran right into her.

"Hello there, neighbor," she declared cheerfully as I stopped dead in my tracks.

Julia, her husband, and two daughters lived just down the street from me in a pretty brownstone they were in the process of rehabbing themselves. She was a petite woman, ten years my senior, with a close cap of blond curls and an intelligent, heart-shaped face. From beneath her gray lab coat peaked the last two inches of a pretty floral dress, and sweet little grosgrain ribbons decorated the toes of her shoes. In one hand she held a Styrofoam cup of coffee and in the other a bagel wrapped in paper. Given a hundred chances, most people would never guess that Julia Gordon was a woman who took dead people apart for a living.

"So what brings you down to doctor land?" she asked.

Julia was an assistant medical examiner at the Cook County ME's office. I'd forgotten that their building was just around the corner on Harrison.

"A little arm-twisting session with one of the Prescott Memorial trustees," I said, figuring that now that we were on the front page of the newspaper, there was no use trying to be coy.

"I won't ask who was doing what to whom." She chuckled. "I seem to recall you going to work on me a couple of times, and there was never any question about who was going to end up on top."

"You wouldn't happen to have fifteen minutes for a little bit of hypothetical arm-twisting now?" I asked as it suddenly occurred to me that this was too good an opportunity to be missed.

"Hypothetical? Does that mean that no bones will be broken?"

"You have my word that it won't hurt a bit," I assured her.

"In that case why don't we go back to my office. If you want, you can have half of my bagel."

"I've already eaten," I lied, falling into step beside her. I don't care how much Muzak and air freshener they pumped into the place, the medical examiner's office was one of the few places that could kill even my appetite.

One look at the new Robert J. Stein Institute for Forensic Medicine and it was clear that if death were a business, in Chicago at least, it would be booming. A low-slung edifice of gray marble and dark, reflective glass, from the street it looked like any other kind of administrative building. But once you passed through its doors, there was no escaping the fact that the dead are an exacting clientele. Chilly even in summer, the temperature was kept at sixty-five degrees because it was kinder on the bodies. The air was thick with the smells of form-aldehyde and decay. We took the elevator to the fourth floor, far from the metal storage lockers and the grisly tile of the autopsy suites with their drains in the floor.

As far as I was concerned, Julia Gordon's office was gruesome enough. Beside the glossy posters of bullet wounds that decorated the walls, the bookshelves were dotted with anatomical oddities floating in jars. On the back of the door there hung another poster, this one dis-playing the characteristic tire marks made by various brands. It wasn't until you looked closely that you real-ized that all the marks that had been photographed were made in the flesh of the victims of traffic accidents.

I looked around at the files and papers that littered her desk. "I hope I'm not imposing too much on your time," I began. "You look busy."

"To be perfectly honest, I'm grateful for the distrac-tion. There's something I have to do this morning that I've been trying to avoid. You're just giving me a chance to procrastinate a little longer."

"What is it?" I asked, wondering what a woman rou-tinely dissecting would view with such dread.

"I have to call a resident at a community hospital out in Park Ridge who made an error. She was on duty when the paramedics brought in a four-year-old girl who'd been struck by a hit-and-run driver. Instinctively, and no doubt out of kindness, she insisted on washing the little girl's body before her parents saw her. I know that she meant to spare the parents, but in doing so she destroyed any evidence that we might have found that would lead to finding her killer. Now, even if an eyewitness were to materialize, I don't think that would be enough for the prosecutor to take before a grand jury."

"You make being a lawyer seem like a day at the

beach," I said, thinking about Claudia's comment about wishing that she had a job where mistakes didn't matter.

"Oh, I don't know if our jobs are really that different," she replied. "After all, what I deal with is the aftermath of people's fear or greed or stupidity. I'm sure that you could say the same about your work. The only difference is that what I do smells worse and is much more interesting."

"How can you be so sure that it's more interesting?"

"Because every life, no matter how tragic or mundane, is a story, and I'm the person who gets to tell the end."

"I guess that's what I wanted to ask you about— hypothetically, of course."

"You and I both know that there's no such thing as a hypothetical question," she replied sweetly, "only people who want to put some distance between themselves and what they want to know."

"In that case I hope you'll wait before you start leaping to any conclusions," I replied, suddenly wondering if this was such a good idea. "I wanted to ask you how you might go about killing off hospital patients."

Dr. Gordon raised her eyebrows and shot me an appraising look. "Assuming you don't want to get caught?" she asked.

"Yes."

"Well, I don't know what I would do, because it's not a question I've ever really considered, but I *can* tell you what's been done in the past. For example, there was a fairly recent case where a male nurse in Oregon was convicted of killing seventeen patients by injecting them with potassium chloride."

"Is that a poison?"

"No, it's a drug that's commonly used in low concentration to control irregular heartbeat. At higher doses it's fatal."

"Why did he do it?"

"I don't think they ever found out. As I recall, there were several witnesses for the defense who all testified that he was a particularly conscientious and devoted caregiver. I believe the theory the prosecution presented to the jury was that his actions were an extreme form of burnout. The defense tried to make the case that the nurse was driven to madness by the escalating demands of managed care."

"What about the others?"

"Well, by far the most famous case was at the Veteran's Hospital in Ann Arbor, Michigan, mostly because the number of patients involved was huge. There were something like forty patients—practically an epidemic—who experienced episodes of cardiopulmonary arrest. I don't know if you are familiar with it, but cardiopulmonary arrest is almost always fatal unless artificial respiration is begun immediately. Fortunately, there was a pair of Filipino nurses who seemed not only particularly vigilant, but highly skilled at the technique. Due to their efforts, out of the forty cases only seven of the patients died."

"So what happened?" I asked, thinking about the sixteen folders in the trunk of my car.

"Well, naturally the sheer number of incidents involved raised suspicions that something abnormal was going on. An investigation was eventually launched, which led to four of the bodies being exhumed and autopsied."

"What did they find?"

"Absolutely nothing."

"You're kidding."

"No, but because the deaths occurred on federal property, the medical examiner was able to send tissue samples to the FBI crime lab."

"Did they find anything?"

"Yes. In every one of the patients they found a drug called pancuronium. It's a neuromuscular blocking agent that's actually a synthetic form of curare. It's most commonly known by its brand name, Pavulon."

"I thought curare was a poison."

"If by that you mean that it can be used to kill people, then half the drugs that are commonly prescribed are poisons. Pavulon acts by inducing temporary muscle paralysis. In high enough doses it stops your heart from beating and your lungs from breathing. It's used in the operating room during anesthesia as part of a mixture of different anesthesia drugs."

"What does it look like?"

"It's a colorless, odorless liquid that resembles water. It's very fast acting, but conversely its effects disappear quickly. That's why the nurses were able to both induce arrest in their patients and then reverse it."

"You mean it was the two nurses who were killing off the patients?" I demanded.

"Yes."

"But again, why?"

"Again, nobody knows for sure. Some people believe that the two women did it to draw attention to what they felt was an acute shortage of nurses. Several psychiatrists were called in to interview them both, and their conclusion was that both women were mentally ill and craved the attention they received whenever they successfully resuscitated a patient."

"What I want to know is why it took forty cases before they launched an investigation."

"I wasn't there so I can't say, but I think in part it was a natural unwillingness to consider the possibility of foul play in a hospital. You also have to take into account that death is not an unusual occurrence in a medical setting. I hope you're not thinking of killing off hospital patients?"

"No," I assured her.

"Then can I ask you what exactly it is that's prompting your question?"

"I'm afraid not," I replied apologetically.

"Then at least promise me one thing," she said, suddenly looking stern. "If your question gets any less hypothetical, you'll come to me first."

CHAPTER
18

In big law firms, light and space are the twin talismans of power. Like some principle of relativity, the closer you are to the top, the more you have. There is nothing subtle about the system. At Callahan Ross you are meant to always know exactly where in the hierarchy you are.

The first thing I did when I got into the office was pay a visit to the bottom rung of the ladder, to the airless, lightless world of the messengers and file clerks in order to drop off the box of Claudia's files. I filled out the rush slip, stopping just long enough to pay tribute to James, the former army drill sergeant who presided over the endless stream of paper that was the lifeblood of the firm.

I decided to climb the six flights of stairs back to my office. I figured it was the only exercise I was likely to get in the foreseeable future. I also knew it was the only time I was going to have to myself that day, and I desperately needed time to think.

What on earth had I hoped to accomplish by spewing out my crackpot theories to Julia Gordon? Did I really think that she would just sit back and wait patiently for more bodies to turn up? She'd probably been on the phone to the police the minute I left her office.

Trudging up the spiral of the firm's internal staircase,

I ascended through the well-ordered precincts of real estate, tax, litigation, antitrust, corporate finance, and international law. With every floor the idea of someone systematically killing off Gavin McDermott's patients seemed increasingly absurd. If the deaths were indeed the result of the acts of a madman, then it truly was a matter for the police. Perhaps if the truth were revealed, the adverse publicity might discourage HCC from pursuing the hospital, just as my mother's outspokenness had soured discussions with the archdiocese.

As I finally arrived at the floor that housed the various corporate departments, including my own, I was struck by a truly horrible thought. Elliott had said that there was a difference between being ruthless and ruthlessly refusing to abide by the rules. Was it possible that Gerald Packman was somehow engineering the deaths in order to deliberately make Prescott Memorial seem less desirable and drive down the price? I didn't like to think that even someone as cold as Packman would be capable of such calculation, but in my experience the higher the stakes, the more ruthless people were prepared to be. Still, if Packman was behind the deaths, then why wasn't the story public?

What was he waiting for?

On my way back to my office I stopped to see how document preparation was going on Delirium. I found Jeff Tannenbaum at his desk, up to his eyeballs in paper, cursing softly under his breath. Preparing the documents for a transaction of the sort that we'd negotiated between Delirium and Icon was a monumental task. Unlike litigation, the skills required were not those taught in law school, where the focus is on fact finding, argument, and the application of rules to facts.

The side of the law for which most people look to

lawyers—planning and getting things done—was learned through apprenticeship. In corporate practice, deals were traded and documented at the speed of a fax machine, and the only way to learn what you needed to know was from someone who was experienced and let you participate in the process. Even so, there was always a moment when you had to let go of your mentor's hand and walk through the minefield on your own. A combination of circumstances had conspired to make the Delirium-Icon deal a closing that Jeff Tannenbaum would have to handle on his own.

As much as I believed him to be ready—if he wasn't, we had no business making him a partner—it didn't make it any easier for me to let go. Most deals are repeats of other deals, with no new ground broken, but the price of error is invariably steep. I asked Jeff if he needed help on anything, and he answered no. It took every ounce of self-discipline I had to take him at his word.

As I walked past Cheryl's desk she shot out of her seat and began gesturing wildly.

"Don't go in there!" she exclaimed, pointing at my office door, which was closed.

"Why not?" I demanded.

"Your mother is in there!"

"Oh, my god," I groaned, collapsing dramatically over the top of Cheryl's cubicle in self-pity. "What's she doing here? What does she want?"

"I don't know. But right now she's in there interviewing another secretarial candidate."

"I don't believe you," I said, making a half-hearted attempt to pull out my hair. "You're making this up just to torment me."

"No such luck. Apparently you never told Mrs. Goodlow that you would be unavailable this afternoon, so she went ahead and scheduled you to interview a job candidate."

"So what's this one like?"

"I didn't really get a chance to talk to him. But he and your mother seem to have really hit it off."

"He?" I demanded, straightening myself up.

"Three strikes, remember? By the way, have you seen Jeff? I saw him in the elevator, and he looked like he was about to throw up."

"What did I look like the first time I coordinated a closing?" I asked.

"As I recall, you actually did throw up a couple of times," conceded my secretary.

"Believe me, you will, too."

"Okay, Ms. Tough-Guy, you'd better go in there and talk to your mommy before she comes out here and kills us both."

"How do I look?" I asked, giving my hair an ineffectual pat.

"Approximately the same color as Jeff," replied my secretary, as I squared my shoulders and prepared to face the music.

I found my mother sitting next to an extremely handsome and well-groomed young man on the leather couch in my office. Their heads were close together, and they were both laughing. Eventually they noticed that I was there, and the man who wanted to be my secretary rose quickly to his feet. He was wearing a charcoal suit tailored to the swooning point, an immaculately pressed white shirt with French cuffs, and a Hermes silk tie. His wing tips had been buffed to a military sheen, as were his fingernails. His teeth were perfect.

I knew immediately that there had to be something wrong with him. Either that, or Cheryl was wrong about

Mrs. Goodlow and her three-strikes rule, and in my experience Cheryl was never wrong.

"Kate, I'd like you to meet Tim Lovesy," declared my mother, as I shook hands with Mrs. Goodlow's latest offering. "He and I have just had the most amusing chat while we were waiting for you to get here."

"I'm very pleased to meet you," he said.

At least I knew that he spoke English. Maybe the problem was that he was illiterate.

I murmured something in reply, completely thrown off guard by the highly presentable Mr. Lovesy.

"I'm sure the two of you will get along famously," my mother assured him, beaming.

"You mean, provided she wants to give me the job," he replied.

"Oh, nonsense," declared Mother. "Of course she's giving you the job. If you can't trust your mother's judgment in these things, who else can you possibly trust?"

As Cheryl took Tim back to Mrs. Goodlow's office to discuss salary and benefits, I told myself that it was all just a bad dream. With any luck, I'd wake up in my own warm bed, ready to start the day all over again. My mother took a seat in the wing chair that visitors sat in, and crossed her ankles gracefully as she launched into a litany of Mr. Lovesy's charms. I listened in utter amazement, wondering what on earth my mother was up to.

"So what brings you to the office?" I asked, as soon as she paused for a breath.

"Well, I've been doing some thinking about this whole Prescott Memorial mess," she replied lightly. "I think perhaps we've been overreacting."

"Don't even think about it," I cut her off, suddenly understanding the motive for her charm.

"I don't know what you're talking about," she replied, somewhat taken aback.

"Yes, you do. You came here to tell me that you've changed your mind, didn't you? They've sued, and now you want to get out of it!"

"I'm afraid it's a bit more complicated than that," she declared. "They've raked up all those horrible old stories about Great-grandfather, and they're feeding them to the press."

Mother handed me a manila envelope. Inside was what appeared to be the draft of a magazine piece entitled "Blood Money." A note clipped to the front indicated that it was slated for publication in *North Shore*, a glossy lifestyle magazine that circulated in the city's affluent northern suburbs. I skimmed it quickly. It was about the purported origins of Chicago's most famous family fortunes and how many of the city's most prominent philanthropists owed their good fortune to an ancestor who hadn't hesitated to rob, smuggle, or even commit murder for financial gain.

While Everett Prescott was featured prominently, his exploits running opium and guns in the China trade were hardly the only misdeeds the article chronicled. I had to hand it to Gerald Packman. There was almost nothing that would mortify my family more than to be pilloried in public, except perhaps knowing that their friends were being subjected to the same treatment on their account.

"Denise says she's received phone calls from reporters at the *Tribune* and the *Sun-Times* saying that they're thinking of doing similar articles," complained Mother.

"I warned you this would happen," I said, trying my best to sound sympathetic. "You have to see this for what it is, a sign that we're getting to them. I told you they would never go down without a fight. Well, this is how they're fighting."

"If they publish this, it will kill your grandmother," declared Mother dramatically. "You might as well just go ahead and order the coffin."

"There is nothing new in this," I said, pointing to the manuscript. "Every single one of these allegations—that Everett Prescott made his money selling drugs and guns, that he kept Chinese women—every single one of them has been in print before. Hell, how else do you think they managed to dig it all up so fast? Believe me, Grandmother will live through it."

"That's easy enough for you to say. You didn't get this in the mail today." Mother reached into the Neiman Marcus bag at her feet and pulled out a package just slightly larger than a shoebox and handed it to me. It felt terribly light.

"It's empty," I said.

"No, it's not. Look inside."

I lifted up the top. Inside was a sheet of white paper on which someone had scrawled in red crayon the single word, BANG!

CHAPTER
19

That night I took Mother's Neiman Marcus bag along with me to dinner. I was meeting Elliott at Brasserie Jo, the pretty French bistro on Hubbard. He'd called while I was in with my mother, and Cheryl had accepted his dinner invitation on my behalf. Unfortunately, she hadn't thought to ask him whether the judge had handed down a verdict yet in the fraud case, so I didn't know if Elliott was back from Springfield for an hour or for good.

A quick call from Cheryl to the personal shopper at Saks solved the problem of what I was going to wear—a dove gray suit with a cropped jacket with a round feminine collar and a short and narrow skirt. There was also a scoop-necked blouse to wear underneath. When I held it up to my shoulders, it looked like it would expose more skin than I usually show at the beach.

I laid it over the back of my chair and took the black Manolo Blahnik pumps out of their box and set them gingerly on top of my desk. They looked so dangerous I was afraid I might hurt myself.

"I'm assuming you're not supposed to actually wear these on your feet," I declared. "I mean, they're really just a form of weird fetishist sculpture—"

"According to what I read in *Vogue* magazine, they

are considered the sexiest shoes made," my secretary informed me. "They're remarkably comfortable, and they never go out of style."

I set them down on the carpet and stepped into them. "You're absolutely right," I said, doing my best to adjust to the altitude in the stiltlike stilettos. "I'm sure the hookers of ancient Rome wore something similar." I didn't like to say it, but they actually *were* comfortable. "What else is there?" I asked as Cheryl dug through the tissue at the bottom of the bag.

She came up holding a lacy black push-up bra and matching panties.

"And who, pray tell, are those supposed to be for?" I demanded.

"Elliott," replied my secretary as she flashed me a knowing smile.

Elliott was waiting for me at the door, still dressed for court in a dark blue suit. Beneath the soft tousle of his brown hair his eyes looked tired and his shoulders seemed to sag. However, at the sight of me he broke into a grin as big and warm as summertime.

"You look beautiful," he said, slipping his arm around my waist and drawing me toward him for a quick kiss. Then he stepped back, looked me quizzically in the eye, and then glanced down at my shoes. "My, Little Red Riding Hood, how tall you've grown," he remarked.

"Cheryl's to blame," I explained somewhat incoherently. "Did you get a verdict? Are we celebrating tonight or drowning your sorrows?"

"Celebrating," replied Elliott. "The jury came back for the plaintiff and awarded us $6.7 million in damages."

I leaned over and kissed him on the cheek. "Ooh," I squealed in my best chorus-girl impersonation. "I'm going to have to start calling you the six-million-dollar man."

"Please, the six-point-seven-million-dollar man," joked Elliott as the hostess came over and showed us to a table for two in a quiet corner of the restaurant. As we sat down he noticed the bag.

"A present for me?" he inquired.

"Actually, it's a message for my mother. I was hoping you might send it out and have it dusted for prints." I went on to describe the package that had been sent to my mother's house and the message scrawled on the single sheet inside it as we took our seats.

"I can't believe she opened it without knowing who it was from," remarked Elliott once I'd finished. "If it really was a bomb, she would have been killed."

"I'm sure that's what whoever sent it wants her to think."

"I'll send it out to our forensics guys and have them take a look at it. But I doubt they'll turn up anything useful after the thing's gone through the post office. So who do you think sent it?"

"Who knows? My mother's been on every TV and radio station in the city the past couple of days. Maybe it's from some Bolshevik who hates rich people or some disgruntled former servant. God knows, you could populate a small town in Wisconsin with the people she's fired."

"That wouldn't explain why it came now, not unless you're a big believer in coincidence. It seems to me like a pretty good bet that this was deliberately sent to scare her off her crusade against HCC."

"In that case it worked. Mother showed up at my office this afternoon to try and wriggle out of trying to block the sale."

"And I suppose you didn't let her."

"You're damned right I didn't let her," I announced, tearing into the warm baguette that had just materialized on our table.

"My mother told me I'd meet girls like you," reported Elliott gravely.

"Girls like what?"

"Girls who like trouble."

"It has nothing to do with liking trouble," I protested. "My mother came to me with this half-baked idea that she wanted to keep HCC from buying Prescott Memorial. I suspected that her motives were truly selfish— she literally didn't want some company out of Atlanta taking away the Founders Ball and all the other Lady Bountiful accoutrements she enjoys as a trustee of the hospital. I got involved because she's my mother and I didn't have the backbone to say no. The only trouble is that the deeper I dug, the more convinced I became that whatever her motives, my mother was right in fighting the sale. There's no way I'm going to let her back down after we've come this far."

"Even if she's being threatened?"

"*Especially* if she's being threatened," I declared. "If you give in to threats, in the end you're just rewarding bullies."

"I agree with you one hundred percent," said Elliott. "But I just love it when you get all riled up like that." I threw a piece of my bread at him. "I still want to know who you think might have sent it."

"Well, for starters, HCC."

"In which case they'll follow it up with something worse if this doesn't dissuade her."

"You're serious."

"If you're going to go around bullying people, you have to be willing to follow through on your threats or else no one will take you seriously. Everything I've found out about Gerald Packman says that he means business and he's not above using force. When he worked for a fried-chicken franchise, he was having trouble with a couple of his food delivery people refusing to unload trucks. Supposedly he was waiting for them at one of the restaurants. As soon as they showed up, he frog-marched the pair of them into the freezer, tied them to chairs, and made them sit there while he unloaded the truck himself. I think one of them ended up with frostbite. Packman fought him tooth and nail in court alleging that the frostbite was his own damned fault, the result of his being too lazy to do his job. Do you think he sounds like a guy who's above sending threats to socialites in the mail?"

"Well, he's threatened the wrong family," I said as our waiter materialized with menus and asked if we cared to order something to drink before dinner. I preempted Elliott and ordered a bottle of champagne.

"Congratulations," I said once the bottle had been delivered and the tall flutes filled. "I know how much you're going to miss the Springfield Ramada."

We clinked glasses and drank.

Elliott took my hand across the white linen of the tablecloth and drew his finger gently up the inside of my arm. Over his shoulder I could see the antique bar of ornately pressed tin and a spectacular arrangement of spring flowers. A pretty woman with long dark hair and an elegant black dress leaned over to her male companion and whispered something in his ear. Whatever she said made him tip his head back with laughter.

I felt the electricity of Elliott's touch, and my skin thrummed like a living thing. I opened my mouth to speak, hesitating long enough to wonder why I was the only person in the restaurant who didn't seem to be able to set aside the problems of the day and just enjoy myself. Then I told him the whole story about Mrs. Estrada, her appendix, and the suit against Claudia.

"Do you think there's any chance that all of these things are somehow related?" asked Elliott once I'd finished.

"You mean the patient deaths and the sale of the hospital? I've certainly thought about it. The only trouble is that it just doesn't add up. If it's someone out to damage the reputation of the hospital, why is it that it's only Gavin McDermott's patients who end up dead? Besides, if HCC was trying to make the hospital look bad, you'd think that they'd have gone public by now."

Our food arrived and we paused while our waiter set our plates in front of us and asked if there was anything else we needed. Once I'd taken a few bites of cassoulet, I continued.

"My biggest problem is believing that a large publicly traded corporation somehow arranged for Mrs. Estrada's appendix to rupture so that they could murder her afterward in order to make either Claudia or the hospital look bad."

"What about the other deaths?" asked Elliott. "Could they be a part of the larger plan to acquire the hospital?"

"I go back and forth," I confessed. "I have moments when I think that Gerald Packman is capable of anything, even murder. Then I stop and wonder if there isn't some kind of medication I should be taking for paranoia. I mean, this is a health care company we're talking about, not the evil empire. I think it's actually much more likely that there's just some psychopath out there killing off patients because the voices in his head are telling him to."

"You know that Packman's not above feeding the

story to the press, if he finds out and decides it's in his interest."

"That's the trouble. He already knows. He brought it up that time I met him, which tends to confirm our theory about HCC having a mole inside Prescott Memorial, someone who's feeding them information. But I still can't figure out why he hasn't used it."

"Maybe he already has," ventured Elliott.

"Meaning?"

"Meaning he doesn't have to make the deaths public if just threatening to do so will accomplish his mission."

"You're talking about blackmail," I whispered thoughtfully. "You're talking about hiring someone to kill McDermott's patients and then blackmailing McDermott into voting in favor of the sale."

"You have to admit it would work."

"It seems awfully risky. I'd think it would be easier to just buy the votes."

"But blackmail is much more cost-effective. I imagine it would take some serious cash to buy a successful surgeon like McDermott."

"Whereas he'd be willing to do almost anything in order to stay successful," I said.

"Exactly."

"The only trouble is, I bumped into Julia Gordon. She rattled off the details of several cases where hospital patients were systematically killed off, and in every case it was some kind of nut."

"She actually used the word *nut*?"

"Let's just say in each case the perpetrator's motivations were apparent only to themselves."

The waiter came and cleared our plates and took our orders for dessert. I took the opportunity to tell Elliott about my conversation with Laffer and the fact that he'd promised to change his vote provided I could bring him proof of HCC's wrongdoing.

"Then I guess you'll want to hear what we turned up on the fab four."

"Who are the fab four?"

"Our four front-runners for HCC mole: Gavin Mc-Dermott, Carl Laffer, Kyle Massius, and Farah Davies. You'll be happy to hear that I finally remembered where I know Dr. Farah Davies from," Elliott said. "It came to me when I was driving back from Springfield tonight."

"Where?"

"She was the third party in a divorce case I was involved in."

"I didn't know you were ever married," I remarked.

"Involved as an investigator," he corrected me.

"I also didn't think you did divorce work."

"I did in the beginning. When I was just starting out, I did anything that would help me make my rent. In this case the client was a doctor who was a friend of mine, so when he asked me, I didn't say no."

"So was Farah Davies the wife or the girlfriend?"

"Neither. She was the wife's girlfriend."

"You're pulling my leg."

"Scout's honor," he replied, holding up his hand in a two-fingered salute while the other held his champagne glass. "Apparently the client's wife had a very difficult pregnancy with their third child, lots of complications, and Dr. Davies was her OB."

"And?"

"Over the course of the pregnancy the two women became close."

"I'm good friends with my dentist," I protested, "but that doesn't mean I'm sleeping with her."

"Let's just say they became closer than you and your dentist."

"So how did the husband find out?"

"Well, he figured there was something going on. All of a sudden the wife starts acting weird, staying out late, going away on the weekends. He was afraid that she was seeing another man. That's when he came to me."

"So what did you do?"

"I followed the client's wife on a weekend trip she was taking to the Kohler spa in Wisconsin."

"And?"

"And it turns out she wasn't meeting another man, she was meeting Farah Davies."

"Maybe they were just going up there for the facials and the massages."

"I guess that's one way to describe what they were doing," declared Elliott with a look of amusement on his face. "If you want, you can look at the pictures yourself and decide what they were doing."

"No thanks, I think I'll pass."

"As you might expect, my doctor friend was absolutely devastated. It's hard enough when your wife is sleeping with another man, but this . . ."

"So did he leave her?"

"No. She left him. Told him that she'd decided that she wanted to live openly as a lesbian."

"What about the kids?"

"That was the problem. Given the circumstances my client felt he should be granted custody of the children. His wife, needless to say, thought otherwise."

"So how did they resolve it? Did they end up fighting it out in court?" I asked, thinking that for all its perceived drama, I actually led a very boring life.

"It never even got that far," said Elliott. "As soon as my client filed his custody petition, two lawyers from one of the big national gay-rights organizations paid him a visit at his office."

"What did they say?"

"They told him that if he persisted in seeking full custody of his sons through the courts, they were prepared to fight him with every means at their disposal. As far as they were concerned, his assertion that he was the more fit parent was a blatant example of discrimination based on sexual preference. They told him that they welcomed the opportunity to turn his custody claim into a test case for lesbian rights, make a public issue out of it, put it on the front page."

"So what did he end up doing?"

"He hired an attorney and quietly negotiated a shared custody arrangement with his ex-wife. It wasn't what he wanted. He didn't think that it was in his sons' best interests, but he was afraid of what the publicity would do not just to his boys, but to his practice. I never met his wife, so I really don't know her side of it, and Lord knows in my line of work you learn not to judge, but I can tell you that for the husband the whole thing was incredibly hard."

"What about Farah Davies? What was her role in all of this?"

"You mean besides starring in some rather hot photographs taken with a telephoto lens? Nothing."

"Are she and your client's wife still together?"

"I don't know. It's not as though Dr. Davies is an openly practicing homosexual. In fact, it's just the opposite. She's publicly dated a number of men, most recently Kyle Massius, the president of the hospital."

"I wonder if she and McDermott were ever an item," I mused. "That would certainly explain his behavior toward her at the party the other night."

"You mean he might have had a reason? I thought it was just because he was a jerk. But any way you look at it, Dr. Davies has some pretty good reasons to not want some parts of her personal life made public."

"Meaning?"

"It probably wouldn't help her practice any if word got out that she was into women."

"Women go to male doctors all the time," I said. "Still, I see your point. Dr. Davies has every reason in the world to want to avoid having her sexual preferences made public, but I don't see how that could possibly have any bearing on the situation with HCC."

"They could be blackmailing her," offered Elliott thoughtfully, lifting a forkful of cheesecake to his lips. "But actually I like her better for the HCC mole."

"Why's that?"

"Well, for one thing she's ambitious. She made no secret of the fact that she wanted the chief of staff job and was furious when she was passed over for Carl Laffer. Not only that, but obstetrics is by far the biggest money-maker for HCC. Whenever HCC moves into a new market, the first thing they do is go around cutting deals with the local obstetricians, trying to get them to send their patients to one of the company's hospitals. If I were Gerald Packman, Farah Davies would be my first choice."

"Except for one small thing," I interjected. "She's not a trustee, which means that she doesn't have a vote. She's only a department head. She's not privy to the kind of financial information that I'd want if I were in Packman's position."

"But if she's close to Massius, he might be passing her information. And she might be able to influence his vote."

"She wouldn't have to," I pointed out. "It would be so much simpler to just make a deal with Massius. He's sick

and tired of running a prestigious but otherwise impov-
erished institution. He'd love the idea of himself at
HCC—a corner office, a seat on the corporate jet. . . . If I
had to pick the person most likely to sell out to HCC, it
would have to be him. Not only is he in the best position
to help HCC with insider information, but he stands the
most to gain from striking a deal with them up front. He
gives them his vote and whatever information they ask
for now in exchange for a big job with an even bigger
salary once they take over.

"Right now he's just an underpaid administrator who
has to not only suck up to everyone who might have fifty
dollars to give, but bow and scrape in front of everyone
from the medical staff to my mother. A deal with HCC
would turn him into one of the most powerful corporate
players in town. People would be standing in line to bow
and scrape in front of *him*."

"Okay," said Elliott, "we'll put him on top of our
list."

"The only problem is that if he does turn out to be the
mole, it puts me in the weakest position."

"How so?"

"Massius is an administrator, not a physician. Therefore he has the simplest relationship with the hospital
and the least responsibility."

"I thought he runs the whole hospital."

"True. But he doesn't treat patients. He doesn't train
physicians. He has no higher level of obligation than a
VP for a department store. He has to answer to his boss
and obey the law, period."

"But if he's slipping HCC confidential information,
that's clearly in violation of SEC regulations—"

"Absolutely. But like jaywalking, it happens all the
time. I'm not saying that if it comes to that, I won't try to
make it sound like a hideous transgression, but in terms

of blocking the sale I'd be much happier if the mole turned out to be McDermott."

"What about Laffer?"

"I'd say if he's willing to change his vote, that pretty much rules him out."

"Even so, he's a pretty interesting character."

"You mean because he's an ex-basketball player who also happens to be an opera fanatic?"

"For starters. You know, in some ways he reminds me a lot of the doctor whose wife was sleeping with Farah Davies, the classic good guy to whom bad things always happen."

"What bad things have happened to Laffer?" I inquired.

"He was named in a big malpractice suit five or six years ago. Your friend Joan Bornstein handled his defense. It was one of her first big, high-profile trials."

"What happened?"

"You know that Laffer and McDermott are partners, don't you?"

"No, I didn't realize that."

"It's not exactly like they're joined at the hip. They're both in a practice group with six or seven other surgeons who share office space, cover for each other on vacation, and take turns being on call. All of them take trauma call at Prescott Memorial, as well. Anyway, around that time, McDermott was going through an ugly divorce, and in consequence he was leaning on his partners pretty hard."

"Meaning?"

"Meaning he was doing a fair amount of drinking and even more feeling sorry for himself. It turns out that wife number two just so happens to be Dale Adelhelm's sister."

"Dale Adelhelm the divorce lawyer? They call him the Jackal."

"Yeah, because he has a knack for picking the carcass clean. Between the two of them they hung McDermott out to dry. The way my investigator explained it to me, Dr. McDermott is going to be the only man in the history of the free world to end up paying alimony after he's dead."

"So she took him to the cleaners. What does that have to do with Laffer?"

"One night while all of this was going on, McDermott showed up on Laffer's doorstep sloppy drunk and crying about all the bad things that his ex-wife was doing to him."

"And?"

"It was a night that McDermott was on call."

"And he was drunk?" Claudia wouldn't have so much as a teaspoon of cough syrup the nights she was on call.

"Shit-faced. So Laffer does his best to be a sympathetic friend, and before you know it, McDermott's fast asleep on the couch. Laffer covers him up with a blanket and is about to go to bed himself when he hears McDermott's beeper going off. Now what he should have done is just ignore it and gone upstairs to bed. But I told you he's a good guy, so instead he calls the page operator and tells her that he's covering for McDermott."

"So what happened?"

"The operator tells him there's a patient being air-evacked to the hospital, a thirteen-year-old boy who'd been hit by a semi. Laffer grabs his car keys and arrives at the hospital at the same time as the boy. The kid's a mess. He's covered with blood from head to toe and has several abdominal lacerations, any one of which are deep enough to cause massive internal bleeding. He also has compound fractures of both of his legs—and that's just what the paramedic tells him in the first two minutes."

"Did the boy die?"

"Laffer had to operate to remove the spleen and repair internal damage, but he was able to save the other organs. An orthopedic surgeon was called in to set the patient's legs, and after six hours of surgery, an exhausted Dr. Laffer walked out into the waiting room to tell the boy's terrified parents that while his injuries had been severe, it looked like there was a good chance that their son would survive."

"But something bad happened," I said, not sure I wanted to know what it was.

"The boy died the next day from a massive brain hemorrhage. Apparently when he was hit, his skull had been literally torn lose from the neck, causing him to slowly bleed into his brain."

"How awful."

"From the trial transcripts it looks like the experts disagreed about whether Laffer should have known. There was one expert who testified for the defense that even if Laffer had diagnosed the head trauma there would have been no way to correct the problem and save the boy."

"I imagine the plaintiff's lawyer had a field day."

"Absolutely," replied Elliott, switching quickly to the badgering tone of voice favored by lawyers during cross-examination. " 'You mean, doctor, that you didn't notice that the poor child's skull had been separated from his spine?' "

"No jury in the world could sit there and listen to a detailed account of what had happened and not want to see someone pay."

"And that somebody was Carl Laffer."

"But what you're saying is that if he hadn't gone out of his way to protect Gavin McDermott, who'd behaved completely irresponsibly by getting drunk when he was on call, it would have been McDermott sitting there in that courtroom getting his lunch handed to him. No wonder Laffer was so quick to come to Claudia's defense during the morbidity and mortality conference."

"Yeah," agreed Elliott. "He knows what it feels like to

have your professional reputation publicly torn to shreds by a bunch of lawyers."

"True," I mused. "But what I was actually about to say is that he knows what it's like to end up being screwed on behalf of Gavin McDermott."

CHAPTER
20

After dinner I asked Elliott back to my apartment. Even though I did my best to make the invitation sound off-hand, I knew I wasn't fooling anybody. It had taken three years for me to make up my mind. There was nothing casual about it.

If Elliott was nervous, he didn't show it. Instead, he spent the ride back to my place telling me about the fraud case that had occupied him for so many weeks in Springfield.

"It would actually make a pretty good soap opera," he began, "at least the civil portion of the case. From the transcripts, the criminal trial actually seemed pretty cut and dried."

"It was insurance fraud, wasn't it?"

"Medical insurance. Two obstetricians with an incorporated practice were convicted of defrauding the government of millions by billing Medicaid for tests and procedures that were never performed."

"But didn't your client say all along that he didn't know?"

"He did. But under the criminal statute it doesn't matter. He was a principal of the corporation and that made him responsible in any criminal proceeding."

231

"But not in a civil action?"

"Dr. Butler, our client, was seeking to recover for loss of income and damage to his reputation caused by his partner's criminal behavior under tort law."

"Do you honestly believe he didn't know what was going on in his own practice?"

"If there's one thing that this case has taught me, it's that doctors can be incredibly naive when it comes to business," replied Elliott. "Their whole training teaches them that medicine is far loftier and nobler than the crass pursuit of the dollar."

"Maybe that's why they hate managed care so much," I ventured. "Companies like HCC rub their noses in the dollars and cents of medicine."

"Oh, I don't know," he countered. "It's not like most physicians have exactly taken an oath of poverty. My client didn't have any problems taking the money—or spending it as long as it was coming in. He says it never occurred to him to question how, with insurers constantly lowering the ceiling on what they're willing to pay for certain procedures and their patient population remaining pretty steady, their practice was making more instead of less money."

"And it really was all his partner's doing?"

"Apparently the partner was having an affair with the woman who was in charge of the practice's billing. After the trial she confessed that it was like being given a license to print money. The other doctor actually argued during the civil case that he hadn't considered what they were doing as wrong. He went on and on about how the government was unfairly forcing doctors to work harder and harder for less and less money. He was just leveling the playing field."

"I get it," I remarked, pulling off Lake Shore Drive onto Fifty-third Street. "It's a variation on the Robin

Hood defense. Only instead of robbing from the rich to give to the poor, you rob from the government to keep the rich rich. I take it the jury didn't buy it."

"Are you kidding? We had a panel of blue-collar workers and retirees from downstate Illinois. They didn't have a lot of patience for doctors complaining about how hard they work and how poorly they're rewarded."

"And yet, you know, I've watched what Claudia's had to go through for her training, and I'm not sure I'd be willing to go through it if I didn't know that at the end of the road I'd be making a shitload of money. She and I were talking about it the other night—not the money, but just what she's had to give up. She's spent whole years of her life in the hospital, turned her back on anything resembling a normal life, all in order to become a surgeon. I'm not saying it justifies fraud, but I do worry that with the way things are going in medicine, we're going to end up with too few doctors and too many investment bankers."

"Now that," said Elliott, leaning over to give me a quick kiss on the cheek, "is a truly scary thought."

When I pulled up to the curb in front of the apartment, Leo was there waiting to pick up the car. He seemed ridiculously pleased that I'd brought a man home. When I introduced Elliott, he beamed and pumped Elliott's hand like the father of the bride.

The movies have ruined so many moments that take place in real life, raising our expectations to impossible levels. But as Leo pulled away from the curb and Elliott slowly enveloped me in his arms, I swear I almost heard the swollen strains of a soundtrack in my head.

I took him by the hand and led him up the stairs to the outer door of the building. There were three doors to go

through to get to the apartment, and three locks on each
door, so that I had more keys than a janitor. As I fumbled
to find the right ones, Elliott kissed the back of my neck,
which made finding the keys difficult. We lingered in the
vestibule, picking up where we'd left off on the street. By
now the old ladies in the apartment building across the
street were probably hanging out their windows with
binoculars, but I honestly didn't care. For once I wanted
to surrender to the moment.

Eventually we made our way up the vestibule steps
through the inside door—more kisses, more keys—to the
first-floor landing. During the day, natural light filtered
down from the third-floor skylight. At night, glass sconces
that had once been illuminated by gas glowed dimly
against the dark paneling.

But tonight what the soft light revealed brought me up
short. The front door of the apartment was open. Not
just unlocked, but ajar. Even Elliott, whose mind was
now firmly on other things, immediately grasped the sig-
nificance of this. Hyde Park is an urban neighborhood
and Chicago is not Disneyland.

We looked at each other for a minute, not wanting this
to be happening.

"Do you think your roommate might have just forgotten to close it?" asked Elliott, but I shook my head.

I felt sick to my stomach, my fear no doubt magnified
by disappointment. All my instincts told me that we'd
been broken into. Leo had even told me that there was a
burglar at work on the street, and I had stupidly down-
played his warnings. While I dreaded the shambles and
vandalism that most likely awaited me inside, I found
myself wishing selfishly that I'd suggested that we go
back to Elliott's place and left Claudia to come home and
pick through the wreckage. I pulled out my cell phone.

"I'm going to call the police," I said.

"Let me just go in and check it out," said Elliott, slipping the Browning from the holster beneath his jacket and flicking off the safety with a practiced hand. "This might be just like the box that was sent to your mother— a message to scare you, nothing more."

"I'm still not so sure that going in there is such a good idea," I protested. "I think it's better to let the cops check it out."

"Come on, one quick look," urged Elliott. "It's probably nothing." Under the circumstances I couldn't blame him for being less than enthusiastic about waiting for the police to show up.

"I'm going with you," I said. "If it turns out that Claudia *did* forget to close the door behind her, then I sure as hell don't want her to drop dead of a heart attack when she sees you creeping around the apartment with a gun."

"Then stay behind me," said Elliott, pushing open the door and stepping inside to listen, keeping the gun in front of him and slowly covering the room.

"Claudia?" I called out. "Are you home?"

The only answer was the silence of the apartment.

We stood for a moment in the entrance hall, listening. The light on the answering machine blinked silently from on top of the table in the dark, indicating that we had messages. The living room and dining room lay to our right.

I fumbled for the switch that turned on the lights in the living room and dining room. Both were exactly as I'd left them that morning. I took a deep breath and followed Elliott as he made his way down the long hallway that formed the backbone of the apartment. He stopped at the arched entryway that opened into the kitchen. I had forgotten to turn off the light that morning, but other than my profligacy with electricity, there was nothing else worthy of notice.

Elliott proceeded to work his way toward the back of the apartment. At each doorway he paused while I groped for the light. Then he stepped inside like a character in a TV cop show to check it out. With every room I felt more and more ridiculous. There was absolutely nothing out of the ordinary in the apartment. My dirty coffee cup still sat beside the kitchen sink, and the towel I'd used to dry myself after my shower lay on the floor of the bathroom exactly where I'd dropped it. A copy of *Clinical Anesthesiology* lay open on Claudia's bed.

Elliott stopped on the threshold of my bedroom, which was the last one at the end of the hall. He reholstered the Browning and turned to me with an enormous grin on his face.

"I guess the only thing the burglars did was trash your bedroom," he said, surveying the tumult of dirty clothes and rumpled linen that was my room's natural state.

"What pigs," I said, slipping my arms around Elliott's waist. "Why don't you go into the living room and put on some music while I clear a path to the bed. Then I'll see if I can find us a bottle of wine in the fridge."

"Why don't you let me get the wine," he said. "It looks like you're going to be in here for a while."

"You'd better leave that to me. Grown men have fainted when they open up the door to our refrigerator. Claudia has been known to store anatomical specimens there."

"In that case I hope you weren't planning on cooking me dinner any time soon," remarked Elliott as he turned to head back down the hall.

"You're safe," I called after him. "I can't cook a thing."

As I shoveled my dirty clothes into the laundry hamper I found myself feeling vaguely uneasy. I might not mind leaving my clothes on the floor, but the lawyer in me abhorred loose ends. While I was convinced that there was an innocent explanation for the front door having been left open, the fact that I didn't know what it was nagged at me.

As I hastily smoothed the sheets on my bed and pulled up the duvet cover, I told myself that Claudia had probably just gotten careless. Lord knows the combination of Mrs. Estrada's death and the malpractice suit was starting to make her come unglued. I figured I could live with the occasional lapse at home, just so long as she didn't start getting forgetful in the operating room, too.

After I was finished, I stopped to survey my handiwork. Elliott had put on music in the living room, and I was intrigued by the fact that he'd chosen one of the CDs from Claudia's collection as opposed to one of mine. It was a digitally remastered recording of Billie Holiday's. For some reason the sound of her voice made me feel as though the evening was back on track. Our Starsky and Hutch interlude already forgotten.

I made a quick stop in the bathroom to tidy up my hair and brush my teeth before making my way to the kitchen. I opened the refrigerator door and was rewarded by the sight of a congealed piece of pizza wrapped in a paper napkin and a sliver of something in a plastic bag that might have been a lemon at some point in the distant past. However, in the back behind the ketchup bottle I spied a bottle of champagne. One of my clients had given it to me when I'd made partner.

"Perfect," I said, and headed to the butler's pantry in search of champagne flutes.

The butler's pantry, like the crown moldings and enormous dining room, was a holdover from the day when cooks cooked and butlers butled. Even though it was bigger than my first office at Callahan Ross, it was really nothing more than a wide internal passageway between the kitchen and the dining room lined with elaborate glass-fronted cabinets for china, as well as having a sink for washing glassware.

With the bottle of champagne in one hand, I put my shoulder to the swinging door to the pantry and was surprised to find it blocked from the other side. In an apartment that old nothing worked right. The doorstop had probably slipped down on the other side, but rather than walk all the way around, I just gave the door another shove.

I don't remember screaming, although I know that I must have. It was the only way to account for the speed with which Elliott found me, with his gun drawn and a look of alarm spreading across his face. But by the time he arrived, I was already on the floor, my knees slippery with blood, grabbing for my roommate's chilly wrist, searching frantically for a pulse.

CHAPTER
21

The outside world went away. If there was any sound, I could not hear it—not Elliott's voice or the locomotive of my own breathing. Instead, there was a rushing sound like steam that filled my skull, and the terrifying realization that I was no longer capable of telling my body what to do. I just sat on my knees in the puddle of cold blood, holding my dead roommate's hand in mine, staring at the black-handled kitchen knife protruding from her neck.

Elliott's strong hands grasped me by the shoulder and pulled me to my feet. In one swift motion he lifted me a few inches off the ground and swung me clear of both the swinging door and the blood, setting me back down on the other side.

"Are you okay?" he asked, drawing me into an embrace that left his white shirt smeared with Claudia's blood. I realize now that I should have been less impressed by his concern for me than the fact that even in the shock of the moment his first thought was to get me away from the body and preserve the crime scene.

I shook my head, unable to find my voice, and buried my head in his neck as if in doing so I could blot out the

239

horror of what was happening. Ever so gently, he pushed me away and led me slowly out onto the sunporch.

I found myself taken back to the night that Russell died. Even though his was a death that was expected—even, during those last days of anguish, yearned for—in some ways it was exactly the same. A part of me felt as though my soul had been torn in two, as if some fundamental part of me had been ripped shrieking from the roots.

And then there was the other part, the automaton that just went through the motions. The one who kissed his forehead one last time and straightened the thin sheet of his hospital bed. The one who slipped the wedding ring off his emaciated finger, clasped it in a furious fist, and walked down the somber hallway of the cancer ward, looking for a nurse to tell.

Elliott called 911 and then joined me in the darkened sunporch to wait for the police. Refusing the comfort of his arms, I stood alone, fighting back a tide of rage and grief, willing myself not to cry. There was still a lot to be gotten through and nothing, absolutely nothing, to be gained by falling apart.

I heard the sirens before I saw the lights of the approaching squad cars. As usual it was the University Police who got there first. They were so much a fixture in Hyde Park that the people waiting at the bus stop hardly glanced at them as they pulled up to the curb.

In the early sixties Hyde Park was a neighborhood in jeopardy, in danger of being ripped apart not by the antiwar dissidents who disrupted so many other college communities, but by the Blackstone Rangers, a particularly vicious street gang. In its rational way, the great minds at the University of Chicago discussed whether it would be more cost-effective to move itself lock, stock, and library to Arizona or to hunker down and defend its turf. Thus was the University of Chicago Police Department born. Operating under a special city charter, they were now the largest private police force in the country. My mind clung to these and other irrelevant facts like a shipwrecked sailor clutching at debris.

It helped me hold my other thoughts at bay, the ones where I replayed the warnings of everyone who'd ever expressed concern about the safety of Hyde Park. All my own jokes about burglars seemed to come back and slap me in the face. I tried to will myself into a sense of numbness, to tell myself that this was a tragedy too big to be absorbed, but still the pain seemed to sear itself into my flesh.

Ironically the deliberate calm of the police, who were now arriving by the carload, reminded me of Claudia, of her surreal detachment while she was trying to restart Bill Delius's heart. It might be life or death, but it was also just a job.

Elliott and I gave our statements to the police. Someone must have turned off the CD player, either that or the disc had played itself through without my noticing. I found that while I could not think, I could at least answer questions, provided that they were simple and the answers clear-cut. Anything involving reasoning or conjecture, like how long Elliott and I had lingered in the vestibule or how long it had taken us to walk through the apartment, was beyond the limits of my cognitive powers.

By the time we'd finished, the place I had once called home had been transformed into a crime scene. I kept hearing the sound of the intercom and the buzzer and the voice of the uniform who'd been charged with the task of letting people into the building.

The neighbors, normally not a gregarious lot, began coming out to investigate the commotion. The graduate students from across the hall stuck their heads out only long enough to gawk, but old Mrs. Leavitt from upstairs, a mathematician's widow, cried softly when she heard the news. Later she insisted that she be let in to bring me a cup of tea in a rose-patterned China cup. She also brought an ancient cardigan, which she laid across my shoulders as if Claudia's death had somehow turned me into an invalid. It had holes in it, and like its owner, it smelled of lavender and mothballs.

I sought refuge in the sunporch at the front of the apartment. There, curled up in my wicker chair in the darkness, I could see the morgue wagon pull up to the curb, and watch as the patrolman urged passersby to keep moving, assuring them that there was nothing to see. Joe Blades arrived at about the same time as the TV minicams. I don't know which I was more surprised to see. He drove up in a Caprice Classic, which he left parked in the bus stop. He stopped for a minute on the sidewalk, straightening his glasses and buttoning his tweed jacket against the wind. Elliott must have called and asked him to come.

Blades was an old friend from the days when they both worked the white-collar crimes unit in the state's attorneys office. Joe was a Princeton grad who'd turned down the chance to go to law school in order to pursue a career in law enforcement, rapidly rising through the ranks to his natural resting place—homicide. Elliott came out to the front steps to meet him. They shook hands, their heads close together, conferring gravely. I forced myself to get to my feet and walked out to meet them.

"I'm so sorry," said Joe, taking my hand in both of his and giving it a quick squeeze. Indicating the man standing next to him, he said, "This is my partner, Pete

Kowalczyk. He and I have been assigned to investigate your roommate's death."

Kowalczyk doled out a syllable in greeting, not enough for me to be able to tell how he felt about being pulled off whatever he was working on to look into a murder on the south side. He was a brick wall of a man, almost as wide as he was tall, with arms as thick as a stevedore's and a thick brush of salt-and-pepper hair above the wide planes of his Slavic face.

I know this has been a bad night," continued Blades kindly. "But if you feel up to it, I'd like to ask you some questions." I nodded as the crime-scene crew brushed past in their dark overalls, lugging their heavy boxes of equipment. "Is there someplace out of the way where we can talk?"

"Why don't you two go into the living room?" suggested Elliott, separating himself from the official police investigation and letting his friend go about his job.

"I'm going to take a quick canvas of the building," reported Kowalczyk to Blades. "See if any of the neighbors heard anything."

Blades nodded, and we went inside. The homicide detective drifted around the room for a bit before he finally settled in Claudia's favorite armchair across from me on the couch. I felt the tears well up in my eyes. Blades dug into his pocket and produced a clean white handkerchief and passed it to me without a word. In his line of work, I figured, he must buy them in bulk.

With efficient questions he quickly took me through the story of discovering Claudia's body. After that, the conversation turned to Claudia, with Blades quickly focusing in on the things most likely to lead him to her killer: her boyfriends, her habits, and her vices. I did the best I could to fill him in on the details of Claudia's life. I told him about her parents, children of the sixties who were both tenured professors at Columbia, and her fellowship in trauma surgery. Then I told him about Carlos.

"Do you know his last name?" asked Blades, taking notes.

"No. But anybody who works in the ER at Prescott Memorial should be able to tell you. Like I said, he's a paramedic."

"And how long did you say they were seeing each other?"

"I'm not sure. Maybe two or three months."

"And you said she broke it off when she found out he was married?"

"Yes. And almost immediately afterward we started getting these hang-up calls."

"Did he ever follow her, do you know? Ever threaten her?"

I shook my head. "You have to understand about Claudia," I said. "She wasn't one of those women who can't wait to run home and tell her best friend all about it. I know it sounds corny, but she was a person of action, not words. She used to say that's what made her choose surgery. She could use her hands to actually make patients better, as opposed to playing twenty questions to figure out what was wrong with them and then writing them a prescription. She said it gave her a charge every time she held an instrument in her hand." I suddenly found myself looking at the world through tears. I got to my feet and started pacing, anything to keep from falling apart.

"So, do you think this guy Carlos is the kind of person who could have done this?" asked Blades. "You said the front door was open. Do you think she would have let him in if he'd come over?"

I thought for a minute before answering. "No," I said finally. "Like you, she was in a line of work where you get to see just how mean the mean streets really can be. I don't think she'd have let Carlos in if he'd showed up, not after what happened the other day."

A voice from the other room announced that the crime lab was done with pictures, and Joe Blades got to his feet. "Thank you for your cooperation," he said. "Would you mind hanging around a little while longer in case we have other questions?"

I nodded numbly. Part of me was hoping that this meant that at least this part of it was over, and part of me was filled with dread at the prospect of what was to come. "Is it okay if I use the phone to make a call?" I asked. "I need to tell her parents what's happened."

I have been the bearer of bad news in my time. I have looked men in the eye and told them that they were bankrupt, I have fired people, and worse. But I would have gladly given up every cent I had, pledged my family's fortune and sold myself into slavery if it meant that I didn't have to make that call, if it meant that I could bring their daughter back.

It was after midnight in Chicago, an hour later in New York. I called directory assistance for the number and took the phone, dragging the cord behind me, into the living room in the hopes of finding a small corner of privacy in my own home. Elliott found me just as the phone was ringing, and sat beside me on the couch.

A sleepy voice answered, a woman's.

"Mrs. Stein?" I said. "This is Kate Millholland." By the time I got my name out, I think she knew. Just those six words at one o'clock in the morning were enough.

Now there was no turning back. "Something terrible has happened. Claudia's been killed."

At that her mother let out a terrifying sob, a plaintive expression of grief, and I felt the words dry up in my mouth. I shot an imploring look at Elliott, who gently took the receiver from my hand. I was out of the room, out of the apartment, on the street in front of the building before I even realized I was moving. If it weren't for the police line they'd set up in front of the apartment, the barrier of blue sawhorses and yellow crime-scene tape, I would have been down the street and halfway to the lake. Instead I just stood there on the pavement, hugging myself against the cold, watching incredulously as life went on along Hyde Park Boulevard.

Eventually Elliott came and found me. "Her father is going to fly out in the morning. He said he'd call as soon as he booked the flight." I nodded, grateful. "They want to talk to you inside," he continued, gently putting his arm around me and leading me back up the steps like a reluctant child.

"What do they want?" I asked. I was close to the breaking point now.

"They want you to look at something, and then they're going to take her away."

I nodded, hearing the rushing sound returning. I did not want to go back into the apartment. Not tonight. Not ever. Silently I started bargaining with myself. I will go in now, but it will be the last time. I will do it and then it will be over. I will never spend another night in this apartment. I crossed the threshold and realized that I was breathing fast, almost panting in my panic.

"What do they want me to look at?" I asked as Elliott led me into the kitchen.

"The knife," replied Elliott as my feet involuntarily slowed to a stop in the hall. "They need you to look at the knife."

CHAPTER

22

Somehow it was worse, knowing beforehand exactly what I was going to see, and yet, strangely enough, it was Claudia herself who gave me the strength to do it. I kept thinking of her composure in the emergency room on the night when I brought Bill Delius in, the calmness of her demeanor, the measured "please" that preceded every request even as she struggled to save my client's life. The least I could do was try to hold myself to the same standard tonight. I owed her that much.

Claudia's body still lay on the floor of the butler's pantry. I could see it just beyond the door, and it held me in a primitive kind of paradoxical fascination. I could hardly bear to look at it, and yet I could hardly force myself to look away.

Everyone had cleared out except for Blades and Kowalczyk. Now that he'd been here awhile, I could see the questions forming on Kowalczyk's face. Most cops were ruled by Occam's razor, the scientific principle that states that the simplest explanation fitting the facts is probably the right one. I could tell the whole thing bothered him—not just the murder, but Claudia, me, the apartment. By now Blades had filled him in on who I was and what I was worth. I could tell he saw me as a piece of the puzzle that didn't fit and that it bothered him.

They wanted to know if I recognized the knife.

I took a deep breath, determined not to disgrace myself, and slowly made my way to the butler's pantry. Blades took me by the elbow and steered me around the blood, which had darkened in the hours since I'd stupidly blundered through it. I crouched down beside my dead friend and tried not to look at anything besides the knife. It was hard. There were little things I hadn't noticed before—the hemostat clipped to the drawstring of her scrub pants, the piece of rubber tubing that peeked out of the breast pocket. Somehow as they'd gone about their work, the police had managed to knock her glasses askew. My hands itched to straighten them.

Of the knife all that was visible was the black wooden handle and about a quarter inch of blade. Whoever had killed her had done their best to ram the knife in to the hilt. Judging from the diameter of the handle and the width of the blade, I could tell that it was a paring knife. It had entered the right side of her neck, roughly an inch and a half below the ear. I forced myself to lean over her body and look, but the tip of the blade did not show through on the other side.

I stood back up and went back to the kitchen counter. All the knives were in their places in the wooden block except for one.

"It looks like whoever did it just took one of the knives from here," I said. "I couldn't tell you for sure without seeing the whole thing, but it looks like the smallest one of the set."

"Pretty fancy cooking knives and not much else in this

kitchen," observed Kowalczyk. "Have you had them long?"

"About a year," I said. "They were a gift from a patient of Claudia's when she was still a resident, a German woman who came from a little town called Solingen that's famous for their knives."

"It looks like he must have come in through that window," said Kowalczyk with a nod toward the shards of broken glass that lay in the bottom of the sink. From his voice it sounded like he'd already made up his mind about what had happened and was relating an established fact. "He must have thought the place was empty, but when he found Dr. Stein at home, he grabbed the knife from the counter and killed her. Then he took off through the front door without taking anything."

"He couldn't have come in through that window," I said automatically, noticing the broken pane for the first time.

"Why not?" countered Kowalczyk, obviously taken aback. "All the rest of them have burglar grates across them. He picked that one because it's the only one that doesn't."

"Don't you want to know why it doesn't have a burglar grille?" I asked.

"Okay, I'll bite," offered Blades, looking up from his notebook. "Why?"

"I'll show you," I said, happy for the chance to get out of the kitchen, away from the body of the woman who had been my best friend. I opened the back door of the apartment and led the detectives out onto the small, dark landing that held the enclosure where we kept the trash. From the landing, stairs ran up and down connecting all three floors of the building. Elliott and the two homicide detectives followed me down the steps single file like a Boy Scout outing. We stopped at the walkway that led between our building and the one next door.

"Look," I said. "None of the buildings on this block were built with the first floor on ground level. They were all designed to sit high up off the street to make them seem more grand. The first floor is actually a full story above street level. Front and back, you have to walk up a flight of stairs to get to the door, and then inside, there are more stairs. And see here where the steps go down to the basement?" I pointed to the concrete stairs that ran beside the exterior wall of the building and led into a deep well like a concrete bunker surrounding the basement door. "Take a look. What's that directly above them?"

All three men looked up at the building. "Your kitchen window," said Blades. "The one without the burglar grille."

"That's why there was never one put on that window. It's almost impossible to reach. There's a twenty-foot drop underneath it. You'd have to put a ladder in the stairwell in order to get in, but it's not wide enough to give you enough of an angle to support a ladder that tall."

Blades pulled a flashlight from his pocket and trained its beam down the concrete stairwell toward the basement door. "And here's where all the glass fell when he broke it," he observed.

"Yeah," said Elliott, "but there's much more glass outside than inside, so what does that tell you?"

"That it was probably broken from inside the apartment," offered Blades. "Meaning that whoever broke it was trying to make it look like a botched burglary."

"Which explains why the front door was left open," I said.

"How do you figure that?" asked Elliott.

"Because Claudia let her killer into the apartment. It was someone she knew. Most likely the murderer left this way, through the back door. That's why he forgot that the front door was open."

"Why would she have left the door open?" asked Kowalczyk, obviously not buying my theory.

"I don't know," I replied. "Maybe she wanted to keep open a line of escape . . . ."

In the end I had Elliott take me to the new apartment downtown. It was closer than his place, and even though I'd never spent much time there, at least it was more familiar than a hotel. Besides, with the doorman in the lobby and security otherwise tight, it was one of the few places where I thought I might be able to feel safe. I just prayed that Claudia had never mentioned the address to Carlos.

If Danny was surprised to see me showing up in the middle of the night with bloodstains on my clothes and a strange man at my side, he was too well trained to show it. He merely touched his gray-gloved hand to the bill of his cap and wished us a very pleasant good night.

Upstairs it smelled of fresh paint and new carpet. Elliott hadn't seen the apartment since it had been finished, and I could tell that even through his fatigue, he liked what he saw. Empty, it had been a beautiful place; now it was simply stunning. But tonight the whole world, no matter how physically perfect, seemed out of joint and beyond my understanding.

There were plenty of beds but no sheets. I really didn't

care. Elliott followed me into the master suite and took off his jacket and his tie. I stripped down to my silk blouse and underpants and curled up on the bed, struggling to keep my eyes open long enough to see Elliott disappear through the door. He came back a few minutes later with the matelasse coverlets that had been ordered for the guest room. He tucked me in carefully and gave me a chaste kiss on the top of my head.

"I'm sorry," he said, lying down beside me fully dressed and wrapping his arms around me.

As I closed my eyes I noticed that he'd put his gun on the nightstand within easy reach.

The next morning I woke up to the smell of coffee and the sensation that someone had come in the night and hollowed out my heart. I opened my eyes and saw Elliott. He was sitting at the writing desk in front of the big arched window that looked out over the lake. He looked freshly shaved and showered and was dressed in a pair of khaki pants and a light blue oxford cloth shirt. There was a Starbucks cup at his elbow, and on the desk in front of him lay the Browning 9mm he always carried and what looked like a box of ammunition.

I propped myself up on my elbows as Elliott came over and sat beside me on the edge of the bed. He handed me the coffee. He must have just come back with it, because it was still hot.

"What time is it?" I asked, my voice still thick with sleep. Every movement was an effort, a battle against the heavy weight of grief.

"Six-thirty," said Elliott. "I hope you don't mind, but I went back to Hyde Park this morning and picked up some clean clothes for you and a couple of other things you might need. I had one of my people stay there overnight—it was Joe who suggested it. In a place like Hyde Park, as soon as word of the murder hit the street, every two-bit break-in artist would have tried to get in and make off with your stuff as soon as the cops had left."

"Thank you," I said. I felt it would be ungracious to explain that as far as I was concerned, the thieves could help themselves. Nothing, certainly nothing I owned, seemed important to me today.

"I've also talked to Claudia's mother. It sounds like she's taking it real hard." I wrapped my arms around my body as if to ward off the cold, but in reality I felt like I was holding myself together. "Her husband's already on his way. He arrives at eight-fifty at O'Hare. I have the flight number. If you want, I'll go pick him up."

"No," I said. "I'll go."

"I brought you some muffins," he said. "Just in case you're hungry. I put shampoo and soap in the bathroom for you. I also called Cheryl and told her about Claudia. She said she'll get in touch with the people at the hospital and let them know what happened."

"Have you talked to Blades? Have they arrested Carlos yet?"

"It's still early, Kate. You've got to give him some time."

"Her father arrives in two hours," I said. "What am I supposed to tell him?"

I stood in the shower and tried to wash away the memory of what had happened. Growing in me like a cancer was a sense of realization, a suspicion bordering on fear, that if I hadn't met Elliott for dinner, or if we hadn't lingered in the stairwell, everything would have ended up differently. But what I couldn't figure out was whether Claudia would still be alive or whether I would have been killed, too.

I closed my eyes but could not get the picture of Claudia's body out of my head. As the hot water rushed over my body, I ran through the entire clichéd litany of grief. I cried and demanded answers from God and from myself, felt the anger coursing through me at the injustice of what had been done. Claudia, who'd worked so hard to save lives, had had hers taken in an instant.

Someone once said that pain is a teacher who must be understood. But that morning I knew that they were wrong. Pain is pain. Sometimes the best you can do is try to keep it from knocking you flat.

Eventually the wave of emotions passed through me, having run its course. Slowly I forced myself to turn to more practical matters. I washed my hair and tilted my head back and let the soap run down my back. My body felt like it was made of lead, and every action seemed to be an effort of will.

I got out of the shower and turned off the taps, drying myself on the pristine hotel towels that Elliott had managed to procure for me. I dressed slowly, like an invalid, in the black pantsuit that Elliott had brought, forcing myself to focus on the details—zippers, snaps, buttons. Then I dug a hairbrush out of my purse along with a big clip, which I used to pin up my still-wet hair. I didn't bother with any makeup. Under the circumstances, what would be the point?

I found Elliott in the kitchen, sitting at the antique farm table, making notes on a legal pad.

I sat down across from Elliott, feeling drained from the effort of getting dressed and making the trip from the bedroom. I didn't know how I was going to make it through this day. Elliott, having anticipated my state of internal disorder, had begun making me a list. On the yellow pad he'd written not just the flight information for Claudia's father, but the name of a Jewish funeral home that would handle the arrangements for bringing Claudia's body back to New York. I had never thought of death as a religious event. Somehow after you were dead, I didn't see how it made a difference. But Claudia's parents, for all their radicalism, had brought her up in synagogue. I hoped that the care that Elliott had taken over these arrangements might bring them some small comfort.

He and Cheryl had also put together the death notice for the Chicago paper. Cheryl had also called my mother to spare her learning about what had happened on the news and to assure her that I was safe. Mother had called the new apartment while I was in the shower and had a long talk with Elliott.

"She seemed very concerned that what happened might in some way be connected to what's going on with HCC," reported Elliott.

For a minute I couldn't breathe. I felt overwhelmed with the feelings of my adolescence, a powerful mixture of helplessness and rage.

"It's all about her, isn't it?" I demanded, unable to control myself. "Claudia is stalked and murdered by her scumbag ex-boyfriend, and my mother is sure it has to somehow be because of her. I really don't give a shit what she thinks," I said, my voice spiraling into the unfamiliar registers of hysteria.

"I was talking to Joe this morning, and he's starting to think that the killer might turn out to not be the boyfriend."

"Was this before or after he talked to Carlos?" I demanded. "Does Carlos have an alibi?"

"I have no idea. I think what's bothering Blades is the lack of overkill."

"What?"

"Usually when a stalker kills his victim, it's the culmination of a long string of escalating events. There's usually a lot of unnecessary violence, slashing, a struggle even—"

"Carlos is a big man. Maybe he just overpowered her."

"Maybe. Or maybe it's really a different kind of crime."

I opened my mouth to say something, but Elliott raised his hand to ask me to hear him out. "Just think about it," he said. "I'm not saying that it happened, but what if whoever sent your mother that package knew enough about you to know that you would never be deterred by that kind of blackmail? What if they realized that it would take much more to stop you?"

"Are you suggesting that HCC had Claudia killed in order to somehow get to me, to make me drop the fight against them?"

"Listen," said Elliott, taking my hands in his across the table. "I don't know who killed Claudia, and I sure as hell don't know why. But I do know that her death has accomplished what no threats could have done."

"What's that?" I asked.

"In your eyes it's suddenly made the whole thing seem unimportant."

Before I left for the airport, Elliott sat me down and made me agree to take the Browning. None of my arguments—not even the fact that my carrying it, concealed without a permit, was a felony—deterred him. Indeed, he refused to let me leave the table until I not only agreed to take it but also showed him that I knew how to use it. I couldn't believe that whoever had killed Claudia had reduced me to this—sitting at my own kitchen table, with a 9mm semiautomatic pistol in my hand.

CHAPTER
23

When I got to O'Hare, I made my way to the United terminal and pulled up to the curb at the departures level. The act of finding a parking space was completely beyond me, so I flagged down a skycap, gave him a hundred bucks, and asked him to keep on eye on my car. As I put my wallet back in my purse I felt the pistol, heavy as a hammer among the rest of the litter in my bag. Uncertain of what to do about it, I threw my purse under the front seat. As I closed the car door I said a silent prayer of thanks that I hadn't forgotten about it and ended up answering questions in the airport security office as a prelude to my arrest.

Inside the terminal I sleepwalked down the concourse, jostled by the passing crowds. Most days I was a part of the hurrying hoard, impatient and focused on my destination. But today my grief seemed to not just set me apart, but also to have made everything seem foreign and somehow sinister. I searched the faces of the passersby and the people whose job it was to serve slices of pizza and hamburgers at eight o'clock in the morning. How many of them were capable of violence? How many of murder?

I found the gate and waited, watching for Claudia's

father. Morton Stein had been a lion in his day, a founding member of Philosophers for Justice, a radical academic organization that had challenged the morality of the war in Vietnam and later embraced a number of other causes in the name of social justice. Claudia's mother, also a philosophy professor, was a friend of Betty Friedan's and an outspoken proponent of the feminist movement. While I'd been hanging out at the country club, Claudia had been marching against nuclear power and boycotting grapes.

I remembered that Elliott had said that Mrs. Stein was taking it hard. I couldn't imagine any other way to take it. How could two people who had devoted themselves to advocating social justice ever even begin to come to terms with the senseless murder of their only child? How could anyone?

Professor Stein was one of the last people off the airplane. For a minute I almost didn't recognize him, he seemed so much older than the last time I'd seen him. It was a shock to realize that it wasn't the passage of time that had wrought the change, but rather grief that seemed to have shrunken him.

He was a small man, like his daughter, with a face that had delighted campus cartoonists for generations. His eyebrows were as thick as caterpillars, and his hair, receding from a high forehead, was white and long enough to reach his collar. But today he just looked like a beaten old man, a refugee from someplace terrible. He'd also developed a new habit overnight, an involuntary shaking of the head, as if mentally he was arguing against some terrible tide that only he could understand. I stepped up and hugged him.

He didn't have any luggage, just a single black duffel that he carried on a strap over his shoulder. As we made our way slowly down the concourse the silence between us was excruciating. Unlike Claudia, her father and I both made our livings from our words and from our wits. Somehow tragedy had robbed us of our gifts.

As we took the escalators up to the relative quiet of the ticketing level I did my best to explain the arrangements that had been made so far. I don't know if he actually heard me. His wife, he explained, was too devastated to make the trip and was in bed under a doctor's care.

The Jaguar was where I'd left it. The skycap gave me back the keys, and I opened the trunk to put in Professor Stein's bag. For a minute I just stood staring at the box of patient files from Prescott Memorial. They were sitting right there, exactly where I'd left them, last night or a thousand years ago, whenever I'd brought the box home to return them to Claudia.

I laid Professor Stein's bag beside it, curious to find that it was heavy. As I slammed the trunk on top of it I couldn't help but wonder what it was that you packed when you went to fetch your daughter's corpse.

Professor Stein said he wanted to go back to Hyde Park and see the apartment. He explained that his wife had made him promise that he would choose the clothing that Claudia would be buried in. Inside I cringed, imagining his pain at going through her things, but I realized that he also might need to visit the place where she had been killed, to see it for himself so that he could understand that she was really gone.

"So," he said after I'd retrieved my purse from under the seat and we'd pulled away from the curb, "do they know who did this terrible thing?"

"The police think she may have surprised a burglar."

"But you don't think so," he replied. I remembered what Claudia had once said about her father, that he was the most intuitive man on the face of the earth.

"It's too early to say," I answered. "We have to give the police a chance to do their job. One of the homicide detectives that is investigating the case is a man I know, very bright, a graduate of Princeton," I added, knowing that to an Ivy League professor that would mean something. "I honestly believe he won't rest until he finds out what happened to Claudia and brings whoever is responsible to justice."

"Justice," sniffed Morton Stein, "now there's a relative term. Of my entire family I am the only Holocaust survivor. Everyone else was lost, killed in the camps. I grew up in Brooklyn with a woman who I called Nana, but actually she's no relation. She was just another survivor from the camps who'd promised my mother that she would take care of me.

"Even though we never talked about it much at home, I think Nana used to tell Claudia stories about the war. I think that was part of what made Claudia choose a career in medicine. She wanted her life to be a force for good."

"She did," I said. "Even though her life was cut short, I know she made a difference. You know, for as long as we'd been friends, I'd never really seen Claudia at work before a couple of nights ago. A client of mine had a heart attack just a few miles from Prescott Memorial, and I brought him into the emergency room. It just so happened to be a night that Claudia was taking trauma call. I mean, I drove a dead man to Prescott Memorial Hospital, and Claudia brought him back to life. There have to be hundreds of people that she saved, people that ended up being able to walk out of the hospital."

"And then just like that she's gone," her father said angrily. "Some animal breaks into her apartment looking for something he can pawn for drugs and takes her away from the world forever." He frowned. "I used to believe that the death penalty was a barbarous perversion of the power of the state. Now . . . now I would like to kill whoever did this to my daughter, with my bare hands. I can't stand the idea of him breathing air, eating food, enjoying the luxury of an uninterrupted night's sleep, while my daughter lies there cold and dead."

I parked behind the apartment in the space reserved for one of the neighbors, a physicist who worked at the university's facility in Argonne. Under the circumstances I didn't think he'd mind. Beside us was Claudia's car, a nine-year-old Honda Civic, just one more loose end that would somehow have to be dealt with.

As I got out of the car I felt suddenly self-conscious, as if there were people watching me from every window. Even in a crime-ridden neighborhood like Hyde Park, murder is not an everyday occurrence. The interest of the neighbors would be intense. It made me feel vulnerable and strangely exposed.

I went around to help Professor Stein out of the car and led him through the narrow passageway, no more than three feet wide, that ran between our building and the one directly to the north. I didn't want him to go in the back way. Besides, I needed the buffer of more time before I made my way into the part of the house where Claudia had died.

Elliott's operative was an off-duty FBI agent named Cecilia Roth, who'd spent the night standing guard in the sunporch of the apartment. She was young but carried herself with the kind of self-confidence that comes from being not just physically fit but heavily armed. Who knows, I thought to myself, maybe Elliott has a thing for girls with guns?

After we introduced ourselves, she made herself scarce. She said she was running out to get something to eat, and I believed her. I knew that a person could easily starve to death on what there was to eat inside the apartment.

"The police are going to want to talk to you," I said to Claudia's father as the door closed behind Agent Roth. I knew that I was just stalling, making conversation so that I could put off doing what had to be done. "I'll take you to the station as soon as we're finished here."

"Why do they want to see me?" he asked.

"I think it's routine for them to talk to the family. He'll probably also want to ask you some questions about the last time you saw Claudia, the last time you two spoke."

"We talked last night," he said, his eyes resting on the telephone on the table in the entrance hall. "She called me when she came home after her shift. I was surprised to hear from her. She usually only calls on Sundays when the rates are low."

"Why do you think she called you last night?" I asked, wanting to know what time it had been and wondering if it might help Blades pin down the time of death. "Do you remember when she phoned?"

"A little after nine. She said she was in some kind of trouble. She wanted to know what I thought she should do."

"You mean about the malpractice suit?"

"Yes. She was very worried about it. Even though she knew that she hadn't done anything wrong when she took out that woman's appendix, she was terribly upset. She was afraid that the whole thing was going to end up ruining her career."

"Did she tell you that she'd hired a lawyer?" I asked. "Did she explain that she was going to fight the suit?"

"Yes. But apparently the hospital people were very angry about that. They were trying to pressure her into agreeing to some kind of settlement."

"What kind of settlement?"

"She didn't say, but I think the hospital just wanted to do whatever they could to make the whole thing go away."

"Did she say who it was who was trying to pressure her?"

"No. But they said that if she didn't agree to the settlement, they'd make the charges against her public. You know she had a job lined up at Columbia's medical school in the fall. She wanted to come back to New York so that she could be closer to us. It's what she'd worked her whole life for. She was worried that the people at Prescott Memorial were out to destroy her."

I took Professor Stein into the butler's pantry just to get it over with. The blood was all still there, though now it mostly looked just dark and brown. He spent a long time standing there, staring at it. It was the last place that I wanted to be, but I didn't feel as though I could just leave him there. The trouble is that there are some things that you can never unsee. I couldn't erase the image of Claudia's body. It was as though it had been burned into my retina. Even if I went blind and lived for a thousand years, there was no way I was ever going to forget it.

And yet the longer I looked, the more I saw what Joe Blades had seen. It was actually a very simple picture— the dark lake of blood, smooth edged and now drying, and the chalk outline of her body on the dirty floor where she had died. Most of the glass-fronted cabinets in the pantry were empty. Detective Kowalczyk had been right. The knife block, the handful of champagne glasses, the few plates and cups and glasses that Claudia and I had between us were all anomalies in an otherwise empty kitchen.

Professor Stein even gave voice to it. With tears

leaking from behind the steel frames of his glasses, he turned away from the chalk outline on the floor. "At least she didn't struggle," he said quietly. Then he started down the hallway to his daughter's room.

She didn't struggle.

I remembered the whiteness of her body and the coldness of her skin. There were no bruises, no cuts, no defensive wounds. Wouldn't she have reached for the knife or even—I hated to think about it—writhed in pain as she bled to death on the floor? Anything that would have disturbed the neat puddle of the blood on the linoleum floor.

Even though Claudia had been tiny, certainly she would have done something to defend herself. Or had she just been paralyzed by fear? I really didn't know about such things, but it almost looked as if Claudia had lain still and allowed herself to be slaughtered.

Lain still.

I reached for the phone on the wall in the kitchen. Then I dialed Julia Gordon's number at the medical examiner's office.

CHAPTER
24

"Oh, my god, Kate!" exclaimed Dr. Gordon as soon as I got her on the phone. "I can't believe it about Claudia. Someone told me about a stabbing when I stopped at Starbucks this morning, but I had no idea that it was Claudia until I got in this morning and saw her name on the day's case log."

"Will you be performing the autopsy?" I asked, trying to push down the thought of Dr. Gordon practicing her grisly avocation on my roommate.

"No, Dr. Sylvestri will be doing her case. As a rule we don't do autopsies on people we know. Of course, Detective Blades was here first thing this morning pushing to have it done right away."

"Have they started?"

"They're downstairs right now. Believe me, Kate, nobody wants to see this one slip through the cracks. Detective Blades says that he's already gotten calls from the University of Chicago—you know how sensitive they are when anything happens in Hyde Park—and the people at Northwestern Medical School because she was one of their fellows, all putting on the pressure."

"Would you be willing to do me a favor?" I asked.

"That would depend on what it is."

"Do you remember what we talked about the other day in your office? Those cases where caregivers were going around deliberately murdering patients?"

"Yes," she replied, a note of caution entering her voice. "Do you think that they could have something to do with Claudia's death?"

"Please, Julia," I said, "just ask them to test for any kind of drug that can cause paralysis."

"When are you going to tell me what all of this is about?" she demanded.

"Just ask them to do the tests. If any of them come back positive, I promise, I'll tell you everything."

After I hung up the phone, I went looking for Claudia's father. I found him in her room. He was sitting on the end of her bed. Beside him was the outfit that he'd chosen for her to be buried in, a red wool dress with a black velvet collar that I'd helped her pick out for her interview at Columbia. In his hands were some snapshots of Claudia that Carlos had taken when she and the paramedic had gone to Galena for the weekend. In them Claudia had looked happy.

I watched from the doorway for a long time, but Claudia's father never looked up, and I couldn't bring myself to disturb him. Instead I went back into my bedroom and packed up some of my own things that I'd be needing over the next few days.

I took my suitcase and the clothes that I needed that were still on hangers from the dry cleaner and put them in the front hall by the door. Agent Roth still hadn't returned, so I took some time to say my own good-byes. Not to Claudia—the time for that would come later—but to the place where we'd lived for so many years. I walked slowly from room to room, remembering. There was really nothing I wanted to take with me. The stereo belonged to Claudia. I'd send it and her CDs to her parents when I packed up the rest of her things. Everything else I would just get rid of.

I walked into the dining room and wondered if anyone would ever want our beat-up table. Maybe I should just leave it for the next tenants—let the tradition continue. I wondered whether Milos, our landlord, would tell whoever rented it about what had happened here. He probably wouldn't have to. The neighbors would be dying to tell them the news.

I sat down at the head of the table in the chair where Claudia had been sitting the last time she and I were together. She'd been poring through the charts of all of the Prescott Memorial patients who had died, looking for a way to save her career, not knowing that it was her life that she was going to end up losing. She'd been looking through the records hoping to find some variable, some thread that linked them together. She had been meticulously listing their attributes on a hand-drawn chart in the hopes of finding a clue to how they'd died. But when I looked at the dining room table, I saw that it was empty. The chart had been there when I'd picked up the box of files yesterday morning to be copied. I remembered seeing it there.

With a growing sense of urgency I began systematically looking through the apartment. I checked on the desk by the telephone in the front hall, thinking perhaps that she'd had it in her hand when she'd called her father. I checked the trash cans to see if by any chance she'd thrown it away. There was nothing.

Reluctantly I made my way back to my roommate's bedroom. I didn't want to disturb her father, but I was convinced that her notes would be there, if anywhere. Besides, I had to know. Something more than instinct, a kind of primal humming in my chest, told me that it was important.

I found Professor Stein neatly folding up Claudia's clothes and putting them into his black duffel. "I think I am ready to go to the police," he said.

"While you were looking through Claudia's things, did you happen to come across some notes that she had written on a yellow sheet of legal paper?" I asked.

"No. I haven't seen anything like that."

"Do you mind if I look around her room? It was something she was working on that related to the malpractice case. I'm just wondering what's happened to it."

Morton Stein shrugged his shoulders and went back to his grim packing. Claudia's room was so tidy it took only a minute to look through it. There was nothing there that pertained in any way to the patients at Prescott Memorial. Suddenly I thought of something.

"Have you seen her backpack?" I asked.

"Her what?"

"Her purple backpack. She carried it instead of a purse. It was the kind I'm sure all your students carry. There was nothing special about hers except that she had a key chain of a skeleton hanging from the zipper."

"I didn't come across it," he said, closing up the bag and hoisting it onto his shoulder, ready to go.

Suddenly I was glad that we were on our way to see Joe Blades. Even though I didn't know it at the time, when he'd asked me if there was anything missing from the apartment, I hadn't given him the correct answer.

I brought Claudia's father to the sixth district police station. It was a battle-scarred edifice that looked like a cross between an office building and a bunker. Inside, the desk sergeant dealt with the public through two inches of bulletproof glass, and the cramped waiting room was furnished with wooden benches chained to the wall. The whole place smelled like the Prescott Memorial emergency room, only without the benefit of disinfectant.

I hated to leave Claudia's father there, but he said he didn't want to inconvenience me any further. Besides, he pointed out that the police would almost surely want to talk to him alone. I left him reluctantly, pressing my office number upon him along with instructions to call me when he was ready to be picked up. From my car phone I dialed Joe Blades, only to be told, just as I'd expected, that he was on his way back from the medical examiner's office. I left a message that I'd called. Then I dialed Joan Bornstein's office.

Fortunately she was in. After I told her that Claudia had been murdered, I waited while she cycled through the normal shocks of incredulity and dismay. But when she started in on the dangers of Hyde Park, I cut her off.

"I don't think she surprised a burglar," I informed her. "I think this is all tied into what is going on at Prescott Memorial."

"You mean the malpractice suit?"

"That or her old boyfriend or the bid by HCC. I'm not sure which, but her death advances too many people's agendas for it to be a coincidence."

"What do the police think?" I could tell from her tone of voice that she thought I was crazy.

"They're doing their job, which is to find physical evidence, interview witnesses, and chase down leads. In the meantime, there's something that I need you to do."

"Anything."

"I'm going to have copies of the patient files that Claudia was reviewing, the patients whose deaths were suspicious, brought over to your office. I want you to get a couple of doctors working on going through them right away."

"What do you mean by right away?" she demanded.

"Immediately. Right now."

"Today? Do you have any idea what I'd have to pay to get a physician to just drop what he's doing and tackle this?"

"I don't care. I'm willing to pay the earth."

"That's good," replied Joan Bornstein, "because that's pretty much what it's going to end up costing you."

When I arrived at the firm, I bumped into Jeff Tannenbaum in the reception room. He'd just come from a meeting with the Icon lawyers. The documents had been approved by both sides, and they would be ready for signatures in a couple of hours. According to Jeff, Gabriel Hurt was not only flying back for the closing but insisted that it take place at Prescott Memorial in Bill Delius's hospital room.

Back at my own office Cheryl seemed surprised to see me. Surprised as well as uncertain. I could see the flicker of wariness behind her eyes, the distance that my grief now put between us. I could also tell she hadn't made up her mind about how to handle this, to handle me.

"I didn't think you'd be coming in today," she said, getting up from behind her desk and following me into my office. "Mr. Tillman just came by to offer his condolences, and I told him that I thought you'd be at home for the day."

"That's the last place I'd want to be," I said.

"I'm sorry, I didn't think . . . ," she stammered.

"That's okay. I ended up spending the night at the new apartment last night. I'm going to get the rest of my things moved in over the weekend."

"Elliott just called. He said you'd be coming in. He's

on his way over. He said he's bringing something you'd want to see—something important."

"Anything else?" I asked.

"A Detective Peter Kowalczyk just called. He wants you to call him back." Cheryl picked the pink message slip out of the pile and handed it to me. I punched in the number. Apparently he was sitting by the phone, because he picked it up on the first ring.

"Kowalczyk," he said.

"This is Kate Millholland, returning your call."

"Joe's in with the vic's—I mean, Dr. Stein's father, but he wanted me to call you and let you know some of the preliminary autopsy results." I could tell from his voice that he didn't much like the idea of sharing information with civilians, especially high-priced lawyers.

"It looks like cause of death was due to a single stab wound through the neck, which severed the carotid artery. No evidence of sexual assault. She didn't have alcohol or opiates on board. We're still waiting for hair and fiber results, not to mention toxicology, but the doc said they'd be releasing the body to the family later in the day."

"Don't you think there's something funny about the fact that it was a single stab wound?" I asked against my better judgment. "Wouldn't you normally expect to see some kind of struggle if she'd really surprised a burglar?"

"Not if the burglar got lucky on the first try," he replied. "Listen, I know you're taking this kinda personal. . . ."

"I wanted to tell you that I realized something is missing from the apartment," I said, fighting down my irritation.

"What's that?" he asked, sounding interested.

"Claudia's backpack."

"What did it look like?"

"Just a purple canvas backpack, the kind that college students carry. Claudia used it instead of a purse. She spent so much time at the hospital, she used to keep a toothbrush in there and a change of underwear."

"What about her wallet?"

"In the smaller zipper compartment, why?"

"Because we didn't find it in the apartment. We just assumed that she must have left it at the hospital. We've got someone over there right now taking a look through her locker."

"Will you let me know if you turn it up?" I asked. I didn't feel like explaining the whole story of the patient charts and the summary chart that Claudia was working on to Kowalczyk. I frankly didn't think he'd be interested in hearing anything that didn't fit into his theory of the case, which seemed to be that she'd surprised a burglar, albeit a lucky one.

"If we find it, we'll make sure that it gets turned over to her next of kin," he replied. "In case you were wondering, that means her father."

"Thanks for clearing that up for me," I said, hanging up the phone.

"Your mother?" demanded Elliott, surprising me from the doorway.

"Worse," I said, waving him in. "It was Blades's partner."

"He may be a hard-ass, but he's also a smart cop. He just doesn't like uppity women."

"I'll keep that in mind."

"Are you okay?" he asked, sliding into the visitor's chair. His jacket caught on the back of the chair, revealing the shoulder holster and wood-grained grip that protruded from it.

"What's that you're carrying, cowboy?" I asked.

"My backup piece. I hope you still have the one I gave you this morning."

"It's in my purse. I promised that I'd keep it with me, and I'm as good as my word. Just tell me you'll come and visit me at Menard after I drop my purse, the gun goes off, and I end up shooting an innocent bystander."

"Every Wednesday."

"Why Wednesday?"

"Visiting day. Where's Claudia's dad? Did he get in all right?"

"He's talking to Blades. I took him to the apartment and met Agent Roth. She's a pretty woman."

"Not to mention a crack shot. She finished seventh at the Nagano Olympics in sharpshooting."

"Cheryl said you had something you wanted to show me."

"Yeah, though now that you're here, I might as well just tell you."

"Tell me what?"

"I had one of my people do a Lexis-Nexis search on each of the fab four, and they turned up something interesting on McDermott."

"McDermott? What?"

"When you and Dr. Gordon had your little chat about hospital killers, did she happen to mention a case at the Bloomington VA?"

"No. What happened there?"

"A nurse was accused of systematically murdering patients. It happened almost twenty-five years ago, but there were a couple of remarkable features of the case."

"Such as?"

"The number of patients involved. We're talking about twenty-six deaths over a fourteen-month period. Not only that, but the way they were killed was pretty interesting."

"Really? How did they die?"

"Apparently the killer injected a drug called succinylcholine into the patients' IV solution."

"What's succinylcholine?"

"It's some kind of anesthesia drug that causes muscle paralysis."

"Say that again?" I demanded sharply.

"It causes muscle paralysis. That's how they died. The drug stops the heart and lungs from working. But that's not the really incredible part."

"No?"

"No. It turns out that the person who was accused of putting the anesthesia drug into the IV lines was a nurse who'd worked at the hospital for ten years. But guess who figured out what she was up to and blew the whistle?"

"I have no idea. Who?"

"A surgical resident named Gavin McDermott."

"Gavin McDermott?" I echoed incredulously. "That is too weird. Twenty-five years ago he discovered a nurse killing off patients with a paralysis-inducing anesthesia agent, and now his patients are mysteriously dying in what appears to be exactly the same way?"

"Sort of makes you wonder why he's never said anything about it at Prescott Memorial. You'd think he'd have figured out what was going on and been screaming blue murder months ago."

"So what about the nurse? Did she ever offer an explanation for what made her do it?"

"No," replied Elliott. "She never did. It turns out that she killed herself before the case went to trial. She injected herself with a lethal dose of succinylcholine while she was out on bail."

"Is that a drug that's still in use?" I asked, wondering

if it was something I should tell Julia Gordon she should look for.

"No. Now they use something else, the next generation of the drug. The action is basically the same, only quicker. Apparently it's marketed under the brand name Pavulon."

CHAPTER
25

The conference room at Joan Bornstein's office had been transformed into a charting command center. Two physicians, both residents at Northwestern who were being paid the equivalent of a month's salary per day in consulting fees, worked at either end of the long table. Neither looked old enough to have completed puberty. Flanking them were data techs working on their laptops, courtesy of Gabriel Hurt.

Having heard of Claudia's death from Jeff Tannenbaum, Hurt had called Cheryl that morning to ask if there was anything he could do. Instead of flowers or sympathy, Cheryl explained that what was really needed was technical support to complete what she'd described only as the research project Claudia had been racing to complete when she died. Four data techs and an MIS specialist from Icon's Chicago offices had arrived within the half hour. So far they'd set up an information paradigm and were busy entering the data as it was culled from the patient charts by the doctors. The MIS expert, a young woman with close-cropped hair and a Han Solo T-shirt that read NEVER TELL ME THE ODDS, was busy writing a program to evaluate the data.

"Can you go through the charts and quickly find the

list of drugs that each patient was given during surgery?"
I asked.

"Are you talking about anesthesia agents?" asked one
of the residents.

"Yes. Specifically I want to know if any of them were
given Pavulon."

"I'm sure they were," the doctor at the other end of
the table answered promptly. His name was Francis Cho,
and as it turned out, he was a surgical resident from
the same program at the University of Chicago where
Claudia had done her training. "Pavulon is part of the
most commonly used combination of anesthesia drugs."

"So far I've got drug lists for all but two patients," vol-
unteered one of the data techs.

He gave the physicians the names of two patients from
whom the data was missing. It took a couple of minutes
to wade through all the paper, but in the end the data
confirmed Dr. Cho's suspicion. All of the patients had
been given Pavulon as part of their surgical anesthetic.

"Damn!" I muttered under my breath.

"Why's that?" asked Dr. Cho.

"It gets us nowhere," I replied. "Even if Pavulon was
found in their bodies at autopsy, there'd be a good explanation for it."

"You know, speaking of autopsies," chimed in the
other resident, a young man with Oklahoma in his voice,
named Larry Spader, "not all of these patients are dead."

"What do you mean they're not all dead?" demanded
Joan Bornstein, appearing in the doorway.

"This one, here, that I've just been going through. She
suffered respiratory arrest, but they were able to resuscitate her. She spent nine days in ICU, but eventually she
went into a convalescent home."

"What's her name?" I asked, feeling the stirrings of

buried memory, but unable to make the necessary connection. "I vaguely remember the night that Claudia answered the code on her arrest. She said she wasn't sure if the woman would ever fully recover."

"The patient's name is Ida Lapinsky," he replied, consulting the chart in front of him. "Apparently she recovered most of her neurologic functions, certainly to the point where she was able to communicate and take part in her own care. I guess the thing that caught my attention is the fact that the neurologist who examined her in ICU made a note that she might be delusional."

"On what basis?" demanded Joan.

"Apparently Mrs. Lapinsky kept repeating the same story over and over again until she became quite agitated. She claims that immediately before she went into respiratory arrest, she saw the devil come into her room, a monster with a big eye, who put something into her IV."

"Who put something into her IV?" I echoed.

"That's all she said," replied Dr. Cho. "The neurologist seemed to think the whole thing was a hallucination resulting from grand mal seizure. Still," continued the doctor earnestly, "if I were really interested in what was going on, I'd want to interview the only survivor."

Before I left, I called Elliott's office. He was out, but I asked to be connected to the lead investigator on HCC. I gave him the address and phone number listed in Mrs. Lapinsky's chart, and he promised to do his best to locate her immediately.

Driving back to the office, I tried to put the pieces together. The only trouble was that I didn't know whether they were to one puzzle or two. What Elliott had reported proved beyond any doubt that Gavin McDermott knew all about causing respiratory arrest in patients using paralyzing anesthesia drugs. But what possible reason could he have for killing his own patients? He gained nothing from their deaths, and indeed, the cumulative result had been a slipping of his reputation and whispering among his peers. I remembered what Julia Gordon had said about these cases usually being the work of deranged individuals. Surely Gavin McDermott wouldn't be the first surgeon to slip off the edge. Perhaps the deaths were part of a systematic effort on his part to free up beds for more critically ill patients? But in the past when Gavin had gotten into trouble, it had been with alcohol. If he were going through some kind of personal crisis, you'd expect him to start drinking, not become psychotic.

And where did Claudia fit into all of this? Was it possible that Carlos was Prescott Memorial's angel of death? It certainly made sense. Not only was he in and out of the hospital with access to all kinds of drugs, but usually it was first-line caregivers—nurses and paramedics—whose burnout manifested itself in homicide. I wondered if perhaps he had some sort of grudge against McDermott, and made a mental note to mention it to Blades.

When I got back to the office, I found a note from Cheryl saying that she'd gone to the police station to pick up Claudia's father, as well as a message to call Julia Gordon at the medical examiner's office. I punched in the number on the message slip and found myself listening to elevator music while I waited on hold for the forensic pathologist to come to the phone.

"Kate," exclaimed Dr. Gordon, coming on the line. From the booming quality of her voice and the sound of running water in the background, I surmised she was on the speakerphone in one of the autopsy suites.

"Thank you for seeing to it that things got moved

along," I said. "I talked to Detective Kowalczyk and he told me that you'd already released the body."

"Yes. The funeral home has already picked it up. I understand the young woman's father is taking the body back to New York with him for burial."

"Yes. All the arrangements have already been made."

"Well, I just wanted you to know that I kept my promise and called in a favor from one of the chemists in the toxicology lab and had him screen for the kinds of drugs you and I talked about."

"And?"

"You'll be interested to know that Dr. Sylvestri noticed a fresh puncture mark on your roommate's arm."

"What kind of puncture?"

"Consistent with a hypodermic injection. It turns out your suspicions were correct. Dr. Stein was injected with Pavulon before she died."

CHAPTER

26

I rocked back in my desk chair and told myself to breathe. Suspicion is one thing. Knowing is another.

"So she didn't surprise a burglar," I said finally.

"No," agreed Julia Gordon, "it doesn't look that way."

"But what I don't understand is, if you were going to inject her with Pavulon, why would you then stab her? What's the point?"

"Perhaps whoever did it was trying to disguise the nature of the crime by making it appear to have occurred during the course of a robbery. Besides, injecting someone with Pavulon probably wouldn't kill them."

"I don't get it," I said, confused. "I thought you told me that Pavulon is a derivative of curare."

"It is. But it's a relatively short-acting drug. It works by temporarily paralyzing the long muscles of the body. Administered continuously through an IV, it causes respiratory arrest, but given in a single dose in an injection would probably only render the subject incapable."

"For how long?" I demanded, as the sickening realization of what had happened slowly began to dawn.

"That would depend on how much was given, as well as the size of the person it was administered to."

"I understand all that, but what would be your best ballpark guess?"

"Somewhere between thirty and ninety seconds."

"Just long enough to make it easy to stab her in exactly the right spot," I declared bitterly, "and then leave her there to die without the murderer so much as getting blood on his shoes."

As soon as I got off the phone I called Joe Blades. At this point I didn't care about HCC and Prescott Memorial Hospital, I didn't even care if my mother never spoke to me again. I was determined to do what I could to help find out who'd murdered Claudia.

I also needed to keep moving, if only to keep myself from dwelling on the horror of what had happened to her. Even as I dialed the number, all I could think of was her lying paralyzed on the floor of her own apartment watching as someone she trusted enough to let into the apartment fetched a knife from the block in order to stab her.

I didn't know if Dr. Gordon had already called Blades and let him know about the toxicology results, but it was clear he was expecting my call.

We agreed to meet at a restaurant called Emperor's Choice, a storefront in Chinatown that was convenient to the sixth district police station where he was assigned. Through the dim light of the restaurant I could make out two heads in the booth at the back of the restaurant, and my heart sank, thinking that I'd have to contend with Blades's partner, Kowalczyk. But when I got back to the table, I was relieved to find Joe reliving the highlights of their most recent police league basketball game with Elliott.

They were drinking Tsing Tao beer and eating hot scallion pancakes. I slid into the booth beside Elliott, grateful for the reassuring warmth of his thigh against mine. A waiter materialized, and I ordered myself a beer, but couldn't stomach the thought of food. Elliott took my hand under the table and gave it a reassuring squeeze.

"When Joe told me that you guys were meeting, I thought I'd come along and make sure he brought the rubber hoses."

"You just heard she was buying dinner and didn't want to pass up a free meal," Joe replied.

"Have you brought Carlos in for questioning yet?" I asked. Usually I enjoyed listening to their gym-floor banter, but tonight I had no patience for it.

"We picked him up at home this morning and brought him in," replied Blades. "It doesn't look like he's our guy."

"Why not?" I demanded.

"Somebody called in sick in his unit, and he ended up pulling a double shift last night."

"That doesn't necessarily mean anything," I pointed out. "Paramedics are like firemen. They come and go while they're on. It's not like they ride around on patrol. Did you check his log? Just because he was working doesn't mean he couldn't have come to the apartment—"

"That's why we're pretty sure it's not him," reported Blades patiently. "He and his partner answered a call last night at seven-ten. A four-hundred-pound woman got wedged into her bathroom and couldn't get out. Her neighbors heard her screaming for help and dialed 911, but by the time Carlos and his partner got there, she was having chest pains to boot. They weren't able to get her stable and out of there until after midnight. The medical examiner puts the time of her death somewhere between nine and midnight, so our friend Carlos is off the hook."

"Shit."

"Why do you say that?" asked Elliott.

"I was working on a theory, and I was starting to get attached to it," I confessed. I went on to tell Joe about the postsurgical deaths at Prescott Memorial and my suspicion that Pavulon had been the agent used to cause them. I also told him about Mrs. Estrada and Claudia's efforts to find a common denominator among the patients and the fact that her notes and backpack had disappeared from the apartment.

"We had them check at the hospital," reported Blades. "They didn't find her backpack or anything like the notes you described. Are you sure you saw them when you left the apartment that morning?"

"Yes. They were on the dining room table. Where did you look at the hospital? Maybe she left them someplace weird. . . ."

"By the time we got to the hospital, the head of her department had already gone in and emptied out her locker and retrieved all of her things. He said he didn't want the sight of them to traumatize her coworkers any more than they already were by her death. It was all boxed up and ready for us. No backpack. No notes."

"So if it wasn't Carlos, who was it?"

"Well, from what the medical examiner's saying, I think we can pretty much rule out a surprised burglar, unless they're starting to carry hypodermics filled with anesthesia stuff around with them," Blades replied.

"Which means that it was premeditated," said Elliott.

"Looks that way," said Blades, "and from what Kate is telling me, we're probably looking at this as a series of related crimes." From the weariness in his voice, I could tell he was less than thrilled by the prospect. "I'm going to go to the D.A. Monday morning and see if I can get him to sign on to opening up an investigation." His beeper went off at his waist, and Elliott slid him his cell phone so that he could call in to the dispatch operator.

He punched in the number and pulled out the little notebook he invariably kept in his jacket pocket. Apparently the conversation was one-sided, because as soon as he'd identified himself, he started writing. When he was finished, he handed Elliott back his phone and said, "Got to go, kids. Duty calls."

"What's up?" asked Elliott.

"Somebody just turned up ten-seven in a vacant lot on King Drive."

"Ten-seven?" I asked.

"Police communication code for 'out of service,' " Elliott informed me as he got to his feet to shake Joe's hand good-bye.

"It's probably nothing. Just a little friendly competition among heavily armed drug dealers," sighed Blades. "I'll take that kind of case any day over a string of mysterious deaths at a highly respected hospital."

After Joe left, Elliott slid into his place so that he could face me from across the table. I kicked off my high heels and slipped my stockinged feet into Elliott's lap.

"You okay?" he asked.

I didn't answer. Instead I picked up a chopstick and started pushing grains of rice around a plate.

"You know that eventually Joe will get this guy, whoever he is."

"I know," I sighed. "It's the eventually part that I don't like. With Joe going to the D.A., you know as well as I do what we're talking about—a massive investigation that drags out over months. Not only will I have to read Claudia's name in the newspaper every day, but also the damage to the hospital will be irreparable. How many old rich guys do you think are going to want their name associated with a place where they let somebody run around killing patients? Now we have no choice but to sell to HCC. . . ."

"I know you've suffered a terrible loss," said Elliott gravely, "and I don't want you to take this the wrong way. But this doesn't sound like you at all."

"What do you mean? I'm just being realistic—"

"That's exactly my point," said Elliott. "Normally I wouldn't expect you to be worried about what was realistic."

"What would you expect me to be worried about?" I asked.

"The Kate I'm in love with would be worried about what was right."

CHAPTER

27

It was strange coming home to the new apartment. It was so big and so empty. Everything in it seemed unfamiliar; I'd picked it all from photographs and fabric swatches. And although I'd studied the decorator's drawings for months, seeing the floor plan sketched out was one thing, while walking through a room filled with actual furniture was another. I was glad that Elliott hadn't offered to come home with me. I wasn't sure I would have had the strength to say no, and yet I knew I didn't want our first night together to be tainted by tragedy.

I bolted the door behind me and switched on the alarm. Then I walked through, turning on every light in the place. On the kitchen table I was surprised to find a tumble of Marshall Field's bags and a note from my mother, who'd apparently taken it upon herself to go shopping. There were sheets and pillows, a terry cloth bathrobe, scented soap, and a pound of coffee and a box of Frango Mints. For some reason the simple kindness of it undid me completely. I sat at the table clutching the folded terry cloth of the robe like a pillow to my chest and wept for a very long time.

When I was finished, I didn't feel better, just exhausted. Even so, I made my way into the little room adjacent to the kitchen that I intended to use as an office. While the rest of the apartment was furnished with valuable pieces about which adjectives like *one of a kind* and *unique provenance* applied, I'd decorated this room myself with a utilitarian computer desk from Pottery Barn and a fabulously comfortable double-wide reading chair upholstered in a cheery shade of red I'd picked out of the Crate and Barrel catalog.

I plunked my briefcase down on the desk and unclipped my hair. I was surprised to find sections were still wet from the morning. I picked up the phone and dialed the extension for the apartment operator. The amenities of my new building went well beyond having a prestigious address. Besides the security and the twenty-four-hour valet and the concierge services that rivaled a four-star hotel's, all calls that weren't picked up on the fifth ring were immediately transferred to the building's own answering service, who took down the messages verbatim in shorthand.

I'd had four calls. One was from Stephen, offering his condolences and inquiring about funeral arrangements. Another was from Cheryl, just letting me know that Professor Stein had gotten off safely and that she'd taken the liberty of giving Carl Laffer my home number. Not surprisingly, the next call was from Laffer asking when it might be convenient to drop off Claudia's personal effects. The last call was from my mother.

I thanked the operator and dialed my parents' number. Anna, the tight-lipped Filipino woman who'd been my mother's maid for as long as I could remember, answered the phone and informed me that "the Mrs., she is out."

I practically had to beg, but I finally managed to convince her to get my mother's personal phone book and give me Gavin McDermott's home number. When I finished taking it down, I looked up at the clock. It was after eleven. "Good," I thought to myself savagely. "I hope I wake him up."

The phone rang twice before Patsy answered sounding groggy and none too pleased. "I thought you said you weren't on call," I heard her say to someone, presumably McDermott, between the time she picked up the receiver and actually said hello.

"Hi, Patsy, this is Kate Millholland. I'm sorry to disturb you so late at night, but I need to speak to Gavin right away."

I waited for so long that I worried that perhaps she'd just turned over and gone back to sleep. I was about to hang up when Gavin came on the line. He didn't sound sleepy at all. Instead he sounded furious.

"What the *fuck* do you think you're doing calling me at home in the middle of the night? I don't care who the hell you think you are. You have a lot of nerve! How the hell did you even get my number?"

"From my mother," I said sweetly.

"Then I suppose you're going to tell me what the fuck you want."

"You and I need to talk."

"About what?" he demanded. His voice suddenly seemed not just loud, but belligerent. He was either drunk or close to it.

"You and HCC."

"No fucking way. This constitutes harassment! I categorically refuse to discuss this with you or anybody else. Of all the nerve—"

"No problem," I said smoothly. "But I just want you to know that I'm going to the courthouse first thing on Monday morning, and I'm filing a lawsuit against HCC, alleging that they made use of misappropriated confidential information in their offer to buy Prescott Memorial and identifying you specifically by name as the person who gave it to them. It doesn't matter to me one way or another if you want to talk or not. I'm just calling you as a courtesy." Then I hung up the phone.

I'd only managed to count to seven before my phone rang. His phone must have had an automatic dial feature.

"I'll see you tomorrow morning at eleven o'clock at Rinalli's—222 South Wabash," he said.

Then the line went dead.

CHAPTER
28

I hadn't really expected to sleep, but McDermott's reaction to my call erased whatever small possibility there might have been. I had hoped to strike a nerve, and I'd succeeded. If I played my cards right, by tomorrow afternoon I would have the proof I needed that Gavin McDermott was the HCC mole. I tried calling Laffer, but whichever number I called led inevitably to his answering service, so I had to be satisfied with leaving messages asking him to call me in the morning.

It wasn't hard for me to imagine McDermott selling out for the money. Even though he made what most people would consider a king's ransom, he had three ex-wives to support and more than a half a dozen children. His eldest, I knew, had just been accepted to Princeton to the tune of $40,000 a year after taxes. And while Patsy had money—she'd played matrimonial roulette enough times—I had no doubt her income and assets had been placed safely beyond McDermott's reach before she said "I do."

The more I thought about it, the more I could also imagine McDermott slipping Pavulon into his patients' IVs. Even though it didn't make perfect sense that he would choose his own patients, perhaps he'd been reluctant to bring that kind of suspicion on his colleagues, who might have insisted more actively on some kind of investigation. It would be just like Gavin to be so certain of the unassailability of his own reputation that he'd naturally assume that suspicion would fall on someone else, perhaps on the nursing staff, instead of himself.

Of course, none of this explained what had happened to Claudia. Had Claudia seen something she shouldn't have? Perhaps McDermott fiddling with a patient's IV? Or had she merely spotted something in the patient data that tied all the deaths irrevocably to him?

I went into the kitchen to retrieve the box of Frango Mints. On the table beside the packages was a pile of mail that I flipped through quickly. Most of it was junk, but there was also a manila envelope that had apparently been hand delivered earlier in the day from Joan Bornstein. I tucked it under my arm and took it back with me to my home office.

As the night wore on I carefully worked my way through both the file and the chocolate mints. On top was a memo from Dr. Cho summarizing the team's findings about the patients who had died. Even after I'd read it through twice, it still seemed like gobbledygook. The only thing that struck me about the data was that the patients had been as a rule elderly. With the exception of Mrs. Estrada, all were without close family. Besides the fact that they were all McDermott's patients, the only other common denominator seemed to be that they were all people who wouldn't be missed.

Mrs. Lapinsky, the lone survivor, was by far the most interesting. Elliott had found her in a rehabilitation hospital in Blue Island, where he was planning to visit her the next day. Reading through the summary of her treatment prepared by Dr. Cho, I wondered whether it would turn out to be a wasted trip. Even before suffering a mild stroke as a result of her cardiopulmonary arrest, Mrs. Lapinsky would have made a less-than-reliable witness. She was an alcoholic with a fourth-grade education who'd spent much of her adult life on welfare. A chronological listing of emergency-room visits offered an encyclopedia of complaints: high blood pressure, diabetes, headaches, ulcers, shingles, gallstones, blurred vision, and boils.

Once, close to the beginning of her rotation, Claudia had told me that the biggest threat to the work of Prescott Memorial Hospital was selfishness. The cruel reality, she explained, is that in any place and at any time roughly 20 percent of the people in society either cannot or will not take care of themselves. It was up to us, said Claudia, to decide if we were going to pick up the tab for the 20 percent, and what we chose to do said more about us than it did about the poor.

When I protested that the uninsured were not turned away from receiving necessary care, I thought she was going to slug me. True the uninsured can take their diabetes, their tuberculosis, their hypertension, and their obesity to emergency rooms where they must be treated free. But Claudia was quick to point out that treating the uninsured by treating them only in emergencies is often the most expensive course of action, the high price we pay for choosing to look away.

An uninsured diabetic is cheap to treat when he is delivered comatose to the emergency room and dies. But a more typical emergency-room visit brings charges of between two hundred and five hundred dollars, while the regular checkups and preventive care that would have avoided the coma in the first place would have cost less than a quarter of the amount.

The question, according to Claudia, was always what

kind of society we wanted to live in. Did we want to live in the Chicago of Everett Prescott's time, when there were people dying in the streets, or did we want to do our great-grandfathers one better?

In addition to his summary, Dr. Cho had stapled a copy of the note the neurologist who'd treated Mrs. Lapinsky after her episode of cardiopulmonary arrest had written on her chart. It was clear from his tone that he thought she was crazy. Delusional. A dried-out ex-alcoholic gabbling out a garbled account of what her shriveled brain had concocted during a grand mal seizure. According to his notes his follow-up took the form of a request for a psychiatric referral, but there was no indication in any of the documents that I had that one was ever done.

I dropped off into a restless sleep, wondering whether Mrs. Lapinsky's devil with the "big eye" meant that she was crazy, or that I was.

The next morning I took a shower and banged around the kitchen in my underwear in a futile attempt to make coffee. My new kitchen was a cook's Valhalla, filled with cupboards of every size and description, including several with built-in hooks or shelves the purpose of which completely eluded me. I had no idea what had possessed Stephen to order them all, whether he'd hoped someday to venture into the kitchen himself or whether, like my mother, he was eternally optimistic that I might eventually reform.

The coffeepot was one of those Italian ones that does everything but curl your hair. After pushing all the buttons in every combination I could think of, I couldn't get it to produce anything other than a kind of hissing sound. I padded back upstairs to the bedroom in frustration, slipped on a pair of jeans and an old Harvard sweatshirt that had once belonged to Russell, and set out in search of the nearest Starbucks.

I didn't have far to look. The doorman on duty directed me four blocks west to the one on Rush and Oak. Standing in line with all the slightly hungover beautiful people who lived and worked in the neighborhood, it occurred to me that instead of Hyde Park, I was now living in the Chicago equivalent of Beverly Hills. As I clutched my enormous latte in both hands and walked back toward the lake, I wasn't sure how I was going to like it.

As I got close to my apartment I was surprised to see a familiar figure being disgorged from a taxicab. It was Carl Laffer, swathed in the Gore-Tex of a serious runner, pulling himself and a couple of big shopping bags out of the back of the taxi.

"I was hoping I would catch you," he said, unfurling his rangy frame and slipping a couple of bills to the driver. "I got your message this morning about wanting to meet, and I thought I'd kill two birds with one stone. Your mother told me I might find you here."

"What's all this?" I asked, eyeing the shopping bags.

"Claudia's things from the hospital. Your mother said she thought you'd be going to New York for the funeral, so I wanted to be sure you had a chance to go through them and take her parents whatever you thought they might want."

"What kind of stuff is it?" I asked, feeling strangely reluctant to pick it up.

"I don't know. I didn't really look." My heart leapt in my chest, thinking that Claudia's notes on the patient charts might be among them. "I was just going for a run along the lake before I stopped in to see my patients at Northwestern. I thought I'd drop the bags by as long as I was in the neighborhood."

"Thank you," I said, not knowing what else to say. I

had wanted to talk to Laffer after I'd had a chance to confront McDermott, not before.

"Would you like me to help you get the bags upstairs?" he asked eyeing the cup of coffee in my hand.

"I'd appreciate it," I said.

We each grabbed a bag as the doorman swung the door open for us, touched his cap, and wished us both a very good morning.

"How long have you lived in this apartment?" he asked, making small talk as we stepped into the elevator.

"Since yesterday," I said. "I bought the apartment almost a year ago and gutted it," I said, deciding to leave Stephen Azorini out of it. I figured if he hadn't already learned the details of our breakup by reading the papers, it wasn't my job to bring him current. "The work was finished a couple of weeks ago, but I'd agreed to stay in the apartment in Hyde Park with Claudia until she was finished with her fellowship."

"I'm sure you didn't want to leave her alone in that neighborhood," he observed.

"I didn't want to leave her, period," I said, my voice tightening up with the unwanted approach of tears. "But she was moving back to New York. It seemed like a natural time."

"I don't need to tell you," said Laffer, with a sad shake of his head, "but your roommate was one of the most talented surgeons I ever had the privilege of working with. She was one of those rare few who, when they looked at something, saw a solution instead of a problem."

I nodded, fighting back the tears, as the elevator came to rest on seven. I squeezed awkwardly past Laffer through the narrow elevator door as he chivalrously hung back and waited for me to pass.

"Only one apartment per floor?" inquired Laffer.

"That's the way the building was originally designed," I told him dutifully. "This particular apartment is actually a duplex. The apartments on seven and eight have been joined together to form a single residence." I wanted to kick myself for sounding like a realtor, but there was something about the shock of losing Claudia that had knocked me off kilter. I no longer had any idea of what was going to come out of my mouth. I just hoped Laffer wasn't the kind to easily take offense. I thought that he and I had gotten off on the right foot the other day, and I didn't want to do anything to change that.

"You must have room enough for a staff in here," he said, as he stepped inside the massive foyer. At the sight of the apartment, I could tell, he suddenly felt less urgent about fitting in his run. "This place looks like it goes on forever."

"Actually, the building was designed with servants' quarters in the basement," I said somewhat apologetically. "When you buy your unit, the co-op board assigns you a corresponding staff apartment. I've just moved in, so I don't have anybody working for me yet, but the apartment is quite nice. You can't beat the location," I added stupidly.

"I'll say," remarked Laffer, drawn in spite of himself to the windows on the far side of the living room and their commanding view of the northward skyline and the lake.

I set my purse down beside the bags in the entryway.

"Would you like a tour?" I inquired.

"If you're sure it wouldn't be too much trouble," he replied, unable to completely conceal the envy in his voice.

"This building was designed by David Adler," I began, leading him through the living room into the library, a fantasy of floor-to-ceiling bookshelves complete with a

CHAPTER

29

Just like Claudia, I found myself alone with the devil. The same devil who had come into Mrs. Lapinsky's room with not an enormous "eye," but an enormous *I* for Indiana basketball. McDermott hadn't been the only Prescott Memorial surgeon who'd been in Indiana at the time of the VA Hospital deaths. Carl Laffer, the man who loved nothing more than opera and Bobby Knight's Hoosiers, had played basketball there as an undergraduate. Not McDermott, Laffer.

What a mistake it had been to think that just because Laffer seemed nice that he was actually kind. Surgeons were, by necessity, capable of ruthlessness, in the operating room and when it came to their own careers.

I must really be my mother's daughter after all, I thought bitterly to myself. I'd been blinded by good manners, tricked into applauding Laffer's ambition as diplomacy and his ruthlessness as pragmatism because he wore a mask of perpetual geniality. What a fool I'd been to think that a hospital would be that different from a large law firm. If I'd bothered to take the time to look beneath the surface, I would have seen that they are both the same—Darwinian systems where survival belongs to the fittest and where leadership, just like in a pride of lions, is earned through successive challenges of nerves and blood. Carl Laffer hadn't beaten out McDermott and Davies for the chief of staff's job by being a white-haired elder statesman. He'd gotten it by being the fiercest and most cunning of the three—something I was afraid I hadn't realized until it was too late.

Laffer had spent his entire career in the shadow of McDermott's superior surgical skills. He'd had the difference in their talents publicly thrown in his face in the malpractice suit involving the ten-year-old boy, and he'd paid a heavy price for covering for his colleague. No doubt when HCC approached him, Laffer recognized the company's plan as not only an opportunity to definitively best his rival, but to finally reap the financial rewards long overdue him.

Laffer was the one who'd cut a deal with HCC, which is why Packman knew all about the patient deaths. Indeed, telling Packman had been the whole point. With stakes that high, Laffer was leaving nothing to chance. He knew what an attractive figurehead Gavin McDermott would make for HCC, the instant credibility affiliation with the famous surgeon would bring to the company's efforts in Chicago.

But Laffer wasn't about to let that happen, not when it was so easy to tip the scales in his own favor. If HCC was successful in gaining control of health care in Chicago, then whoever they chose to be chief of medical services would wield tremendous power not just over patients, but physicians in the system. My guess was that that was the deal that Laffer had cut with HCC—appointment as chief of medical services in exchange for handing them Prescott Memorial Hospital on a platter. I didn't think that he'd commit murder for anything less.

The killings themselves had been easy. Surgeons spend the best part of their lives up to their elbows in gore.

They deal in the currency of life and death every day. For most, like Claudia, it makes them appreciate the value of human life, but for a much smaller percentage, their familiarity cheapens it.

No, for Laffer, the tricky part had been maintaining an equilibrium. On the one hand, the deaths of McDermott's patients had to be public and conspicuous enough to insure widespread whispers about something being amiss. On the other, he had to avoid any kind of public inquiry that might sour the deal between HCC and Prescott Memorial. No doubt he figured that as chief of staff he'd be able to control any kind of investigation in the guise of overseeing it. What he hadn't counted on was Mrs. Estrada.

The identity of undercover patients was, of necessity, a closely guarded secret. Only Kyle Massius and Farah Davies knew the true circumstances of her admission. And while Laffer was undoubtedly aware of the existence of such patients, they posed no threat to him, since their complaints invariably "cleared up" prior to their actually having to go through surgery. Even someone as calculating as Carl Laffer could not have foreseen an undercover patient legitimately requiring emergency surgery, much less the set of circumstances that led to its being performed by someone other than McDermott.

I'd signed my roommate's death warrant the day I'd told Laffer that Claudia was my roommate. He knew then and there that there was no way the hospital would be able to pressure her into accepting the blame for Mrs. Estrada's death, and Joan Bornstein would never rest until the facts behind the other deaths were fully revealed. I'm sure he figured he had no other choice.

Just like now.

I was surprised to hear my own voice saying something about the cornices of the bookshelves and how the wood had been imported from Italy. I tried desperately to focus on what Laffer was saying, sickened by the sudden realization that the man who had stabbed my roommate in cold blood had no doubt come to try to silence me.

Laffer didn't seem to notice. He was talking about Claudia and her love of books, and how we really needed to plan some sort of memorial service. The people who had worked with her needed a forum in which to express their grief.

Killing Mrs. Estrada had been Laffer's only mistake. Not only did he have no way of knowing that she wasn't what she seemed, but he didn't find out that it was Claudia who'd done the actual operation until after he'd slipped the Pavulon into her IV. His sympathetic treatment of Claudia at the M&M conference hadn't anything at all to do with compassion, but rather the desire to not deflect blame from McDermott.

"Do you think she would have liked the idea of a rabbi officiating?" he asked.

I wanted to tell him that she would have preferred to be alive and see him dead, but what I managed to say was, "I don't think it would have mattered to her one way or the other. I think she would have just liked the idea of all the people she'd worked with coming and paying their respects."

"Maybe just the hospital chaplain then," Laffer mused. "He's new, but a nice young man. I'm sure he would be happy to oblige."

"Would you mind excusing me for a moment," I said, trying to make my voice sound natural. Instead I was afraid that I sounded like a terrified ingenue uttering wooden lines in her first play. "I'd just like to run to the ladies' room for a moment. But go ahead, make yourself at home. Look around. I'll come and catch up with you."

Instead of heading to the powder room, I quickly made my way into my little office adjacent to the kitchen. I closed the door behind me and, with trembling hands, picked up the receiver and dialed Elliott's cell phone number. The call went through, but instead of Elliott answering I got a voice-mail recording. My terror made it difficult to breathe, but I managed to rattle off a message explaining that I figured out not only who the mole was, but the identity of Claudia's murderer. From the other room I heard the shrill cry of Laffer's beeper, and I hastened to finish off my message to Elliott with an explanation of where I was.

Just as I was about to hang up the phone, I heard the soft, yet unmistakable click of an extension being eased into its cradle in some other part of the apartment. Suddenly I was afraid. Not nervous, or anxious, or filled with foreboding, but flat-out, in-your-face, the-metallic-taste-of-adrenaline-running-down-the-back-of-your-throat afraid.

I told myself to breathe, as I rapidly calculated the odds. My purse, and the gun, were by the front door in the apartment. I stood a better chance of slipping quietly out through the kitchen and making a run for it down the back service stairs. I told myself that with any luck I'd be safely in the basement before Laffer even realized that I was gone.

As quietly as I could, I turned the handle of the study door and cautiously stuck my head out. The apartment seemed quiet, the hallway empty. Breathing something very close to a sigh of relief, I stepped through the doorway, turning toward the kitchen.

Carl Laffer's hands, meaty like hams, grabbed me from behind and pulled me off my feet. I felt the wind go out of me as I hit the floor, heard the hiss of profanity as Laffer grabbed me by the scruff of the neck and shook me like a doll. I tried to scream, but I could not find my voice. Instead I kicked and clawed with all the strength that I had, miraculously managing to kick free of him. I hit the floor in a disorganized pile and rolled over onto my hands and feet into a kind of impromptu runner's crouch, meaning to take off toward the service exit in the kitchen, but Laffer's legs were in front of my face, effectively blocking my escape.

I rolled over until I was facing the other direction and took off at a dead run, not knowing where I was going but blindly trying to put any kind of distance I could between myself and Claudia's killer. After a couple of seconds I realized that I was in the main hall of the apartment, heading toward the front door—the front door and the gun.

For a minute I thought I'd made it, I felt I was almost clear, I *was* clear, but even as I thought that, I felt my legs go out from under me as Laffer hooked me from behind. My head hit the hard marble of the entrance hall, and I saw stars, but I still frantically clawed along the ground, hoping to make it to my purse.

For a fraction of a second I felt Laffer's grip loosen, and my fingertips touched the soft leather of my purse. I rolled over on my back, groping blindly in the dark recesses of my bag. As my fingers grappled with lipstick tubes and packages of tissues, my mind registered the syringe in Carl Laffer's hand.

I felt the sting of the injection at the same moment I felt the hard barrel of the gun in my hand. I scrabbled desperately to get it turned around, groping for the pistol's walnut grip. As I turned the gun in my hand my brain registered quite calmly the fact that Laffer had injected me with Pavulon. Indeed, I felt the blackness of paralysis starting in my thigh and working its way up my left side. I watched him stand up slowly, put the cap back on the syringe, and tuck it into the pocket of his warm-up jacket, waiting for the drug to take effect. It was only a matter of seconds before I was completely helpless. I thought about the pristine block of Henckel knives on the counter in the kitchen. I wondered whether he'd risk it or if he'd brought something with him to do the job.

I knew that I was almost out of time when I squeezed the trigger. I managed to get off three rounds through the bottom of my purse before the blackness enveloped me completely like a kind of dark ice. I realized with horror as Laffer collapsed noisily on top of me that the drug was not going to make me lose consciousness. Instead I was going to lie there and watch Carl Laffer's sightless eyes staring into mine as his warm blood oozed over me and as every oxygen-starved molecule of my body screamed out for air.

I remembered thinking that this is what drowning must be like. The agony of running out of air was unbearable. I felt the darkness closing in around me like the aperture of a camera closing down and knew that this is what it must feel like to know that you are about to die.

CHAPTER
30

Another Monday morning, another press conference on the courthouse steps. This time my mother wore a telegenic suit of fuschia silk. I was dressed in black.

I'd spent the night at Prescott Memorial under observation for shock and any possible adverse effects from having been injected with Pavulon. Elliott had stayed the night in the armchair beside my bed, and when the sleeping stuff they'd given me wore off, he'd come upstairs with me to say hello to Bill Delius.

This morning Mother was triumphant. Not only had she announced to the assembled reporters that the board of trustees of Prescott Memorial Hospital voted to refuse to sell the hospital to HCC, but they had agreed to join in a class-action suit with Northwestern Memorial Medical Center and the Archdiocese of Chicago against HCC. Among other things the suit alleged that the company had engaged in unlawful business practices.

She said nothing about Carl Laffer. When I asked Elliott about it, he said that Blades had already spoken to the D.A., who'd agreed to handle the whole thing with a minimum of publicity. That was fine with me. I figured I'd already had about as much of the spotlight as I could handle.

If you liked
DEAD CERTAIN
by Gini Hartzmark,

don't miss the other Kate Millholland novels.

PRINCIPAL DEFENSE
The First Kate Millholland Novel

Although she's an heiress, Kate Millholland works hard for her money as a mergers-and-acquisitions lawyer in Chicago. When Azor, the high-tech, high-profit pharmaceutical company founded by her sometime lover, Stephen Azorini, faces a takeover, Kate will do anything to stop it from happening.

The stakes rise even higher when Stephen's teenage niece, Gretchen, is killed. Everyone knows that if Gretchen's shares go to the corporate raider, Stephen will lose everything.

by GINI HARTZMARK

FINAL OPTION

When lawyer Kate Millholland arrives at the home of Bart Hexter, one of Chicago's most powerful players in the futures market, she finds him behind the wheel of his Rolls-Royce, clad only in a pair of red silk pajamas, with two bullets in his head. This scheduled meeting with the dead man places her at the top of the suspect list.

BITTER BUSINESS

At the request of a colleague, Chicago attorney Kate Millholland agrees to represent the Cavanaugh family's company, Superior Plating & Specialty Chemicals—and discovers that the family is as corrosive as the chemicals it produces.

FATAL REACTION

For Chicago attorney Kate Millholland, navigating the male-dominated legal profession was a piece of cake . . . until Danny Wohl's brutal murder. Head of the legal department at Azor Pharmaceuticals, Danny was in the midst of pivotal negotiations with Tokyo investors. Now Kate dives into the billion-dollar deal midstream and finds the water filled with career sharks, secret affairs, lethal chemicals, and one cold-blooded killer.

ROUGH TRADE

Pro football is a new business for Chicago attorney and deal-maker Kate Millholland, but one meeting with the Milwaukee Monarchs convinces her that the team is in deep trouble. The move that could save the once-great team—a transfer to L.A.—is vehemently rejected by owner Beau Rendell. But soon Beau is out of the game— murdered, the police say, by his own son and heir. While the press and the fans go wild, Kate runs with the ball and collides with an opposition that plays to kill.

by Gini Hartzmark

Published by The Ballantine Publishing Group.
Available at your local bookstore.